MW01706683

TwoBlackEyes
AND THE UNFINISHED SCRIPT

Also by Tyler Trafford

Almost a Great Escape
Alexander's Way
The Métis Girl
The Story of Blue Eye

TwoBlackEyes
AND THE UNFINISHED SCRIPT

TYLER TRAFFORD

Frontenac House

Copyright © 2017 Bradley and Dena Flock
All rights reserved, including moral rights. No part of this publication may be reproduced or transmitted in any form or by any means, electronic or mechanical, including photocopying, recording, or from any information storage retrieval system, without permission in writing from the author, publisher, or ACCESS copyright, except by a reviewer or academic who may quote brief passages in a review or critical study.

Book design: Neil Petrunia, Epix Design Inc.
Cover Image: Mary Haasdyck
Author photo: Monique de St. Croix

Library and Archives Canada Cataloguing in Publication

Trafford, Tyler, 1949-, author
Twoblackeyes : and the unfinished script / Tyler Trafford.

Includes screenplay by Brandon Flock with a modified ending
by Tyler Trafford.
Issued in print and electronic formats.
ISBN 978-1-927823-70-5 (softcover).--ISBN 978-1-927823-71-2 (PDF)

I. Title. II. Title: Two black eyes.

PS8589.R335T86 2017 C813'.54 C2017-903351-4
C2017-903352-2

Frontenac House gratefully acknowledges the support of the Canada Council for the Arts for our publishing program. We would also like to thank the Government of Alberta Multimedia Development Fund for their support of our publishing program.

Canada Council for the Arts Conseil des Arts du Canada

Alberta Government

Printed and bound in Canada
Published by Frontenac House Ltd.
1648 Bowness Rd. NW
Calgary, Alberta, T2N 3J9, Canada
Tel: 403-263-7025

www.frontenachouse.com

TwoBlackEyes and The Unfinished Script is dedicated to everybody who crosses the River of Doom into the Land of Ground Thunder Running.

~Tyler Trafford

CONTENTS

ACT I

KAYDEN

Kayden Montgomery is the beginning. TwoBlackEyes is the ending.

Before Kayden there was Elbow Park where our house is busy on a late summer afternoon. The gardening crew are giving the cotoneaster hedges a flattop haircut like Dad's school photo from the early 60s. The crew boss says, "Good afternoon, Mr. Nathan," when I stop to admire his work. I give him a thumbs up on the trim. I wouldn't dare tell him it looks a bit lopsided. Mom will do that.

Inside, the cleaning ladies are vacuuming and washing floors. They call me Mr. Nathan too. Slightly embarrassing. I am only 17. I smile at them politely and make them smile by returning the undeserved formality: "Hello to you, Miss Roslyn and Miss Jackie."

My nonstop parents Rick and Julia Munro are out of town until late tomorrow. I have the house to myself.

I'll probably go over to Reese's for a while. She lives a few blocks away beside the Elbow River. She texted to let me know her parents were going to a cocktail party at the neighbour's. Reese is a very creative and assertive person. She's very organized in bed. She could write a manual about ways to have sex in new places in her house. She likes to be in charge and to tell people I belong to her. I don't mind. She is following the real estate market closely and knows which families are headed for divorce and will sell their homes, most likely after the kids have moved out. She expects we will be in a position to make an offer right after we graduate from university and are recruited by major corporations. She's a planner.

I'll walk home while the streets are turning shadowy black. The long August evenings are a rare opportunity to be alone with scenes from my Palaeolithic life.

When the light is just right, softly quiet, I watch The Great Bull Hunters leaving camp. I like the ease with which they disappear into the whispering night, crossing the river into the Land of Ground Thunder Running.

There's no easy explanation. I suppose my private school counsellor would have told me it's my desire for adventure. But that wouldn't be right because I know my Palaeolithic life began 20,000 years ago. I am a descendent of the hunters whose handprints you see today on the walls of the Lascaux caves in France.

School has been pretty much a waste of time for me, other than a grade eight art class when the teacher showed a film about the paintings in the Lascaux caves. And there they were: four black bulls, or aurochs, running across the plains – the ancestors of today's cattle – but twice as big, faster and more aggressive.

Bison, horses, birds, rhinoceros, hunters. I barely noticed them. I could only hear the bulls running.

And I would have given all the money my parents were paying in tuition to see those caves and feel the red pigment blown against my hand. But it was not my money, and it was not my life to control. But those hunters and those bulls have been with me for four years and are sounding louder every day.

I know ... I shouldn't say school has been pretty much a waste of time, but if all you want to do is press your hand where another hand pressed red 20,000 years ago and say I, too, am a hunter, then what does your heart care for school? What does your heart care for anything else?

You just go along.

I met Kayden in Film Studies at Western Canada High School. He'd started there in grade 10. I started this year, in grade 12. Everybody knew Kayden. Nobody knew me, except kids from my Elbow Park neighbourhood. Or they thought they did because they knew the street I lived on. In Elbow Park, if you tell somebody the street you live on, they will guess your whole story. Especially how much money your parents have.

Most of my growing up friends were finishing grade 12 at my old private school where they were getting a good education. Academics wasn't why I left that school. I wasn't in trouble or anything. I left because I was starting to daydream scripts about my friends' lives. How they would go on to university and become lawyers and accountants and engineers and doctors. How proud their parents would be. How they would fall in love and get married and have kids and get stock options in oil companies and take the whole family on cruises and own recreational property on a lake in British Columbia. Those scripts were my first drafts. In my next drafts I would throw in the lie, cheat, and steal twists, and a few along the way broken hearts. I always finished with happy endings. I liked to write happy endings.

They were obvious stories. One dimensional. Immature. Judgmental now that I look back. And sad sometimes. For me. I made them up because I envied my friends and their films. They had what I wanted. Documented destinations. Obvious futures. I thought of myself as a secret screw up, going along with other people's choices because I didn't know what I wanted to do. Other kids didn't have to go along. They liked their futures. They already had their careers picked out for them. I didn't. I didn't know screenwriting was a career choice. All I had was Palaeolithic dreams I couldn't talk about.

Even though I could write other people's films, I couldn't write my own. My following in my parents' footsteps script didn't have a plot, a storyline. Anybody reading my draft would say, "When is this going to get interesting? When's this guy going to do something with his life?"

My script needed a turning point. I remember watching *The Graduate* with my parents. We did everything together when Dad was home.

I didn't expect to have a Mrs. Robinson turning point in grade 12, but I liked how her character rocked Benjamin Braddock's storyline. She had a special way of waking him up.

I suppose my film chatter gives away why I had always signed up for drama class. I would have preferred to take Film Studies except that's not a private school honour student choice. Theatre is still more mainstream than film. No future in film, the counsellors would have said to young Shakespeare who would have ignored them and gone on to collect Best Screenplay Oscars and Spielberg size paycheques.

As far as actors go, I'm a Johnny Depp fan. I liked his Captain Jack Sparrow in *Pirates of the Caribbean: The Curse of the Black Pearl.* I like action, adventure, and boy meets girl.

The only close to film choice I had in private school was signing up for drama to audition with the we're so different haircuts for a Macbeth part. "Drama's an appropriate supplement for Nathan's C.V.," the counsellor told my parents. The major accounting firms prefer applicants who are well rounded and serious about their career ambitions.

Luckily there wasn't a symphony course. Symphony, he said, attracts a wealthier crowd than theatre. A symphony fundraiser is the ideal career advancement opportunity.

I got the comedic role of Porter in *Hamlet* even though I didn't have any acting experience: I was a natural at bumbling my way through a scene. I always got a laugh. I wanted to do it Jack Sparrow but he's not the Shakespeare that parents pay tuition to see.

The entire cast had to attend rehearsals, no matter how small your role, so I had a lot of time on my hands. One thing led to another: I actually went to the trouble of studying playwriting. That's when I discovered the Three Act Structure. The fundamental format for telling any story – from a five star Oscar to a zombie spine chiller.

Act I creates the setting by describing the main character's routine life, one that is apparently going nowhere. Act II presents a challenge – will the hero (or heroine) dare to give up his comfortable situation and risk everything by crossing a symbolic barrier into an unknown adventure? Of course, the answer is yes. In this dangerous territory, the hero makes new friends who show him he owns powers he didn't know about. He'll need those powers and all the Obi-Wan Kenobi help he can get to accomplish a seemingly impossible deed of bravery and sacrifice.

Act II contains the big climax scene in which the impossible challenge is overcome, and the hero must return to everyday life, transformed by his experience and knowing who he really is. That's the part I don't get. Sounds like the way kids talk after they go to family therapy, "I'm learning to be brave enough to express my uniqueness." You bet.

I'm one of those people destined to stay in Act I's routine life.

If you recognize the Three Act structure in a film, you'll see it in every film. The first 40 minutes of *Pirates* has a classic Act I describing Jack's ridiculous life as the worst pirate captain ever – no ship and no crew.

Act II is the adventure. Jack and the beautiful, innocent Elizabeth have to save her Prince Charming (Will) from the evil Barbossa, the meanest pirate captain ever, with a real ship (the Black Pearl) and a crew of cutthroats.

Act III brings closure to all concerned. Barbossa and his cutthroats die vigorously. Will and Elizabeth are together again and happy. Jack completes his quest by capturing the sublime Black Pearl thanks to his innumerable acts of bravery and self sacrifice. However, despite his good deeds, he must always live in the shadow of the gallows rope. He must always be a pirate captain. I suppose the message there is that Jack has grown as a pirate and is able to feel more positive about himself, now that he has discovered who he really is – a gentler, more supportive cutthroat. But, once a pirate always a pirate, and the hangman will never quit scheming to put a noose around Jack's neck.

Thank you, Macbeth rehearsals!

After that discovery I had a secret ambition to write a film script. I had an idea for one, sort of. Actually, all I had was a list of characters: mostly family and friends with different names. But no setting and no plot. Sounds lame, doesn't it? As if I were going to write a thinly disguised script beginning with my personal Act I. Good luck, Nathan. No Act II and no pirates in sight.

It took a while to talk The Commotion into taking me, their only child – their pride and joy – their dream coming true – out of an expensive private school where I was really fitting in and getting straight A's and sending me to a public school for grade 12. It required promises on my part: I had to prove myself worthy by making the grade 11 honour roll. Plus, I could not attend just any public school. I had to go to where my dad went – Western Canada High. Routine. Tradition.

They had sound reasons for allowing me to go there, and I had my own reasons for wanting to. They wanted me to be an all star business student, a straight to the bottom line accountant. They wanted me to fit in. I wanted to try something unacceptable. I was restless. Not that Western was much different than the private school. Parents at both schools believed their children would live exceptional lives as captains of industries, not pirate ships.

I was born qualified for success, starting as an honour roll baby: a cute blue eyed curly haired blonde with a wide smile and white teeth; a child model signed to an agency just like Mom and Dad.

I had always fit in with after school programs, going to the members only Glencoe Club with friends where we charged french fries and Cokes to our parents' accounts and swam or played tennis or fooled around until it was time to go home. Extra sports coaching was part of our program.

Making a team was a goal. Swim team, soccer team, hockey team, ski team. Being on a team was important. Teamwork taught us to have the right attitude. The important life skill of not letting parents, coaches and teammates down. Being labelled as not coachable was the end of the road. Sorry, your son doesn't fit in. How embarrassing is that for parents?

The Commotion intended for me to continue drama in grade 12 at Western, and anticipated family applause for me in whatever Shakespearean remake the drama department chose. Without telling them, I crashed the conformity line signing up for Film Studies, a provisional course that had a regular length Tuesday class plus a triple Friday afternoon class. The counsellors warned me that if the course and the teacher didn't work out, it would be discontinued. Take it at your own academic and career risk was the message I got. I could hardly wait for the class to start. For the first time in my life I saw myself as living dangerously. Film Studies!

The future of the course looked precarious: only two students had signed up, Kayden Montgomery and Nathan Munro. If the rest of the grade 12 class had seen the teacher, Miss Emily Arbutus, more desks would have been filled. Day one was a blur because the moment I saw Emily Arbutus I decided I would cast her as an Act I sensitive girl in glasses who was overshadowed by the cute girl. In Act II there would be a makeover and Emily would emerge with her strawberry blonde hair cut long like Cameron Diaz. She'd be wearing scarlet lipstick. Sexy but different than Cameron because she looked like she could have starred in my Palaeolithic film, sort of the way Raquel Welch starred voluptuously in *One Million Years B.C.* (I'd found Dad's poster of barely bikinied Raquel rolled inside his 1978 *Superman* poster.)

I tried to imagine what Emily did on weekends. Attend book readings? Did she have a boyfriend? Did she hope to discover a student with hidden talent? With only Kayden and me in her class that wouldn't happen.

Kayden had short dark hair, deep set brown eyes and a no fat physique like a soccer player. Just about the opposite of Nordic blonde, slightly chubby me.

In our first class, I was talking enthusiastically about Johnny Depp when a student volunteer knocked on the door and told Kayden to go to the principal's office.

Ten minutes later he came back. For somebody who had just been ordered to the principal's office he didn't seem too concerned. To me, a visit to the principal's office meant trouble: at school and at home. Maybe I'd be called next. Maybe the counsellors had informed my parents about my risky decision. Sorry, Nathan. No Film Studies for you. Back to *Macbeth.*

That's when I saw how difficult it was to read Kayden. I can usually read people pretty well, or at least make a good guess. Being smaller than average and awkward at sports taught me how to read the people trying to push me around.

I would see later that nobody could read Kayden. That made him intriguing to me. He didn't give anything away and didn't offer anything unless asked. He had no persona. That's a theatrical term to describe a role or character assumed by an actor. In real life, too. Most of us try to project an image of ourselves, our persona. Something that we think is an improvement on who we are, or covers up a weakness. My persona is fitting in and being responsible: polite, sincere, and positive. Definitely not a scriptwriter.

After Film Studies, I walked with Kayden to the parking lot. I felt out of place beside him. Him being the one everybody in school knew and me tagging along as if we were real friends.

"What did the principal want?" I asked. "You don't have to say. I'm just curious."

He bumped me with his elbow. "Does Jack Sparrow," he said with a grin, "want to know if I'm going to be court martialled and flogged?"

I was surprised at that. He didn't seem to be an interested in pirates type. Or films, really. It was hard to know what interested Kayden, or why he was taking Film Studies.

I gave him my wobbly Johnny Depp act. "That's '*Captain* Jack Sparrow,' if you don't mind."

Kayden leaned against his pickup, the only one in the school parking lot. "The principal wanted to know why I didn't sign up for the sports teams this year."

"What's the big deal about that?" I asked trying to sound as if getting asked to sign up for sports teams was routine in my life.

"I'll show you." He opened the truck door and took out a football.

"Watch." He pointed to a group of grade 12 boys laughing and pushing each other by the picnic tables on the far side of the parking lot.

"Hey, Gerry," he called out waving the football above his head. The tallest one looked over. "Start running!" Kayden shouted to him.

The boy began jogging. Kayden leaned back and threw. The boy caught the ball over his shoulder mid stride.

"That's the big deal. Gerry almost scored a record number of touchdowns last season because I was throwing to him. He dropped a couple or he would have had the record. He doesn't know I'm not playing this year."

Gerry tried to throw the football back, but it fell short and Kayden had to walk through the cars to find it.

If I could throw a football like Kayden I definitely would have signed up for the team. Who would I rather be, the awkward Porter in the school play or the good looking quarterback?

After that, we started talking regularly on the way to the parking lot after Film Studies. Then he'd drive away in his truck.

"I'd better get going," he'd say. He never said where he went, where he lived, or what he did after school. I invited him to our house once.

"The Commotion will be there," I told him when he said he'd come. "They're having a bridge tournament at our house tonight."

"Sounds like serious cards."

"Very."

My mom's blue eyes opened wide when Kayden walked in with me. I knew she thought I was about the best looking guy around. Even so, Kayden gave her second thoughts on that. And she didn't waste any time finding out about him. She's got nerve, that's for sure. And I got a message too. If any girl wanted to choose between Kayden and me, I wouldn't stand a chance. I'd seen the way girls at school checked him out, but the effect he had on my mom couldn't be mistaken. He was what she called a prize catch. Not that she was really interested. She's not a Mrs. Robinson. Her friends are. I know that for sure about one of them.

My dad tells everybody my mom was a hot number in university. I believe him, although she doesn't act like she knows she is still hot. She's all blonde curls and love, as irresistible as Reese Witherspoon in *Pleasantville.* A lot of neighbourhood envy is hidden behind polite smiles when dads of less hot Elbow Park moms give Julia a once over.

I think handsome Kayden, built like a man and showing up without references, fascinated her. For sure she was curious. Normally she's multi tasking on the phone, reading a recipe, organizing everybody and getting carried away with bigger plans than she has time for. But she stopped everything when she saw Kayden.

"Do you live around here?" she asked as she began her quest to define him in a social context. Mom's Holy Grail is to know as much as possible about everybody I know.

"No, ma'am," he answered. Like he was being quizzed by a policewoman. "I live with my aunt during the school week. On the weekends I live with my grandparents on the Rockin' R Ranch outside Longview."

"What about your parents? Where are they?"

That's a typical Nosy Julia question. What if they're dead?

"They died when I was in elementary school."

For a moment, Julia looked like she was going to cry. She's very sympathetic to tragedy.

Dead parents. Living with an aunt. Grandparents own a ranch. No explanation. Very different from Elbow Park where people embellish everything. The positive stuff, that is.

I think that Longview ranch interested my mom the most: it was a potential cocktail party sharing detail to which she could connect. My dad's family were pioneers. Loved horses and cattle. Probably rode broncs in the Stampede.

"Nathan will be enrolling in Commerce next fall," Mom told Kayden. "He's going to be an accountant like his father. Are you planning to go to university?"

"I have to. My parents left me the Rockin' R, but only if I get through university."

"I'm sure you will. You seem like an ambitious young man." That was a Mom compliment.

"Thank you."

"Call me Julia, please."

"Yes, ma'am." She smiled, probably wondering who the right girl would be for this prize catch.

She excused herself and went back to her chaos. I knew she'd be onto Dad as soon as he came home. She'd prime him with a bunch more questions for Kayden. If Kayden was coming into her world, she'd need a full background check.

Kayden and I went downstairs to where I lived.

"Goddamn," I said. "Was that true about your parents dying and the ranch and living with an aunt?"

"Yes."

"Do you have a horse of your own?"

"A couple."

I threw myself on the couch. "Holy Jesus. I could write a Disney film script about you."

"Not if you're going to be an accountant. Maybe they'll let you write the financial statements."

Not funny.

"I could," I said with a little hurt in my voice. "If I had a chance."

"You'd have to know the ending first."

What was that supposed to mean?

"Do you think Emily Arbutus would help me?" I asked.

"Maybe."

"If I were to write a movie about her, I'd give her super powers."

We played video games for a while. Then Dad came down. My friends call him Uncle Rick. He's the father every boy wants. Software genius. Great athlete. Speaking role in the 1978 *Superman* blockbuster filmed in Calgary! A poster signed 'To Rick' by Christopher Reeve. Knows everybody. Travels a lot. He's dark and angular like Al Pacino. Except Dad has the smile of a mischievous boy, not a gangster. He was my DC Comics hero in elementary school.

He asked Kayden a bit about the ranch in Longview and whether it was near a ranch his grandparents, my great grandparents, had owned a hundred million dinosaur years ago before there were cars and colour television and the internet. A couple geological eras before my Palaeolithic life.

Kayden promised to ask his grandparents about it.

"Thanks," Dad said. "I'd like to know. For the hell of it." That was the conversation, and different from what I expected. He usually gets me and my friends involved in his action movies. He loves thrills. A weekend plan might start out with just us going skiing, but by Friday night he's got five of my friends and two cousins loaded in his Suburban and on the way to our cabin in Canmore and a day of helicopter skiing.

That's all fine, except he's a really good skier – my friends and I can barely keep up without breaking something and then Mom gets involved and is all commotion about my supposed fragility.

"It's going to be great!" Dad always says when he plans an excitement for us. Sometimes it is. Sometimes it isn't. He only remembers the times when it is. He doesn't remember the other times. Arguing with him is like fighting a blizzard. You can yell and kick but the snow keeps coming. Dad's "Isn't it going to be great!" is relentless.

He took me to the top of Mount Norquay when I got my first skis. He thought it would be a good experience. "Don't tell Mom." Personally, I think the mountain should be declared an illegal nightmare. It is one steep pitch so long that the lodge at the bottom looks like a Rice Krispie square. And nothing except moguls, ice, and broken legs in between.

Great!

When I got to the bottom I was so mad I wouldn't go in the lodge. I sat outside on a bench by myself and shouted, "Dad's an asshole!" He thinks that's a hilarious story.

Legendary.

I think he saw something when he met Kayden that didn't respond to commotion or legendary. Kayden was polite and listened, but my dad could tell Kayden made his own plans and there was no point in even suggesting he change them. Maybe that was the same no point in asking again realization that the principal had when he asked Kayden to sign up for the sports teams.

Kayden left as the bridge players started to arrive. You'd think he was Steve McQueen the way the baby boomer mommas checked him out.

A lot of the couples in the group had kids my age so they knew me, some so well they thought they could quiz me at the door about how switching from a private school to a public school would affect my career plans. I didn't want to talk about plans I didn't have.

Reese's parents were there. They had never liked me after they caught Reese and me in bed when we were meant to be studying. They were ready to blame me if Reese didn't get an A in Canadian History.

Reese's parents were pleased when I started at Western, away from Reese. They didn't know she was a schemer, and parental disapproval was just one more complication she had to negotiate to get her way. She was going to be a terrific lawyer.

One of the bridge players cancelled at the last minute, and I had to sit in. It would have been awkward if I had to partner either of Reese's parents. They weren't very good players. Knowing them, if we lost it would have been all my fault. I'd grown up with cards and knew what I was doing. All my extended family – who I summarize as my Aunts and Uncles and Cousins – played. Every family gathering ended up in a card game and argument of some sort. I know how to play everything from poker to bridge.

The bridge that evening was ruthless so there wasn't much drinking. Mom was up and down all evening being the hostess. Dad was competitive but polite. In the hands I played against him he treated me like any other player, complimenting me after a hand when I took a trick that surprised him. Best of all, he didn't point out my mistakes. He noticed them and I knew he did. He's naturally positive. I've an uncle who is considered to be inappropriately critical all the time: Dad's brother, my Uncle Spencer. My cousin Aubrey calls him The Mean Uncle.

During the breaks I helped Mom. I wasn't interested in hearing about how well everybody's children were being coached for their futures – they already had professionally written resumes with CEO references.

I didn't want to hear their modest bragging because I didn't want to think about disappointing Mom and Dad who had their hearts set on their expectations for me. I shouldn't have been feeling guilty about that possibility because my marks were always good thanks to Mom being non stop supportive about homework and studying.

There was plenty of boring adult career advice available that evening and I managed to avoid all of it.

While we were cleaning up after the guests left, Mom thanked me for helping out with the bridge. "I wouldn't have asked except I didn't see many school assignments on your desk. I'm worried that Western isn't challenging enough for you."

"I'm studying after school, before you get home."

Dad said he was proud of the way I handled the evening. Very adult! That meant he loved me. He liked being friends with me. Maybe we were becoming Adult Buddies. He has a good way of making up nicknames. Mom is The Jewel. He has a hilarious one for Mom's sister, my Aunt Christine: The Sister Wife. She and her family come with us on Dad's Adventures, mostly so that The Jewel has somebody on her side when Dad comes up with a really dangerous idea.

I know I've been raised well, and I appreciate it. There are some pretty spoiled kids in the neighbourhood who Mom and Dad don't like having over, and don't want me being friends with. Mom says these kids are used to having maids cleaning up after them. She says nobody's taught them how to look after themselves. Dad says it doesn't matter. They're going to inherit money and will always have maids to put their dishes in the dishwasher and pick up their clothes. He laughed his can't hold this back laugh that erupts before he says something pithy, such as: "One day the kids of those maids will be running things. They're the ones learning how to work."

People who don't know better think all Elbow Park kids are spoiled. I don't know if we are. But I know we don't all laugh at kids whose parents can't afford to buy them cool clothes and cars. As if they were stupid for driving a Ford. That is, unless they need a truck driving level of kid for something, the way they need Kayden as a quarterback.

Anyway, I know I'm lucky to have Julia and Rick. She says we live in Camelot. I say we live in Commotion. Mom believes we are living the perfect life and I'm her prince. The Little Prince. Dad gave her a gold ring when I was born. That's me. The Prince who is going to grow up, vanquish the dragon, marry a princess, and be the accounting king of a Gold Ring Realm. Nice to know what the perfect future is, I suppose.

Mom's version of our Camelot film is based on the Kennedy family story. The magic time when JFK was king and before people started getting assassinated. For me, Camelot is about the Holy Grail, which always involves a big Act II adventure/quest. A quest is nice, if you get one and recognize it. I expect it's hard to think of your life as having a mythical quality if you're just going along.

We were all tired so I said goodnight, hugged Mom, and went downstairs. Dad would leave early in the morning. Mom would have breakfast for me, and then she'd drive me to Western if she was heading that way. Otherwise I'd catch the bus. In our neighbourhood, riding the bus to school is stupider than driving a Ford. That got me thinking about Kayden and his pickup truck. Would tall, catch a pass Gerry think Kayden was stupid this year for not signing up for the football team? Probably.

I fell asleep dreaming about The Great Bull Hunters leaving camp. Twenty hide covered huts circle a fire at dusk. On one side of the camp a group of hunters are binding flints to arrows, and sharpening spears and knives.

Amongst the men are three teenage boys and a girl led by Kayle. A fourth boy, Norn, is sitting alone. He's small and looks weak compared to the others. The men begin arguing with the teenagers, glancing constantly towards Norn.

The tallest of the teenage boys leads the others to Norn's side. The older hunters turn their backs on them and walk into the night.

"Stand up," Kayle says to Norn, his voice confident.

Norn, still sitting, looks up. "Aren't you going to hunt with the men?"

"We're going on our own. You're coming with us."

Norn, still sitting, shrugs. "No. The hunters are right. I'm not strong enough."

"Stand up. We're going to the Land of Ground Thunder Running." He offers Norn a spear. Norn stands.

The teenagers push Norn into the darkness. Kayle has already disappeared into the night.

A mother begins to cry. We hear her footsteps racing across the camp. She stops on the edge of the firelight. Her son has crossed the river into the Land of Ground Thunder Running.

I can't write as well in real life as I can in my Palaeo dreams. I wish I could. Writing takes more work than I normally apply to anything. Maybe if I worked at it, I could write as well as I did in that dream. I'm very good at wishful thinking.

The next morning I trudged through my classes, half promising to catch up with friends at the Glencoe after school. Making a few new acquaintances. Noticing the girls.

I smiled my magazine model smile in the hallways and said hi to anybody who looked friendly. Like always, I made sure I was paying attention in class so the teachers would know I was a serious student: maintaining priorities, focussing on my academic goals.

Miss Emily Arbutus asked us to call her Emily during class – although not in the hallway. She wanted Film Studies to be an open discussion, and calling her Emily would help Kayden and me express ourselves. I'd always considered expressing yourself as dangerous because you might express yourself in the wrong way. I assumed there was a list of right ways in the teacher's guide to express yourself, when appropriate. Emily put that assumption in doubt.

Today, Emily asked us why we were taking the class. "We're getting to know each other a little through our discussions. Let's talk about why you signed up for Film Studies."

"For the extra credits," Kayden answered. Obviously nobody had taught him that revealing personal information is a positive way of engaging with others, i.e. building contacts.

"I've been in honours programs for 11 years," I said to reveal details about myself that a teacher would use to build up a personal profile on me. "Now I want to add a new dimension to my studies." That showed I was serious about choosing the right path.

"This isn't an honours course," Emily pointed out.

"Even better," I replied. My closest to honest answer so far.

She asked me how I had got interested in films.

"I think about them all the time. I read reviews. I go to films and rent DVDs. I'm self schooling."

"Good for you," she said with a smile that made me glad I'd signed up. "Tell me what you've learned about screenwriting."

She shouldn't have asked because for the rest of the class I spilled my guts on the Three Act Structure and how I would use it if I were a scriptwriter which I said I wasn't planning on being, so don't ask, okay.

I'd never done that before in a class, just started talking and not caring whether I was saying weird stuff or what marks I'd get. Emily Arbutus and Kayden Montgomery seemed genuinely interested.

I think I provisionally fell in love with Film Studies and Miss Emily Arbutus that day. I swore myself to secrecy on that. Try to imagine what it felt like for me to have a Miss Emily Arbutus actually interested in what I had to say about films. Plus, no career counselling. So not Elbow Park nosy. It was a new experience for me.

I usually passed Kayden a couple of times between classes in the mornings and said hi. He wasn't taking any honours courses so we only had Film Studies together. I still wasn't sure if what he'd told Mom about the ranch and his grandparents was really true. Even if it wasn't, it would make a great Act I opening for a film. I would start the camera panning across the mountains, over a creek and then zooming in on a lone rider: Kayden, trailing home a herd of cattle. Storm clouds on the horizon would hint at a dark shadow approaching. His ma and pa are dead. Car accident? He's alone. Carrying the weight of the ranch on his young shoulders. We glimpse his quest. Save the ranch from approaching evil. Signs of hell coming are hinted at by storm clouds unleashing lightning bolts. The barn doors slam. A banker pulls up in a chauffeur driven limousine. Trouble. Act II has arrived. Will Kayden meet his destiny? Will he pass through the wide open doors and into the electrically charged night?

Kayden introduced me to Stevie in the hallway outside Film Studies. "She signed up this morning."

Stevie shook my hand. She had a grip. And callouses. "I'm going to be a mechanic," she explained when she saw me flinch. "And I like movies. Kayden promised this would be an easy pass. Mostly discussion. Marks for participation."

"If you call them movies you won't pass," I said with a photo smile. "Calling them films says you understand the deeper meaning."

She turned to Kayden. "This is going to be fucking great. A whole semester with a cowboy and a pretty boy."

She gave me an appraising look. She couldn't hide the contradiction of her wide, slanted hazel eyes and her mechanic's handshake. Confusing.

Mom wouldn't have liked Stevie's self confident attitude. It was borderline disrespectful.

"Kayden says you want to write movies. That true?" Stevie asked me.

"Maybe."

"Maybe? Got something better to do?"

"Sure. I'm going to be an accountant."

"Great. I always wanted to meet one. My life's complete."

In class, when Emily asked her what kinds of films she liked, Stevie said, "Porn."

Emily tried to calm our laughter down by being serious. "And what do you like about porn?"

"The deeper meaning."

Say goodbye to my hopes of having informed class discussions. This wasn't going to be film festival sophisticated. I didn't know what it could be, never having experienced a Miss Emily Arbutus before.

After the class, Stevie said she liked Emily. "She's smoky and mysterious."

Kayden nudged me. "Nathan thinks she's got super powers."

Stevie laughed. "I think Pretty Boy wants to be Teacher's Pet."

Emily's homework was one DVD a week. This week she handed out two. We didn't argue. Better than two physics assignments. We got *The Birds;* Hitchcock's black and white film that, of course, Stevie and Kayden didn't know; and *Flipped,* a new independent film directed by Rob Reiner that Emily told us was about eight year olds in love.

"I hope she meant 18 year olds," Stevie said. "Otherwise it's probably kiddie porn and we're getting arrested next week."

"It's supposed to be adorable," I said, reading the cover.

Stevie punched my arm. "Perfect for you!"

In the parking lot she asked Kayden if he was going to the ranch for the weekend.

"Where else? Are you coming?"

"Try and stop me! And I think we should bring The Chosen One. Show him the deeper meaning of ranching."

"Want to come?" Kayden asked. Not much detail to the invite. I didn't care. All that mattered was that Kayden and Stevie wanted me to hang out with them.

"Yeah," I said. "But I can't say for sure until I talk to my parents. They might have plans for me."

"Momma's boy," Stevie said.

"Do you do everything you want?" I said. "Don't your parents care?"

"I'm adopted," she answered. "My parents got no expectations." She pointed across the parking lot. "Gerry's my brother. They had him themselves when it was too late to send me back. He's got all the expectations."

She waved to him. He saw her with Kayden and me and turned away.

"He heard you're not going to quarterback this year," she said to Kayden. "Says you're a loser for letting down the team."

I wondered what it would be like to have people want you to be on their team and then be mad at you if you don't join. In my life, only The Commotion cared.

Mom and Dad were pleased I was going to spend the weekend with Kayden. I didn't mention Stevie. Mom would want to meet her. By then, Mom had done her research on the Rockin' R. She said the weekend would be a learning experience for me. The Three R's, Dad said. “Ridin’. Roundin’ up. Ropin’.” Even better than Billy Crystal’s escapades in *City Slickers.* Dad and I revised a few lines of the *Rawhide* song after we had watched the film:

“Mom’s eyes have started rollin’,

Dad’s ass is gettin’ swollen,”

Even Mom laughed whenever we sang it. We were her boys!

REESE

Reese expected me to come to her 18th birthday party the night before I was going to Longview with Kayden and Stevie.

I don't know why people say Reese reminds them of The Jewel from whom I inherited my blonde curls. Dad says Reese is a dark haired Celtic pixie with a magic wand that controls me. Ha. Ha.

Elbow Park parents organize their children's coming of age parties. And invite parents as well. Everybody shows up and gets involved, mostly by keeping an eye open for unacceptable behaviour, parents' behaviour not included.

Mom said Reese's parents had asked a lawyer friend if serving alcohol was alright even if some of the guests weren't quite 18.

Mom was impressed with the answer. The lawyer said no alcohol could be served without the parents' consent, but – and this is the genius of it – Reese's mom figured out a way around that ... tell the kids if they want to come and drink they have to bring their parents! And, even better, bring their grandparents too.

What's wrong with sidestepping a law or two if the grandparents are involved?

A pink path of ribbons and balloons led guests from the Connelly's driveway to the perfect princess setting by the river: lights, a tent, and a fountain with carnation coloured water.

Mom and Dad dragged me over to say hello to Reese's parents. You'd think public school was an unusual experience, an adventure. Like I had really crossed a line.

"Of course you must already know some of the students there. From your elementary school days."

"I recognize a few from the old cellblock. No murderers or terrorists."

End of conversation. Dismissed. I was about to wander into the crowd to find Reese when Mom grabbed my hand. "Remember. Only two beer."

"Okay."

The first person I recognized was Jed from my grade 11 class. He'd already had his two beer limit. And probably a few more.

"Hey Nathan. Mr. Computer! How's it going, my man? Showing them up at Western?" He was talking about my thanks to Dad computer award last year. My moment of fame.

"Nope. Not taking any computer classes this year. I passed the grade 12 course last year. Mostly math and business this year."

"Gonna be a big time dealmaker like your old man, eh? Goddamn good guy. Took us skiing last year. Goddamn good guy."

Jed handed me an unopened Budweiser from his jacket pocket. "Got this for somebody else. I don't know where she went. It's yours."

Reese found me after Jed wandered off in search of a girl he'd heard about in a low cut dress.

"Want to make out with a mature woman?" Reese asked after she gave me a hug and a wet kiss on my neck.

She leaned back, her arms still around my neck. "Nathan, Nathan, Nathan. Every girl's dream. Blue eyes. Sparkling white teeth and a little boy smile." She twisted a lock of my hair in her fingers. "Are you using that crème rinse I bought you?" She'd had a few drinks. Mrs. Connelly was watching us.

"Listen Reese," I said quietly. "Your mom's giving us the evil eye. We'll hook up later, okay?"

Reese stepped back and shook my hand formally. "We have the rest of our lives." She said it like our script was already written.

It didn't take long before the beer got me going and I began having a good time meeting up with friends from grade 11. Then a couple of private school football players cornered me.

"We heard you're hanging out with Kayden Montgomery at Western. That true?"

"He's in one of my classes."

"We heard you were hanging out with him and Gerry's sister, Stephanie."

"Stephanie?"

"You know … Stevie … the lesbian with the weird eyes."

"Oh. She's in one of my classes too."

"That Kayden's a dick. He walked out on his football team. It's an honour to be on a team and he's pissing on it. And Gerry's sister shouldn't be hanging with him after he jerked over her brother. Gerry could miss his scholarship because of that jackass."

The other guy put his arm over my shoulder as if we were pals. He reeked of weed. "We love you, man. But we gotta warn you. That Kayden's bad news."

They walked away, proud of themselves. I finished the Budweiser and got another. Jed found me again and pushed me toward a laughing crowd of my remember the time friends. Ben. Jeremy. Blake.

We kidded each other about how often we broke the rules and got caught, or didn't get caught. The time we smoked a couple of joints. We had four years of each other's mistakes in common. Four years of good time memories.

Feeling so comfortable with my friends, I almost forgot I was going to Longview the next day. When Blake vomited orange puke into the cotoneaster hedge I went to find Reese. She was tormenting one of the football players. I moved on.

By this time the parents had their own party going in the house. They had started by seriously enjoying the food and appreciating the Connelly's efforts as hosts who didn't scrimp when it came to hiring a caterer and servers. The servers were getting bumped around a bit.

This was becoming a big party. The TV room was a scotch bar, the living room a wine bar, and the master bathroom's bathtub a giant champagne ice bucket. Just help yourself beer for the kids stockpiled in coolers outside.

Mom said the Connellys had invited 200 friends of the family. I guessed the other 100 were Reese's.

The eating that had turned into drinking had turned into dancing when the DJ turned up the volume. Parents were standing on the chairs singing and dancing to the songs. Then came the HSD moments – High Surface Dancing. Countertops. Food spilling. Grandparents line dancing to *Cadillac Ranch.*

"You've got Great Parents!" Jed slurred as he piled meat and cheese on a sandwich. "Goddam great. The Jewel and Rick are partying like they're still in their thirties. Everybody's checking out your mom's ass. I mean dress. Sorry."

"No problem."

"Lucky goddamn you Nathan. You've got it made. They're doing everything for you. Totally made."

Jed set the sandwich down to open a beer. He drank half, pocketed another, and then swayed back into the garden leaving his sandwich behind. He would make a forlorn character in a film. Already a serious drinker.

The school would be gossiping for a week about Reese's 18th. Then it would be somebody else's turn.

I expected The Commotion were already planning my 18th. Mine would be legendary if Dad had his way. Never to be forgotten. He and Mom would love it, the way they loved me. I am their life experience. Their reason. Their everything. And I feel bad knowing I'll be happier for them at my 18th than I will be for myself as I am space shuttled into adulthood. Orbiting Elbow Park ambitions forever.

THE ROCKIN' R

We drove in Kayden's pickup to the Rockin' R. Stevie sat in the middle, her legs straddling the four on the floor gearshift. It was a little sexy. I was probably the only one who thought about it.

Stevie's tough girl persona still intimidated me. But her description of Emily Arbutus as smoky and mysterious made me think there was more to Stevie than I was seeing. I figured that lesbian stuff I'd heard at Reese's party was gossip. Most people would call Emily hot. Stevie's smoky and mysterious says not to rely on your first impression. To me, for sure, Emily symbolized the type of teacher I had been hoping to meet for a long time. That's mysterious. I didn't dare think about the smoky part.

Stevie, I suspected, was in love with Kayden and I don't think he knew it. They were talking about giving his truck a tune up and oil change. "We could buy everything we need and do it ourselves at the ranch one Saturday," she said. "That'd save you some money." Sounded like a date to me.

I didn't know anything about tune ups other than Julia and Rick took their cars to the dealership for servicing every spring and fall. I'd never thought about the people who work on cars. I didn't know any. Now I was sitting beside Stevie who'd be starting an apprentice program next fall. She might be working on our cars.

I looked out the side window while they talked. We passed the abandoned oil fields and refinery outside Turner Valley. Dad had told me his father roughnecked in those fields as a teenager during the Depression, bringing in enough cash to keep the family ranch afloat. Kayden and Stevie could have done physical work like that. They wouldn't be afraid. Their hands already had callouses. They had lots in common. It made me wonder why they had asked me along. I didn't have callouses. Mom gave me manicures.

We turned west toward the Rockies at Longview after stopping to get coffee at the Navaho Mug, the old renovated church that Ian Tyson rents out.

"*Eighteen Inches of Rain,*" Kayden said. "His best song."

Stevie smiled at me. "Cowboys, eh. You wanna get a big hat?" she asked. "Or are you always gonna be a suit and tie man?"

"I don't know."

"Maybe you'll go to Hollywood and write scripts. You'll have to grow a Spielberg beard." She rubbed my cheek. "Smoooth. Very smoooth. What do you think, Kayden? Does he look like he could write scripts?"

"Nathan looks like he can do anything he wants."

That surprised me. Kayden and Stevie looked like they could do anything, not me. "Why do you think I can do anything I want?"

Kayden shifted gears to climb a winding hill. "You're an honours student. You can be an accountant or a screenwriter. You can do anything you want when you graduate. Your parents will back you."

"What if I'm no good at screenwriting? It takes a long time to make a name for yourself."

"Good idea. Quit before you start."

Stevie pretended to reach behind me and I found myself in a headlock. "Don't think so much," she laughed as she added pressure. "You're not even 18. Wait for the ending or I'll twist your head off."

When I didn't answer, she really turned it on and I started to choke.

"All right," I whispered. "I'll wait for the ending."

"Louder."

"I'll wait for the ending!" Whatever that's supposed to mean.

We started to laugh and joke around after that so I didn't take Stevie seriously when she told Kayden to stop at the highway turnoff to the ranch. There was a rusting bridge a few meters ahead.

The lopsided wooden sign on the other side of the Highwood River was more of a warning than an invitation.

Rockin' R Ranch
Est. 1902

It might just as well have said: Play it safe. Stay on the other side.

"This is where we cross the threshold," Stevie said to me, "and into the dangerous world of no cell phone service. No more secret calls to Momma. If you get scared when the thunder booms, you'll have to use the phone in the kitchen – and we'll all listen."

"So make up your mind," she said with enough steel in her voice to scare me a little, the way older kids did when they pushed me into the Glencoe pool when the lifeguard wasn't looking.

"Do you want to leave your whiney pants at home?" she asked. "Can you cross the River of Doom?"

"Check your own pants," I answered.

She ruffled my hair. "Golly, Sesame Street! You're talking back!"

Kayden drove us down a long hill, swerving around most of the mud holes and bouncing Stevie between us.

The ranch wasn't Calgary Stampede romantic. The house was a mobile home with chipped brown paint. We stopped at a metal garden gate, bent and dragging on the ground.

"Grab your bag and I'll introduce you to my grandpa and grandma," Kayden said to me.

They were waiting on the narrow porch. Kayden hugged them, one arm around each. His grandfather was the first to pull away. He reached out to Stevie.

"Good to see you Sweetie," he said. "I've been waiting all week."

Sweetie?

"What's broke down now?" Stevie said putting her arms around him.

"When you're 79 it's all broke down," he answered.

Stevie let him go and said, "You look like you got a lot of warranty left."

"That's because of you kids visiting. That's why you're not doing any mechanicing this weekend. Time to be young."

He was thick shouldered and tall, two sizes larger than Kayden, with short grey hair pushed carelessly aside as if appearances were an inconvenience.

Kayden unwrapped himself from his grandmother. "This is Nathan," he said to them. "He's in one of my classes."

"Call us Grandpa John and Grandma Lillian," his grandfather said reaching out his hand. "That's what everybody on the ranch calls us."

"There's only me and you and Kayden on the ranch," Grandma

Lillian said. "That's your everybody. It's not like we got a lot of hired help."

She was as tall as Kayden and had the same tightly curled dark hair, but had sharp features and black glistening eyes. She looked as old as the rusting tractor and truck in the yard behind us.

"You've got friends who want to help," Stevie said. "Young and strong. You've just got to ask."

"Got ourselves dug deep enough in a hole without bringing in a bunch of know it all kids," she replied.

"If you don't quit that crazy old lady talk," Stevie interrupted, "I'm going to throw you in the creek."

"I can whip your behind little girl," Grandma Lillian replied. "And probably whip this cute fella's too."

She frowned at me, her dark eyes measuring me. "You don't look like you're used to hard work. You're not planning on being a lawyer, are you? We've enough lawyers."

"Nathan's going to be an accountant," Kayden said. "Or a screenwriter."

"Well, we've had a few movie people around Longview making westerns so I suppose there's money in it. What kind of movies do you write?"

"Nothing so far. I'm just thinking about it."

Grandma Lillian gave me a hard, no smile look. "Better get going. Nothing writes itself."

"Welcome to the R n R," Kayden said to me. "Rest and Relaxation."

Grandma Lillian put her hand on my shoulder. "Teasing Kayden's no fun. He doesn't care. So we pick on his friends. Don't take it too hard."

Grandpa John led us into the house. "We'll saddle the horses as soon as you've changed your clothes."

"One room for you and Cutie Pie. One room for Stevie," Grandma Lillian said to us. "That's the rules. No arguing. Catch you in the wrong room and you'll sleep in the barn. Supper's at six so don't go riding too far."

Kayden found me a pair of his outgrown boots and a jacket. He pushed a brown felt hat onto my head. "Let's get ridin'."

Grandpa had four horses in a corral for us. He pointed me towards a sleepy grey. "We'll get you started on Fatso. Stevie can ride Sunshine."

I almost dropped the heavy saddle carrying it out. Grandpa John was patient, showing me how to place the saddle pad on Fatso then swing the saddle up and onto his back.

"Settle it down to where it sits naturally," he said.

Kayden and Stevie were already on their horses by the time Grandpa John boosted me onto Fatso.

"Won't be long before you can get on by yourself," he said slapping my leg softly. "Don't worry," he added guessing my concern. "Kayden or I'll be there to make sure you don't get on backward." Kidding was part of ranching, I figured.

We walked the horses along a trail toward the mountains. I liked Fatso's no hurry attitude. When the others got ahead, Kayden would call back to me. "Get that lazybones moving, Nathan. Trot him up here." The first time I kicked Fatso he just kept walking. So I kicked him again. He trotted.

"Good going Cutie Pie," Stevie said when Fatso pulled up beside Sunshine. "A couple more years of riding and you might let go of the saddle horn long enough for us to get some work out of you."

"Thanks, Sweetie," I said and made her laugh. "How'd you learn to ride?"

"I've worked for the ranch for a couple of summers. I pull wrenches more than I ride, but I've learned to be useful on a horse. And, by the way, if you call me Sweetie again I'll twist your head off."

I ignored that. What I didn't ignore was her 'to be useful' comment. 'Useful' was a way of measuring yourself I hadn't heard before. I knew about accomplishing goals and being coachable. I don't think anybody had ever asked if I was useful.

Everything that afternoon was turning out to be different than I had scripted. I had expected more of a Robert Redford film money setup, not old machinery and sagging corral rails.

Grandpa John showed me how to take the saddle off Fatso and where to put it in the tack room. "If you keep coming here, that saddle and bridle will be your responsibility." He handed me a brush. "Get to work on Fatso's back and girth. Thank him for not bucking off a beginner like you. I'm going inside to help Grandma with dinner."

He tapped my hat down over my eyes. "You're going to be okay."

Kayden and Stevie were waiting for me when I finished brushing Fatso.

"Come with us and we'll show you why we're really here." I

followed them along a dirt road to a new steel arena big enough for community hockey.

Kayden swung open a door. "Have a look at the Rockin' R's future!"

A set of bright white bucking chutes like you see at the Stampede lined the far end.

"Grandpa and I designed all this. We shipped our beef cattle two years ago and used the money to build it. We're going to start selling rodeo bulls next spring."

Stevie patted Kayden on the back the way people do to encourage them to talk. "Tell him everything Mr. Reluctant Star."

"I'm a bull rider. This is my first year of riding professionally. I could have started earlier, but I was playing team sports and didn't want to get hurt." That explained a few things.

"You ever seen a bull close up?" Stevie asked me.

"Just from the grandstand."

"Let's go have a look."

I don't know how many bulls and calves and cows I saw in the pens behind the arena. Dozens. Blacks. Dark greys. Three or four with big Brahman humps.

I was surprised to see the bulls standing quietly together in one pen. I expected them to be separated, so they wouldn't fight. They reminded me of resting gladiators. Russell Crowe, 2000 Oscar for Best Actor. Their horns had been cut to blunt stubs, but left long enough to be weapons. The pen had a sweaty don't mess with us smell.

They stood with their heads down, patient. Snoozing in the autumn sun. A couple swished their long ears half heartedly at me when I rested my hands on the pipe fence. A Brahman with a hump on its shoulders pawed the ground and turned to face me. A string of snot hung from his nose and he slung his head. The snot swung through the rails and landed on my shirt. I could read the body language, the primal challenge, and instinctively backed away from the fence, brushing the snot off me. My response bumped me backward into Kayden.

"You're smart to be scared," he said. "They're unpredictable. Especially him. We call him TwoBlackEyes."

I could feel the bull's challenge lingering in my stomach as we walked back to the house. TwoBlackEyes was more than a confidence building obstacle on a school motivational program. He was my Palaeolithic fear, the controlled panic of a hunter sidestepping the running horns of a Great Bull. Ground Thunder. Aim your spear. Slash and jab. Kill or be killed.

I phoned home from the kitchen before dinner. Mom answered. I told her I was having a good time. I'd ridden a horse. "Yes, I was being careful." I turned my back to the kitchen and whispered. "No, my allergies are fine. Yes, I have my inhaler."

"You know how to play cards?" Grandpa John asked me after we'd cleared the table and washed the dishes.

"Sure."

"Good. Do you know how to play whist?"

"You bet."

"Sweetie only plays if we make her, and that's hard to do. I haven't beaten her in an arm wrestle for a year. So you're going to volunteer to be the fourth tonight – unless you want to test your arm against Sweetie's."

"Got your inhaler?" she asked not even looking up.

"I'll play. Let's draw for partners," I said. I got Grandma Lillian. She was a ruthless card player. Whist looks like a simple trick taking game with not many rules. Once you understand how to count cards and read the signals from your partner's leads and discards, you begin to see the complexity. The cards are dealt out and the dealer plays the first card. The others have to follow suit. If they can't, they can discard or trump. With good players, the 13 tricks are usually split 6 to 7. You can't make mistakes.

Grandma Lillian didn't make mistakes. After a couple of hands she gave me a glance to let me know I was keeping up with her. I liked impressing Grandma Lillian at the card table. I expect she'd heard about my hanging onto the saddle horn riding style.

Kayden was the weak player. Counting cards didn't come naturally to him and he made wrong leads and discards. He and Grandpa John took their loss like good sports, insisting we give them a chance for revenge the next night. People can get personal about cards. My family has had its share of evenings that ended in front doors slamming.

When Stevie heard the score, she stood behind me and put me in a headlock again. "You cheated, didn't you?" she asked as I tried to pull free. "How'd you do it?"

Grandma Lillian wasted no time jumping up from her chair and putting Stevie in a headlock. "Don't hurt the boy's brain," she warned

Stevie. "It's all he's got. Looks don't last forever."

Stevie released me and begged Grandma Lillian to let her go.

"Not until you promise to quit beating up the newcomers."

Stevie promised. She rubbed her neck afterwards. "Jesus, Grandma Lillian, that hurt."

"Good. Now you know why boys are scared of you." She looked at me. "You're not going to cry, are you?"

"No," I answered.

When we were sitting on the couches and armchairs, I asked Grandma Lillian if she knew anything about the Munro Ranch, saying my dad thought it was around Longview. "He heard the family sold it in the 50s when his grandpa wanted to start a drilling company."

"Smart man. I expect he made more money from drilling than he would have from ranching," she said.

"Enough to put his family through university."

"Good for him." She leaned back on the couch and closed her eyes. "Let me think a moment."

When she sat up, she turned to Grandpa John. "Weren't there a couple of Munro boys ahead of us in school?"

"Two. Jack and Alfred. Quite a few years older than us."

"Jack was my dad's father," I said. "He died eight years ago. Alfred was killed in the war."

"I was too young to know where those boys lived," Grandma Lillian said. "Maybe there's an old timer or neighbour around who knew the family. I'll do some checking."

My riding the range film ended that night in a reality TV show. The shower didn't get more than warm. The taps and toilet leaked.

Kayden woke me in the morning. "Grandpa John and Stevie are having breakfast. If we don't hurry they'll leave without us."

"I can't tell if you shaved or not," Stevie said as I sat at the table. She reached over and rubbed my cheek. "Nope. Still an accountant. No sign of scriptwriter stubble."

"Maybe he'll be a bull rider," Grandpa John said. "He did okay on Fatso."

"No," Grandma Lillian said. "He's a good boy. He's not the type to be wiping bull snot off his ass."

Stevie pushed a cup to me. "Have a coffee. You've got a long day ahead of you." Mom recommends I drink decaf. I took the cup, wanting to look manly. Mom didn't have to know.

"What are we doing today?" I asked.

"Kayden, Sweet Stevie and I will be gathering yearlings," Grandpa John answered. "You'll be trying to stay on your horse."

I laughed along with them. Grandma Lillian passed around a plate of sausages and eggs and sat down. No yogurt and fruit smoothies here, I supposed.

"Don't you ruffians get this boy hurt," Grandma Lillian said. "And no goddamn bull riding. His folks will want him home in one piece." She turned to me. "Don't go falling on your head. We got a card game tonight."

Stevie banged her fist on the table. "I knew it. Grandma Lillian's taken a liking to Nathan. I was right. He's a momma's boy. And a granny's boy."

I swear Grandma Lillian blushed a little. "That's nonsense. I know how a mother worries. I don't expect your mother does."

Stevie was quick. "Oh, she worries about me all right. She worries that I'll never get married."

"Don't talk like that Stevie," Grandpa John interrupted. "You're confusing to your mother, that's all. She's old fashioned, I expect."

"I told her I'm not a lesbian."

Then I said something awkward that I regretted right away. "Does that mean I've got a chance?" A dickhead remark.

"For sure. We'd make a glamour couple. We could open a truck stop. I'd fix the diesels and you could fix the books."

Kayden nudged me with his elbow. More than a nudge really. "Handsome guy like you probably has a girlfriend."

"Just one."

"You mean your secret one – Emily Arbutus?"

Sometimes Kayden can be a real conversationalist. I stood up. "Let's get going."

We rode hard all morning. The ranch grazed about 1,000 yearling steers over the summer for feedlot operators, and now it was time to sort them by brands for the operators to pick up. We started by riding south and then pushing steers back north toward the sorting pens. Fatso and I had the job of scrambling through the brush and creeks to keep the leaders moving while everybody else gathered stragglers behind us.

By lunchtime, Grandpa John said we'd found all we could that day. We'd sort what we had after lunch. Tomorrow we'd gather the ones we missed.

We unsaddled and hobbled the horses, and sat on the grass to eat our sandwiches.

"Nice riding, Nathan," Stevie said.

She meant it, so I didn't call her Sweetie. "Thanks."

Of course I knew I wasn't much help. I lay back on the grass. I'd never met people like the ones resting on the grass around me. They accepted the flies and brush and stubborn steers. They did what they had to and got the job done. Their lives were an inspirational documentary reduced to two words: Be Useful.

Grandpa John chose me and Fatso to stand at the back of the pen and drive the yearlings forward into the sorting alleys. He ran the main gate, shouting out the brands to Kayden and Stevie working the gates further along. "Move 'em up again," he'd call to me, and Fatso and I would press the herd ahead.

The sorting went fast. Fatso didn't break a sweat. I got a swollen ass. Rawhide.

"We're done for the day," Grandpa John told us at mid afternoon after he chained the gate closed. "They have enough water and feed for the night. Let's see if we can buck Kayden off a couple of bulls."

A black Dodge welding rig swung into the yard as we unsaddled the horses. Two lightly built cowboys got out and waved to Kayden. They carried heavy canvas bags over their shoulders.

"Head over to the arena," Kayden called to them. "We'll be there in a couple minutes."

After I had brushed Fatso, Grandpa John asked me to go to the house and tell Grandma Lillian things were starting in the arena. "She won't want to miss the fun."

She must have heard the Dodge arrive because she was pulling on her boots when I got there. "I'm expecting to see those slick Jackson twins hit the dirt," she laughed. "They win a couple of buckles and they act like they're world champions. A couple of real show offs."

Grandpa John and Kayden were behind the chutes, opening the gates for the bulls.

Stevie introduced me to Jimmie and Alex Jackson. They shook my hand. "Nice to see we drew a crowd," Jimmie grinned. I couldn't tell the twins apart, other than Jimmie wore a dark blue shirt and Alex wore a blue and white check one.

"Too bad there ain't gonna be much action," Jimmie continued. "These bulls got no experience. We'll ride 'em all. Guaranteed."

Stevie punched Jimmie's arm. "You losers got to start believing in your dream. You need to sign up for some self confidence coaching. Be all you can be."

"When you're as good as Jimmie and me, all you need is bull ropes and spurs. You don't need no self confidence," Alex said.

Stevie's soft slanted, hazel eyes crinkled at the corners. "If you know that, you're a goddamn astute cowboy," she said. "But you should have known we expected you here earlier. We could have got some work out of you. There's a couple of chute gates that need welding."

Grandma Lillian turned to Stevie. "Quit teasing the rod burners. How many bulls is Kayden loading up?"

"Three each."

"Alex and Jimmie can't handle two each. They won't ride three between them."

"Now hold on," Jimmie said. "I don't want to brag or nothing, but I'm 7th and Alex's 8th in the national rankings. I expect we can ride a couple of your beginner bulls no trouble."

"You're all mouth," she replied pulling a $100 bill from her shirt pocket. "Here's the bet. I pay you $33 for every bull you pair ride over three. You pay me $100 if you don't make three between you. Can you figure that out?"

The twins turned away and whispered briefly.

"We got to ride three between us, that right?" Alex asked Grandma Lillian. "Only three out of six. Or we owe you $100?"

"And you pay us $33 for every bull we ride over the three," Jimmie added.

"Good figuring astronauts," Grandma Lillian replied. "Do we have a bet?"

The twins nodded. "Stevie holds the money."

"Not me," Stevie said quickly. "Too complicated. Let Nathan hold everybody's money. He's gonna be an accountant."

Being picked as the accountant at a bull ride felt good. Like being picked as the mascot at a baseball game.

Grandpa John called everybody to the front of the chutes.

"Here's the deal. We're bringing in nine young bulls. We've got them all chute trained, tested with the mechanical dummy and they've been bucked at least once with a rider.

"I'll be in the arena. I'll do my best to get you out of there if you have trouble. And I'll decide if a bull doesn't perform and you deserve a reride.

"Stevie will handle the gate. And you'll pull each other's ropes and take turns spotting when you're getting on. You wear helmets, mouth guards and flak jackets. Everybody okay with that?"

The riders nodded.

"How are we drawing the bulls?" Alex asked.

"We'll use chutes one to three. When the bulls are loaded, you'll draw numbers from my hat. You'll ride the bull in the chute you draw. You'll draw again after each round."

A whiteboard on the wall listed the ranch's bulls. First on the list was "2BlkI's." Clever. He wasn't marked down to be ridden today.

Grandma Lillian and I stood on a protected walkway beside the chutes. Stevie and Grandpa John ran the bulls into the arena alley.

The ground rumbled.

Grandpa John and Stevie chased the first three into the chutes. The bulls kicked and jammed their horns against the clanging steel rails.

"The smart ones get used to waiting. They figure out what's coming," Grandma Lillian said. "Some never stop kicking the crap out of everything."

I could see the riders stretching their legs on the rails as they wrapped leather straps over their boots and ankles, and tightened their spurs. "They've got to have everything tied on solid," Grandma Lillian explained.

They buckled their chaps and began running their gloves fast up and down their ropes. "They're heating up the rosin. It makes the ropes sticky."

Grandpa John held his hat out and they each took out a playing card. Alex got the ace. He'd go first. Kayden the deuce, and Jimmie the trey.

For all their bravado, the twins worked slowly and cautiously as they looped their ropes and bells around their bulls' girths.

When Alex had his rope settled in place, he eased himself onto the bull's back. Kayden stood at his side, pulling the rope tight until Alex was ready to wrap the end into his gloved left hand, his riding hand. Jimmie was the spotter, balancing his brother's upper body between his hands as the bull kicked when Kayden tightened the flank cinch.

"You don't want a rider falling inside the chute," Grandma Lillian said. "These boys may act like they're not scared of anything, but when they're close to the bulls they take good care of themselves."

Alex pulled himself up against his glove, leaned forward and nodded.

Grandpa John released the gate latch and Stevie threw her weight against the long rope attached to the gate. It swung open. The small black bull jumped out, head high.

Alex was straight up when the bull's head came down. He read the next move perfectly, shifting back as the high kick came. Then the bull fooled him, turning to the right and kicking high again before jerking left. Alex got caught off balance. The bull spun and Alex couldn't hold on. His leg swung out, his free hand dropped down, his other spur lost its grip and he was off.

Kayden lasted four seconds and was off over his bull's shoulder.

Jimmie rode his bull right handed, his left hand high. Even I could tell it was an easy ride with the bull bucking straight across the arena.

He got bucked off two grey Brahmans in the next rounds. Alex made both his bulls, giving the twins their three rides. Kayden hadn't ridden any. I was disappointed for him.

"It's a draw," Lillian said to me. "Give those wannabe bull riders their hundred back. And tell everyone there will be No Buck Burgers and beer at the house when they've cleaned up."

I thought the cowboys would be disappointed, only riding three of nine bulls that afternoon. They didn't seem to care. Jimmie was more interested in arguing with Stevie's hazel eyes. Alex and Kayden argued about who had the rankest bull.

"That little black one damn near tore me apart," Alex said. "I knew I was gone when I left the chute. That has to be your best bull. Got to be part Mexican Fighting Bull. I bet he makes the Stampede next year."

"Our Brahman crosses will be better," Kayden argued. "The black is a fast learner. He bucks harder every time. The Brahmans take a couple of times to develop a pattern. That's when they start to shine."

I gave Alex his money and told them about Grandma Lillian's offer of burgers and beer.

"Sounds good," Alex answered.

I had a million questions about bull riding and got most of them answered by Alex who unloaded his duffle bag on the porch to show me his equipment. I thought the spurs would be sharp.

"They're made to grip. Bull's got tough hides. These spurs can only annoy 'em. They can't hurt 'em," Alex said as I ran my thumb over the dull rowels. They were locked and wouldn't spin. That explained how the riders used them to hang on.

He let me try his riding glove and wrapped my hand in the rope. He pretended he was a bull and jerked on my hand. I couldn't hold on.

"You have to lift weights. You can have all the natural balance you want, but you've got to build up your arm."

"Why do you ride left handed and Jimmie right handed?" I asked. "Do you change hands for different bulls?"

"Nope. We're both right handed. Except I just naturally ride left. Same as Kayden."

He made me walk along the edge of the porch. "Put your right hand over your head. Swing it around. Now try your left. Which feels the best in the air?"

"My left."

"Okay. That means you'd ride right handed."

Kayden was watching.

Later, when the No Buck Burgers and beers were finished, Jimmie shook Grandpa John's hand. "Thanks for the practice. Those are tough bulls you've got. Alex and me'll talk them up around the rodeos."

Alex stopped Kayden by the twins' Dodge, lettered on both sides with 'Jackson Brothers Welding.' "You coming to the Claresholm ride next weekend?"

"I'm entered."

"Ride like you did today and you might win a go round."

I couldn't figure that out. Kayden hadn't made 8 seconds on any bull.

I went into the house and asked Grandpa John what Alex meant.

"That's the way Kayden is. He never rides safe. All he thinks about is making the perfect ride. He takes every chance he can to score the perfect 100. It's probably impossible, but that's all he wants.

"At rodeos, he's either one of the high scores, or bucked off. Nothing in between.

"He's happy if there's a few seconds in each ride that are what he calls right. Maybe one day he'll put them all together for 8 seconds of perfection. He believes he can do it."

"Maybe he'll do it at Claresholm," I said. "I'd like to see it."

"Maybe."

I watched Kayden balancing on the edge of the porch. His right arm swaying in the air like a conductor directing an orchestra. His left hand holding a rope. Making music. Kayden music. He had thrown Gerry a long pass right handed. I guess he did everything his own way.

Only halfway through the weekend and I was tired. Grandma Lillian and I barely won at whist. I dozed off on the couch afterwards. Stevie woke me and sent me to bed.

"Nighty night, Pretty Boy."

We scoured the pasture Sunday morning. I looked back once and saw Kayden riding with his right arm up, conducting. That's when I got whipped by a poplar branch that tore fingernail scratches across my neck.

"People will think your girlfriend got too excited," Stevie said when she saw the scratches. "Turn around and I'll do your other side the same. You'll be the envy of the whole school tomorrow."

I ignored her.

We finished sorting by lunchtime.

Grandma Lillian heated two cans of tomato soup and dumped a box of crackers onto a plate with a block of cheddar and a knife. "I'll make toast for anybody who wants it," she offered. We all did. I imagined how Mom would have made a commotion out of having guests for lunch. She'd have driven to the deli and bought cold meats and different kinds of cheeses. She would have served home made soup. Food would have been a discussion.

Grandma Lillian plugged the toaster into an extension cord and ran it over to the table. She ate her soup with us and dealt out the toast slices as they popped up. "Got enough there, Stevie?" she asked holding out a fresh slice as if she were a blackjack dealer. "Or do you want me to hit you again."

"I'll stay," Stevie said. "I'm holding a nine of cheese under my ace of crackers. Beat that!" She always had an answer.

"I made a couple of calls about your Munro folks," Grandma Lillian said to me. "Sounds like they had a bad time ranching. Lucky they got into the drilling business."

"Did you find out where their ranch was?" I asked.

She paused before answering. "It's a coincidence. The west pasture you and Grandpa John will be riding this afternoon – that was their homestead quarter. I called a friend in the Turner Valley library. She looked it up for me in the local records. She said the land got sold a couple of times before we bought it or I would have recognized the name."

"The pasture I'll be riding?"

"That's right. If you keep your eyes open you might find the old foundations. Probably near a creek or a spring."

"What about the rest of their ranch? Dad says they had a lot of land."

"I didn't hear anything about a ranch. Only the homestead quarter. That's all most families had in those days."

"Thank you," I said. "Mom and Dad will go nuts when I tell them I was riding on the Munro Homestead."

"If I find out more I'll let you know."

I think she liked me.

We saddled our horses again and rode into the west pasture. "Freddie Cuthbert always reserves this grass," Grandpa John explained. "He pays extra not to have his heifers run with steers.

"By the end of October, the owners will have hauled everything home or to feedlots. Then the ranch is clear until spring and we can get our bulls ready for the rodeos."

He rode with me while Kayden and Stevie loped further south to find any heifers hiding in the brush. I don't know much about how cowboys ride, but it seemed that Kayden made it look easy with that straight back of his.

Fatso hadn't minded poking along behind the others after we left the barn, and didn't mind my bouncing when he trotted. Kayden told me Fatso had more whoa than go. I wasn't ready to ask for a better horse like Stevie's Sunshine. I was happy to be riding one that would whoa if I fell off and wait for me to get on again.

"You're getting to be helpful," Grandpa John said, holding his horse back to let me catch up. "Your parents should be proud of you."

"I've got try and no talent," I said. "Kayden's got talent. If I could ride bulls and horses like him I'd think I had it made in life."

"Try's good," Grandpa John answered. "Talent's good too. We all got something going for us. What matters is knowing what you want to do, and knowing who can help you."

He had a Jeff Bridges' talking style, the Rooster Cogburn one he used in *True Grit.* Dad says John Wayne's version of Rooster was better. He says everything was better back when he was young. I think he is mostly talking about his reflexes and hair.

Grandpa John turned his horse toward me. I expected he was going to say something I should listen to.

"I want you to ride west until you hit a fence. Then start pushing any heifers you find south until you meet up with Kayden or Stevie. I'll keep moving everything that way from here."

Thanks, Rooster. Very mentoring of you.

I'd never ridden on my own. I looked a question at Grandpa John but he was already trotting away. I doubted if he paid any attention to the fact that I knew about shopping centres and traffic, and not about heifers and the trail home. Mom would have told him to act like a responsible adult and not abandon me. But she wasn't there and I wasn't wearing my whiney pants. I'd crossed the River of Doom.

So there I was. Alone. Riding the old Munro Homestead and not too sure which way was south. I didn't want to get lost and have anybody, especially Stevie, searching for me. And I wasn't going to go trotting after Grandpa John and ask him if I could stay with him.

"Straighten your back," I told myself. "Figure it out. You know you're west of Longview and the mountains are even further west. If you can see the mountains, you'll know which way is west and then you'll know south."

I gave Fatso a kick and sent him up the side of a knoll. There I could see the mountains. Snow on top. A cold September skyline. Alberta blue. I used to think Alberta had to be filmed as screaming Stampede crowds and pumpjacks grinding out barrels of oil money. I'd never thought of a silent soundtrack. The real one.

"We got it sorted, Fatso," I said. "We'll head to the mountains and turn left at the fence. Let's hope we don't find more heifers than we can handle."

I admit I felt satisfied with myself and *Young Guns* picturesque as I cruised along on Fatso wearing Kayden's old boots and chaps and a crumpled felt hat. I was helping out my friends. My new friends. On the Munro Homestead. I was in new territory.

"It's the four of us cowboys today," Grandpa John said when we ran the last of the heifers into the pens. Cowboys! He'd included me.

"We've got a few hours of afternoon left. Let's get Kayden on some more bulls." He paused and looked at me. "Should I load a couple steers for you and Stevie?"

Holy Jesus! What a day. And the best was yet to come because that would be a day I'd remember for eternity. It would be the day I saw Kayden riding TwoBlackEyes. Right hand high. Conducting sky music.

It would be the day I rode my first steer. Or, at least tried to. The day I saw Stevie make 8 seconds on a fast black one.

Grandpa John and Stevie watched as Kayden pulled the rope tight under my black steer's belly and over my gloves. Beginners use both hands. I gripped the handhold as hard as I could while he wound the tail end of the rope over my palms a second time.

For a moment I considered changing my mind. But there was Kayden. Helping me. My first time on a steer. I wasn't going to let him down.

"Lean ahead a bit and pull yourself onto the rope," he said pressing his hand against my back. "He'll probably buck forward and up coming out of the chute. Don't let him throw you back."

"Then what?" I could feel my throat closing. I sounded scared.

He pointed to my boots. "Get your spurs on him."

He gave my helmet a tap. "Ready?"

Stevie smiled at me from the chute gate. She made me feel brave just for trying.

I nodded yes, the way real bull riders do.

Stevie swung open the gate.

I lay on my back beside the chute as never forgotten emergency room fear pounded my chest. I fought until I pulled in a breath and tasted dirt.

"Good ride Nathan," Kayden said pulling me to my feet. "You lasted one jump." They were all laughing.

Grandpa John dusted off my butt with his glove. "The steer turned left and you didn't. You went straight over his head. A perfect somersault."

I undid the snap on my helmet and slid it off. I didn't want them to know how rattled I was.

"You okay?" Stevie asked. "You're pale. Did you get the wind knocked out of you?"

I nodded, bent over and puked.

Kayden rested his arm over my back making me feel even more like a goddamn wimp. He had muscles like a man. I could feel his bicep rolling over my puny shoulder.

When I finished heaving he walked me to the arena boards. "Sit here while we run that steer into a pen."

I settled onto my heels and tried to collect my thoughts. One little jump and I'm off. How fucking embarrassing! And I had puked.

Grandpa John came over. I could see his boots. I had tears in my eyes. I didn't want to look up.

"What do you think, son?"

I clenched my fists hard. "Can I try again?"

He didn't hesitate. "You can try all you want."

By then Kayden had chased my steer into the holding pen and had loaded a steer for Stevie.

She looked like a boy with her long hair tucked under a black helmet, and a flak jacket strapped over her chest. Jeans. Boots. Spurs. Confident. As if she could do any goddamn thing she wanted.

Kayden helped her the way he had helped me. Grandpa John pulled the gate. Her black steer bucked fast, straight and even. No high kicks. She rode him until Grandpa John shouted to let go.

"Time to stand up, Nathan," Kayden called to me after chasing Stevie's steer into the holding pen. "We're running in the bulls. Your turn to help me. Grandpa will stay in the arena in case I get bucked off and start puking. (Big laugh from the rails.) Stevie will pull the gate."

I pushed myself off my heels, using the boards for leverage. My back ached and didn't want to bend. But I forgot about that as soon as I was on the high walkway behind the chute looking down at TwoBlackEyes. If riding my steer was like getting hit by a car, riding this bull would be like colliding with a cement truck. The huge Brahman hump over his shoulder quivered. His shark eyes rolled toward me. Black and psycho. He flicked a horn. He knew he had me scared. His breath pumped furnace hot and sour into the chute. The sticky strings of snot hanging from his nose smelled worse than my puke.

"He might be a good one," Grandpa John said to me through the rails. "He was born with a mean streak. I don't think our Kayden will ride him today."

Kayden flashed his open hands, thumbs folded under. Eight fingers. 8 seconds. "Wait for the ending," he whispered. He fed his braided rope and bell between the chute rails and the bull. He stepped over the top rail and pressed lightly on the bull's back with one boot. "I'm here," he warned the bull. The bull flinched but didn't kick or try to hook back with his horns. He was thinking. I swear.

Kayden eased down until he was sitting on the bull's wide back, balancing his feet on the lower rails as he began taking his first pulls on the rope. I would see him do this hundreds of times. Always the same ritual. Religious almost.

He handed me the tail end of the rope and I pulled until he said to stop. He rubbed his glove on the rope to heat the sticky rosin. Then he adjusted the rope and bell until his handle was slightly to the side of the bull's spine. Where he liked it.

"Another pull," he told me.

Kayden then adjusted the rope a second time. "Again," he said.

I pulled hard, straining my back and legs against the rope. Kayden reached over with his right hand and helped me pull.

Then he wrapped the loose end over his glove, behind his hand and around so he could clench the wrap under his fingers. His bicep bulged. The bull's hump shook.

Kayden nodded. Stevie swung the gate open. The bull balked.

"Spur him!" Grandpa John shouted. "Get him out!"

Black eyed hate glared at Grandpa John.

His first stiff legged jump was up and to the right. He straightened, then jolted left, circling in front of Grandpa John and into Kayden's grip. His hooves hammered the arena dirt. Spinners would always be Kayden's weakness. The hardest for him to ride. The most dangerous.

I watched Kayden and forgot the clock. Him leaning forward as the bull's shoulders rose with each rear. Him transferring all his weight back with each high kick. Always balanced, always straight, countering the centrifugal force of the spin.

I glanced at Grandpa John. He was waiting, ready if Kayden fell into the centre, his hand twisted under the rope. Tangled and tight. Hung up. Dangling inside the spin. Kicked. Dragged. Beaten up.

Kayden rode the spin, spurs grabbing. His free right arm rocking above his shoulder. That was when you could see his marvellous balance and timing. As if he were in control.

"Off!" Grandpa John shouted. "Now!" He stepped forward just as Kayden slid into the spin, his riding hand caught under the taut rope. Hanging him in the air.

Grandpa John slapped his hat at the bull and straightened him.

Kayden rolled his hand free and dropped to his feet. Unconcerned. Like he was stepping off the porch.

TwoBlackEyes turned and pawed the ground. Head down. Challenging Kayden. Grandpa John waved his hat again. The bull turned and trotted to the end of the arena.

"I could have spurred him harder," Kayden said.

"He won't be so easy next time," Grandpa John said. "He's just started to figure this out. He never made those stiff legged bucks before."

My hands were shaking and sweaty with adrenalin and stress. Puke rolled up my throat again. I clenched it down.

I knew that moment I wanted to be a Great Bull Hunter like Kayden. I wanted to live that way. The Palaeolithic life. I wanted to be a man not a boy. I didn't want to puke again.

When I think back to that Kayden moment, I knew that was when I made a choice I could never go back on. It would be the day I chose to become a hunter in the Land of Ground Thunder Running – the 10,000 years ago side of my life.

I got on two more steers that afternoon and got bucked off both. I didn't care. Kayden got on three more bulls. He rode one. One didn't buck. One bucked him off. Stevie rode two more steers. Easily.

"I hope your mom won't be upset when she sees your bruises and scratches," Grandma Lillian said to me as we were packing the truck to drive back to Calgary.

"I won't tell her about the bruises," I answered.

She looked at me straight on. "That's your business."

I phoned Mom and Dad to say I was on my way home. I'd forgotten that Sunday night meant we were having The Aunts and Uncles and Cousins over for dinner. She reminded me and, from the background noise, I could tell they had started to arrive.

"Kayden is ready to leave. I'll be there in an hour," I promised. I'd thought she'd be mad at me for being late but she wasn't. "I only put the roast in a few minutes ago," she said. "We'll wait. We're dying to hear about your ranch weekend. Would Kayden like to eat with us?"

Typical Mom. Invite everybody. Open House.

"We smell like ranch," I answered. "We haven't changed or showered. And there's somebody else with us. Stevie."

"Invite him too. The Cousins will want to meet some cowboys. Got to go. See you in an hour." She hung up.

"You're invited for dinner," I told Kayden and Stevie.

"Accept it," Grandma Lillian told them. "From the look of Nathan's pudgy stomach his mother must be a good cook."

"I don't know," Grandpa John said giving her shoulder a warm rub. "It would be hard to beat your tomato soup."

"Don't complain," she warned him, "or you'll be opening your own tins."

They shook my hand goodbye. "Come again." I knew they meant it.

"There's something I need to ask you," I said at the last minute. "My mom may phone you. She likes to know everybody I know."

Stevie smiled and I expected her to say something about me being a momma's boy. She batted her eyelashes innocently at me. I tried to ignore her.

"If she calls," I said avoiding Stevie's eyes, "please don't tell her about me riding the steers. Or trying to. Or puking. She'll worry."

"I guess we can keep that to ourselves," Grandpa John agreed. "I'm sure we'd worry if we knew everything that Kayden got up to in the city."

"You should worry about Kayden," Stevie said. "He's signed up for Movie Club. We're a wild bunch."

"It's Film Studies," I corrected. "not Movie Club. Part of the Drama curriculum with credits. It's a discussion class."

"Right. Real serious. The deeper meaning," Stevie said with feigned seriousness. "None of us can figure life out for ourselves so we're supposed to get the answers from Walt goddamn Disney."

"Out," Grandma Lillian ordered as she pushed us through the door. "Drive safely."

I could hardly stay awake on the drive home. Once I slumped against

Stevie and she elbowed me. "What's wrong with you?" she asked. "You sure get tired easy."

I didn't answer. No point in talking about something you can't do anything about.

Mom was watching for us from the window and opened the front door as we parked.

She swallowed a gulp of shocked air when she saw the scratches on my neck. "Who did this to you?"

"Could have been worse," Stevie said, her girl voice coming from under her felt hat. "Pretty Boy here was getting high school flirty so I gave him a little taste of what happens when a real woman takes control. You ought to see his back."

The chatter in the living room quit. Stevie's ad lib humour had caught Mom off guard. She was looking at ready for anything Stevie as if she were seeing Hilary Swank boxing in *Million Dollar Baby.* Not that Mom would ever watch that movie.

"Hi, folks," Stevie said taking off her hat. Her dark hair spilled over her shoulders. "I'm Stevie. This hunk of cowboy is Kayden. As soon as we get our boots off and Nathan's mom quits guarding the hallway, we'll say hello properly."

The only ones smiling were my cousin Aubrey and Uncle Spencer.

"And I'm Nathan," I said introducing myself to break the tension. "And no, these aren't fingernail scratches. I just rode too close to a poplar branch. My fashion future is not in jeopardy. No scars. Mom can breathe again."

Everybody relaxed. I was good at that. Making people feel comfortable.

"Don't worry about me," I told Mom. "I'm okay. It happened yesterday. Grandma Lillian had a look and said not to worry."

"Grandma Lillian?" she asked as if I'd been prescribed hog fat and chicken brains.

"Kayden's grandmother. She said she's seen worse."

I could tell my mom was torn between pulling me into the bathroom to inspect my back for fingernail scratches, and getting in on the introductions.

By then Dad had introduced himself and was taking Stevie and Kayden on The Family Tour. You're not allowed to be quiet or shy in my family, and Stevie felt right at home. Kayden, as usual, answered questions politely without offering more information than necessary. The family were fascinated and that meant endless questions. They'd met cowboys at the Stampede, and even knew a few of the chuckwagon drivers. But a bull rider! This was forget Jewel's dinner exciting.

"I thought you were going to university?" Mom asked Kayden, as if he'd lied to her.

"If I get in," he answered. Not a Munro concern. We always get in.

Everybody wanted to know all about rodeos, and wished him luck when he said he would be riding at Claresholm next Saturday. They'd go to watch, they said, except they already had plans. They weren't making up excuses. In the Munro family, every weekend is planned a month ahead. Relaxing needs to be scheduled – sports, card tournaments, concerts, Europe, anniversaries, weddings. Endless ways of cramming too much life into not enough time.

I'm an anomaly in my family, sports wise. They were born being good at everything they tried. They didn't hardly have to try. They didn't know average. For me, being average is lookin' good. I warmed the bench for every team I tried out for. Mom and Dad signed me up for lessons in any sport they thought I had a chance.

Naturally, the Munros fell in love with smart talking hazel eyed Stevie and hard muscled Kayden. Aubrey couldn't take her eyes off him. Mom noticed that. And she noticed the way Stevie didn't give a damn about anything, swearing and not concerned about her arena dirty jeans. Looking neck scratching sexy. So appealing. So not appropriate. So dangerous. So not for me.

"No discounts," Stevie was telling Uncle Spencer. "You bring me your car next week and I'll check it over. You look like you got money. What are you? A lawyer? You can afford to pay."

Uncle Spencer laughed that shoulder shaking way of his. "I'm an accountant." The giveaway about understanding Uncle Spencer is his hands. They're wide, as if he should be six foot two instead of five foot ten, and loose on his wrists. They're hands that suit somebody with fast reflexes, as if they could grab a line drive out of mid air. That's Uncle Spencer. Loose limbed agile and as fast on his feet as he is at turning your emotions upside down with a biting remark. An accountant with attitude.

"Jesus Christ," Stevie said. "I'm at a directors' meeting. A couple of accountants and Nathan the wannabe accountant. Even Kayden says he might give up bull riding and go to business school. Is anybody irresponsible around here?"

Then she floored them. "You sound like you could be best ever neighbourhood friends with my family. They live around the corner. The Alberts."

Mom was right onto that. "The Bill and Anne Alberts? The ones on 40th Avenue?"

"That's them."

"Of course we know them. Doesn't your brother Gerry go to Western? I think he plays football."

"Got that right. Kayden knows him. Kayden was the quarterback last year."

"Now I understand," Mom said slowly. "You're Stephanie Albert."

"That's me. The bad influence. And no, I'm not a lesbian. I'm a regular horny teenage girl stuck with a bunch of high school boys who think first base is a safe hit."

Another speechless moment. Stevie was the only person my age I'd seen stop my Mom – and she did it twice. Aubrey laughed.

Dad helped Mom out by asking Kayden if he planned to play football this year.

"No sir," he answered. "I'm not a great student and I've got to focus on my classes while I'm at school."

"Well, good for you," Dad said. "Playing football won't get you as far as a degree. You should be proud of your choice. And I wish you'd quit calling me Mr. Munro. Call me Uncle Rick like all of Nathan's friends. I've got some influence with the business school. Let me know if you need somebody to put in a good word for you."

Mom chose Uncle Spencer to carve the roast. Aubrey eased over to Kayden.

"Most guys would give their right arm for a football scholarship," she said squeezing his right bicep. That little straight smile of hers curled at the corners.

"I'm going into Kinesiology next year on a soccer scholarship," she told him. "You must be good at football. That would get you in."

"Lots of competition, and I can't take that chance. I've got to get accepted on my grades. Besides, they'd expect me to play if I got in and

I doubt if I could keep up with the classes. Then I'd be out."

"What about your bull riding?"

"I just like to see how well I can ride the toughest bulls."

"That doesn't make sense. Don't you want to win?"

"Come to the ranch one afternoon with us. Then you might understand."

I felt awkward eavesdropping on their conversation, but not enough to move further away before I heard how this worked out. They looked good together. His dark curls, her straight smile and no dress up style ponytail. Any modeling agency would sign them just on their photos. I doubt if either of them would bother applying.

Aubrey glanced from Kayden to Stevie. "Did you know Nathan has a manager? Her name's Reese. She calls herself his girlfriend." Very oblique, I thought. "Are you and Stevie hooked up? She's got great eyes." Direct.

"No," Kayden answered. "We've been hanging out together since grade ten. She fixes Grandpa's machinery on weekends and makes Grandma laugh."

"What about Nathan? Why do you hang out with him?"

"He's in Movie Club with us."

I saw my cousin's cute straight smile lifting again at the corners. "Movie Club?"

Nobody takes me seriously about films. I kept listening, afraid Kayden might mention my dream of becoming a scriptwriter. He didn't. He never says anything unnecessary. He didn't even ask Aubrey about my manager, Reese.

When we sat down to eat, Aubrey couldn't hold back. As expected. "So I've been trying to figure out what you three late arrivals have in common besides your smell. It can't be riding bulls. Nathan wouldn't last an eighth of a second. Not repairing cars. Nathan is more of a computer frail. What could it be?"

She looked around the table. "Can anybody guess?" Nobody answered.

"They're all in Movie Club!"

Boy, did she ever think she was stand up. And so did everybody else, including Kayden and Stevie.

"It's Film Studies," I shot back. "It's part of the Drama Curriculum."

"Didn't we agree you were going to enrol in a drama class to develop your acting skills?" Mom interrupted.

"The rehearsals would take up too much time," I answered casually, as if switching classes was nothing to talk about.

Dad, who can't resist an opportunity for stand up, slipped into his Jimmy Stewart impression, giving Mom his best 'I Love You' line:

"Go easy on the lipstick, 'cause you're gonna get kissed." When she smiled I thought there was a chance I wouldn't have to talk about drama class again.

Then Aubrey got a laugh from Kayden with her hands on hips John Wayne impression: "Talk low, talk slow, and don't say too much." Kayden liked it. She liked him.

All very amusing. When the fun wore out, I told them about the Munro homestead. I can be very entertaining, especially when I have a story to tell. This was a good one and I built it up starting with my ride on Fatso. I described – embellished a bit – how riding through the brush and meadows made me feel like I had been there before. Déjà vu.

Dad could barely control his excitement. "I knew it!" he said pounding his hands on the table like a demented A.D.D. kid.

"I knew it all along. Fantastic!"

I suspect in the back of his mind he had always wondered if the Munro ranch had really existed.

"Nathan's great grandfather made and lost a fortune after he sold that ranch," he told Kayden and Stevie.

The rest of us knew this saga front to back. It would be rewritten tonight.

"Old Bill Munro bet everything he owned or could borrow on the drilling business. People said he was crazy. That was the start of the Turner Valley oil boom. The first big one in Alberta and he was right there in the middle of it.

"Then the boom crashed. Bill died almost broke. My dad Jack had to start over. He got it all back and more in the 50s with another drilling company. But he was a gambler, a wildcatter. He put his own money into the wells. He was a helluva driller but he didn't know anything about hanging onto his money. If it hadn't been for my mom's store, none of us would have gone to university. That was her dream for us."

He reached over and rubbed me on the shoulder. "And that's my dream for you Nathan. University. A career."

Apparently I was not a wildcatter. Could I be a Great Bull Hunter? That would surprise him.

Whenever Dad gave me his "This is my dream for you son," lecture I listened politely, knowing that he was really just a Munro gambler, even if he was a chartered accountant. I'd heard him tell his friends about how he'd got a call in the mid 90s from a start up company named Netscape. They had this idea for the first web browser and needed his help. When my dad says his dad was a gambler, I feel like reminding him an Internet start up is a gamble, especially if you have a ten year old boy named Nathan to support. Mom and I didn't see him much back then. It was like he disappeared. I pretended he was Superman trapped in Netscape's kryptonite cave.

Dad made a ton of money wildcatting with Netscape. They owned 90 per cent of the browser market until Microsoft launched Internet Explorer. Dad escaped the kryptonite cave with a boxcar of money. Before Google showed up.

Mom wasn't satisfied with only hearing about the homestead. In her mind, the Munros had always lived there, and it was time for her to renew old acquaintances.

She started questioning Kayden again about his grandparents and the ranch. This had commotion potential. She was going to get involved.

"Do you think they'd let us have a family picnic on the homestead?" she asked Kayden.

"Probably," he answered.

Mom didn't push it. Grandpa John would get a phone call tomorrow. She likes to get her own way especially when she can say it's for the good of the family.

I started coughing and was trying my best to pretend I only needed a glass of water.

All I could think was, "Not now. Please, not now."

Mom took control, rushing round the table and leaning over my chair to rub my chest and back. I heard her whispering to Dad, "Call the ambulance."

"No!" I said. "I'll be fine."

"Let us know if you want help," Dad said.

Mom kept rubbing my back. I flinched as she pressed on one of my worst bruises, and she stopped abruptly. Probably suspecting fingernail scratches.

Stevie didn't miss it, and kidded me. "Got a sore back Nathan? I wonder how that happened."

"Don't worry about me," I said to Mom, and changing the topic. "I'll be fine in a couple of minutes."

Anxious Mom started explaining for the hundred thousandth time how her Camelot Prince had been born healthy but had started to lose weight. Didn't eat. Doctors. Hospitals. Nobody knew why. Mom had the story down pat. She never gave up until her research pointed to Kawasaki Disease. Whoever heard of that? A children's disease that attacks the heart. Very rare. Usually in Asian families. Definitely no Asian blood in the Munros. She found the right doctor for me. Then my respiratory problems started. Asthma. Pneumonia. Allergies. Pulmonary edema.

Mom teared up at the table, the way she can when she talks about how much she worries. "We always have to be so careful with Nathan."

Maybe my broken lungs would kill me one day. I could accept that. I just didn't want my parents to worry about it. That's what I always thought when I got the coughs. The Commotion won't sleep tonight. Because of me.

I did what I had to do. I sat up like a man and smiled. "See, Mom. I'm better. It's over."

It was humiliating though, to sit a table and be the only wimp. To know you are weak and your parents stay awake at night worrying.

"Jesus, Nathan. I thought you were going to croak," Stevie said. "And your mom hasn't even served the blueberry pie. That would have been disappointing. Try playing that sympathy card one more time and I'll have to take you down again."

Mom glared at her. Joking about my health was inappropriate.

"That's right, Stevie," Uncle Spencer said. "I had my heart set on pie too. You almost screwed up this evening for us, Nathan. Don't do it again. Try to be more perfect. Or there will be consequences."

Mom didn't think Uncle Spencer was funny either.

I could tell he liked Stevie. He probably sensed that she was as tough as him, but in a nicer way. You didn't want to be a screw up around either of them. You'd hear about it.

Kayden and Stevie offered to help with the dishes before they left. Mom refused and guided them through the front door, easing Kayden past Aubrey who didn't miss the chance to give him a look that said call me. No mistaking it.

Mom cornered Aubrey by the door. "Don't get any ideas," she warned her. "Those two may look like fun, but you deserve a better life than they're going to have."

Aubrey shrugged. "He's a bull rider. How sexy is that? And that Stevie ... those eyes give me impure thoughts starting with a kiss."

"Quit it! I won't have talk like that in my house. Think of your future. Your reputation."

Aubrey glanced at me for support. I backed down. I knew Mom wasn't warning Aubrey about Kayden. She was warning me about Stevie. Unnecessary, because Stevie wouldn't be interested in a Pretty Boy like me.

The Aunts, Uncles and Cousins left after the dishes were done. Uncle Spencer was the last to leave. "Don't forget our golf game Saturday afternoon," he said to me. "I've got a tee time booked. I'll call you Friday."

I'd forgotten about it and was planning to go to Claresholm Saturday to watch the bull riding. It didn't start until the evening. I could make it after golf if I could get somebody to drive me.

"You bet, Uncle Spencer. I'll be ready."

"Good. We'll make a day of. Maybe we'll go for a steak afterwards. What do you think?"

He didn't miss much. He knew what I wanted to do. He might be the smartest persona reader I know.

I locked the bathroom door and was showering my scratches and bruises before my parents could pester me with questions. I didn't want to spoil Dad's imaginary rambling log homestead with white fences and horses grazing over green pastures and a creek of lazy trout. I didn't want to spoil Mom's imaginary close personal relationship with Grandpa John and Grandma Lillian. I didn't want her telling them her worries about me.

I wanted the Rockin' R for myself, with its weathered trailer, leaky plumbing, and falling down fences. A place where I was strong. I wanted TwoBlackEyes to breathe hot on me. I wanted to stare down his shark eyes. I wanted the bull riding arena to be where I lived. I wanted to hunt bulls with Kayden and Stevie and Jimmie and Alex. I wanted to play whist with Grandma Lillian. I wanted to ride horses with Grandpa John. I wanted to write screenplays. I wanted to watch Johnny Depp films with Emily Arbutus.

I wanted my Palaeolithic life.

I didn't want to worry about The Commotion's pain if my lungs said goodbye. So I went to bed.

The next morning Dad had a big grin as he watched me eat my cereal. "You'd better keep your shirt on around the house," he said. "And I'd stay away from Reese for a while if I were you."

WILLIE

Nobody knew much about Willie except that he lived with a foster family, and ate leftovers from trays in the cafeteria. He was scrawny and pale and tall and probably cut his own red hair. The rumour I heard was that his parents had been drug dealers, probably bikers. All that would have been barely noticed if it hadn't been for his undeservedly cheerful half dancing gangly walk punctuated by shuffles skips and dips.

Willie, probably the least Elbow Park kid in the school, had joined Movie Club a few days after Stevie. He was good at film facts and quick to supply them. He must have had a memory chip in his brain.

"This is a discussion class," Emily would tell him. "You can't give us film facts all the time. You have to participate."

I had begun to notice Emily was letting us direct our discussions ourselves. She didn't seem to care if we tore apart Hollywood blockbusters. I guess with only four students in the class she was taking the provisional aspect of the course for granted and not worrying about directing our critical attention to the curriculum genres. The film festival winners bored us.

Stevie and I had been doing almost all the discussing up until Willie joined the class, and it didn't look like that was going to change. Whenever I made what I considered an insightful point about a film Stevie would tell me she thought everything I said that was serious was really bullshit. She kept telling me I was making up life, not experiencing it. "Until that happens, you'll just be a bullshit guy."

That was when she was being easy on me. "You're a Pretty Boy," she would tell me other times. "Life's easy for you. The only trouble you know about is running over your parents' credit card limit. You need to get your ass kicked a few times before you can talk about how movies reflect life."

That dagger went deep, and she wasn't finished.

"Remember the scene in *Get Shorty* where Chili Palmer beats up Bear, the stuntman turned bodyguard?"

"A little," I said. "Isn't that the one where mobsters think they can make movies?"

"1995," Willie offered, "based on an Elmore Leonard novel. Starring John Travolta as Chili Palmer, a film aficionado loan shark, and Gene Hackman as Harry Zimm, a B movie producer/director."

"Thanks for the facts, Willie," Stevie said. Then back to me: "Remember when Chili tells Bear he can do a lot better for himself than working for a loser mobster?"

"I remember," I said.

"Then think about the praise Chili then gives to Bear: 'You were a stuntman. What's Bo ever done that he can talk about?' And that goes for you, too, Nathan. What have you ever done you can talk about?"

She kept the pressure of her slanted hazel eyes on me.

"I'm thinking," I replied.

"Don't think. Do something you can talk about."

She really knew where to stick in her dagger.

Emily interrupted. "Stevie's got a good insight into this film. She's saying there are two types of characters: the ones like Chili Palmer who can live up to their claims, and the ones like Harry Zimm who only pretend to be as tough and self confident as Chili."

The class discussions went on like that and we got used to Willie's encyclopaedic memory for film details, and the way he would walk his cheerful half dance with us to the parking lot after class.

The first time Willie said anything that wasn't fact related was the day Stevie showed up for Movie Club with a purple bruise turning black under her right eye.

"Don't ask," she said as we waited for the class to start.

I half expected Emily would feel it was her duty as a teacher to find out what had happened to Stevie. But all she did was glance at her once and then begin the class as if everything were okay. I could tell she had decided it was none of her business. She knew Kayden, Willie, Stevie and I were friends and that we would take care of this. It was our business.

Emily was right, but she probably wouldn't have guessed Willie would be the one who knew what to say.

"Stevie should tell Kayden and Nathan who hit her," he said to none of us in particular when we stopped by Kayden's truck in the parking lot after class. "She can trust them. They're her friends. It's wrong to give people black eyes."

He turned and walked back to the school.

Tears dripped onto Stevie's cheeks. "Goddamn that weirdo," she said.

We waited.

"Okay," she said back in her tough girl persona. "I'll tell you what happened. But don't go telling anybody else or you'll be wearing one too.

"After Kayden dropped me off Sunday night my mother started to yell at me about the ranch clothes I'd worn to Nathan's. She was drinking. Nathan's mom had phoned her to make sure I got home safely. It was well intentioned but a bad idea not knowing my circumstances. That's how my mother knew where I had been. She said I had embarrassed our family by going to Nathan's house dressed like a cowboy.

"I told her my life was my own. And a few other things. Then she hit me." Stevie rubbed her tears onto her sleeve. "It's all screwed up now. I'm supposed to phone Nathan's mom and apologize."

I wanted to help her but if I took her home with me, who knows how The Commotion might interfere. Dad might call the police. Mom might feel it was her responsibility as a concerned parent to phone Stevie's mom again and get the family into counselling.

"Don't worry," Stevie said, guessing my thoughts. "My mom usually passes out for a few days after something like this. Then she'll be good for a month. I'll find Gerry and go home with him. His car's still in the parking lot. I'll wait for him there."

Kayden drove off and I walked home. I unlocked the door and went straight downstairs to my room. It was hard to figure out what had happened to Stevie. You see films about this sort of bad stuff, but you don't break apart inside watching a film the way I was breaking apart for Stevie. Willie was right. It's wrong to give people black eyes. I suspect he'd got a few.

Stevie was right, too, about me. I'm a bullshit guy. What have I ever done to talk about? Lots, but only if you count the stuff my parents were involved in. What had I done for myself that I was proud of? Just for me? Nothing.

"I'm going to ride a bull," I promised myself. It wasn't a surprise.

I'd been thinking about it since I'd seen Kayden and the Jacksons riding. It wasn't so much the riding, though. It was more that I wanted to test myself. To see if I was really a Momma's Boy, or if I could do something worth talking about. I was tired of being told what I could and couldn't do. If I could ride a bull, I could do anything. Nothing and nobody could stop me after that.

Mom came home and said Dad would be working late. She said she had enjoyed meeting Kayden and Stevie. "And it is so exciting about the Munro Homestead. Imagine that. You were riding there."

She gave me a tight hug. She stepped back when she felt me pull away but still held my hands while looking into my eyes. "Is everything okay? You've been distant lately. Are you feeling tired? Was the ranch too much for you? Do you think you had an allergic reaction?"

"I'm fine," I said, which is what she wanted to hear. Not that I'd decided to become a bull rider.

She stroked my cheek softly. "I've got a sales seminar to prepare. I'll be done by dinner. See you then."

"Wait a minute," I said before she got to the door. "You might get a call from Stevie. Her mother was upset after you phoned her. You must have made a comment about Stevie wearing ranch clothes to our house. Stevie has to apologize."

"Mothers want to know how their children present themselves to other people. Stevie could be attractive if she tried. Mothers are responsible for their children's behaviour."

"Except Stevie's not a child."

"Yes, she is."

That made me one too.

The entire school knew Stevie shared a cafeteria pizza with Willie the next day. A whole pizza.

"Willie's a math whiz," she told me in the hallway. "The principal is recommending him for Harvard."

"Did Willie actually talk to you?"

"We had quite a conversation about the deeper meaning in films. He agrees with me. Waste of time."

"What's he watch?"

"Same as me. Porn. We're going to ask Emily to bring in *Deep Throat* starring Linda Lovelace. It's a classic. Great cultural commentary. It revolutionized the porn industry. Loaded with social context. Medium quality camera work."

"You're making all this up, aren't you?"

"Doesn't matter. It sounds pretentious enough to be credible. People love hearing it and repeating it later."

She dropped her see through you persona for a moment. "It's kind of cool," she said, "the way Willie is so genius and he talks to me as if I were too."

How Emily handled their presentation impressed me. She must have known that everything they said was reworked intellectual nonsense. She could see the irony in what they were doing, and she went along with them, taking their proposal seriously.

"This is an open discussion class," she reminded Willie and Stevie. "You researched the topic and presented solid reasons why this film deserves to be considered." She asked us for a show of hands on *Deep Throat,* for and against. All for.

"Okay. I'll have to let the principal know the list has been changed."

"Where can we get the film?" Willie asked.

Surprise. Emily had a copy in her home library.

Emily moved higher in our estimation when we glimpsed her ivory thighs as she slipped into the passenger seat of a tinted window Porsche in the teacher's parking lot.

Willie grinned. "Miss Emily Arbutus has a hot date! A 911 Carrera. Easy hundred grand. Flat six engine. Pumps out 315 horsepower at 6800 rpm." Willie started strutting like a tough guy.

"Teacher is gonna get some extracurricular!"

"Smoky and Mysterious," Stevie said.

When I saw those secret power grown up thighs, I couldn't help hoping the Porsche would run out of gas. Soon.

I offered to let Stevie move into our house that evening after her mother kept drinking. When I told Mom about Stevie coming to stay with us, she wanted an explanation and pried unsuccessfully on my conscience a bit.

"If Stevie wants advice, she'll let you know," I told her. "And please don't make any more phone calls."

"Not your business," Stevie said when Mom met her at the door. I didn't know if Stevie's mind your own business no questions greeting or her black eye surprised Mom the most. Whichever it was, it worked because she never dared to ask anything.

Dad had probably seen enough shiners in his day to know that this one didn't need a lot of attention or discussion. Maybe a little kidding around. He saved that for me.

"Don't run into any more branches," Dad said to me with dramatic seriousness before I went to bed. "Any more scratches in the morning and Mom will get suspicious."

Ha ha.

Gerry phoned Friday to tell me Stevie could come home: their mother had sobered up and was sorry.

I phoned Uncle Spencer and arranged to meet him at noon Saturday, play 18 holes and then go to Claresholm for a steak dinner and Kayden's bull riding. When I told him Stevie and Willie wanted to come, he offered to pick them up after we golfed.

Mom says Uncle Spencer is a hard marker. He doesn't give anybody an easy pass and doesn't believe in participation ribbons. That doesn't make him popular with parents. But I like him because you always know where you stand.

I expected to get an earful from him on Saturday about my golf swing that never improves, and then two earfuls when he met Willie. Willie may be a math whiz kid but, bottom line, he's a misfit. Uncle Spencer has no time for misfits of any sort, except me and I don't know why.

The only way I could see the Claresholm evening working out would be if: Willie would talk normal in the car; Kayden rode at least one bull; and Stevie's black eye didn't get discussed. It was probably too much to hope for.

I waited on the sidewalk in my golf clothes Saturday morning, knowing Uncle Spencer would appreciate that. He was always on time. Once he had to come in the house and wake me. That was an unforgivable start to the day.

He clicked open the trunk of his BMW and I loaded my clubs beside his. I threw in a day bag with a pair of jeans and a cowboy shirt for the bull riding.

Uncle Spencer is annoyingly competitive. He has a cupboard full of trophies that he never looks at. Bridge trophies. Ski trophies. Golf trophies. I have one computer trophy. He can focus his mind so hard it hurts just to be around him. He doesn't have coughing fits.

On the golf course he gets impatient with slower players and that puts him off his game and that makes him more impatient and then he plays even worse and by the end of the round he acts like he wishes he'd never picked up a golf club. I've played with some of Dad's friends and they're long past the age of caring. Golf is a long walk to them. Their scores never get better and they don't care. They joke about them. Uncle Spencer doesn't joke about golf or bridge. I'm not sure why he invites me to golf with him.

"Let's not keep score today," he suggested.

Yikes. Uncle Spencer not keeping score?

"We'll only keep track of our good shots. Whoever has the most good shots is the winner. Bad shots don't count."

His first drive went straight down the fairway. "That felt good. I'll take it," he said. "Now your turn."

My first shot went straight but about half as far as his.

"Not bad," he said. "What do you think?"

"I can do better."

"Fucking right," he said as we started up the fairway.

I made a great putt from the fringe on that hole. "Count it," Uncle Spencer called to me. "We each have one good shot so far."

My next drive was right up beside his. He laughed. "Now all you have to do is repeat that swing 70 or so more times and you'll be going around in par."

He sounded like Grandpa John telling me about how Kayden only had to connect all his right moves in one ride – 8 seconds of doing everything right. 70 good golf strokes in a row. That's all it takes. Good luck doing that, Nathan. In anything.

Par is the nirvana goal line to Uncle Spencer. Shooting better than par permits you to be inexplicably peaceful until the next round.

Occasionally over the next holes Uncle Spencer made a suggestion that might improve my swing. He wasn't bossing me around or being parental. It was like he was helping a friend. I felt grown up. I couldn't help wondering why he was treating me this way.

"You did a lot of things right today," he said as we changed in the clubhouse. "And you screwed up a few things. It was good to see your right ones."

"You helped me," I said. "I'm focussing better."

"Focus is paying attention to your situation, not to anybody else. You can listen to other people's advice, but you have to make up your mind what you're going to do and how you're going to do it. Then do it. You have to take responsibility for your swing."

I didn't know where this talk was going or what I was supposed to say. Luckily, he didn't continue.

Willie was nervous chatty when we picked him and Stevie up outside a Safeway. Willie didn't want us to know where he lived and Stevie didn't want to meet at her house. He was wearing a shiny blue satin white fringe cowboy shirt, jeans and beat up cross trainers. Stevie looked all practical cowgirl in her felt hat, western shirt, jeans and boots.

"Sick wheels, Mr. Uncle Spencer," Willie said from the passenger seat. "2003 BMW. M3 coupe. 333 horses. 6 cylinders. 6 speed manual. Zero to 100 in 4.9 seconds. Black on black. Clean. You could ask 40 grand for this."

"Thanks Willie," Uncle Spencer answered.

"I saw your bridge score online. Want to play cards?" Willie asked after we were out of the city.

"Not while I'm driving."

"Play in your head. 52 card blackjack. I'll deal. Two bits a hand. You got a ten of spades. I've got a seven of hearts. Second card. You've got the eight of diamonds. I've got the queen of hearts. You win.

"Next hand. You've got the five of hearts. I've got the jack of spades. Second card. You've got king of clubs. Lots of face cards showing. I've got the four of spades. Not good. Want another?"

"Hit me," Uncle Spencer said.

"Five of diamonds. I'll take another too. Nine of hearts. You win. Again."

They played through two imaginary decks by the time we got to Nanton where Uncle Spencer stopped to buy gas.

Willie gave him $2.25 saying, "You count cards pretty good, Mr. Uncle Spencer. Didn't think you could beat me."

"I didn't think I could either," Mr. Uncle Spencer answered, acknowledging Willie's skill. "Next time I probably won't."

When Willie went into the Husky I asked Uncle Spencer about the game. "How does Willie do it?"

"He's got a few decks memorized and plays them. I've met guys like him before. He's young though. Most of them are in their thirties."

"How do you know they don't cheat?"

"First, it's always two bits a hand. Nobody cheats for two bits. Second, pride. They like to test you."

Uncle Spencer bought us dinner in a Claresholm diner and then we went to the community arena, basically a hockey rink with bucking chutes and rails in front of the boards. I saw Kayden's grandparents in the bleachers and we climbed up beside them. Uncle Spencer is bowlegged and getting just a bit creaky like my dad. He could have passed for a retired bull rider climbing the bleachers to watch the young fellas. Somehow, he always fits in. I think it's his self confidence more than his bowlegs.

Stevie hugged the grandparents. "Quite a shiner you've got there," Grandpa John said to her. "Call me OneBlackEye," she answered. He didn't ask any questions.

Uncle Spencer didn't show any concern.

I introduced Uncle Spencer and Willie to the Montgomerys.

"Nathan told us about you getting him on a horse last weekend," Uncle Spencer said. "Made a big impression on him ... and on his mom and dad."

"I know," Grandpa John replied. "Julia phoned to thank us for looking after her boy. I told her we had no choice. We needed an extra hand and he was the only man available."

Uncle Spencer laughed. "Good to know he was useful."

"He was useful."

Grandpa John explained to Uncle Spencer how the competition would be run. Twenty five riders. After the first round, the top ten would move on to the finals. The highest total for the two rides would decide the winner.

"Riding two bulls in a row is tough," Grandpa John told him. "The bulls win more often than the riders. Half won't make 8 seconds in the final round. That's when they bring out the best bulls."

Willie leaned over. "Adriano Moraes rode ten out of ten at a world final."

Grandpa John nodded in agreement. "He's a natural."

The bulls running into the chutes and clanging their horns against the steel rails fascinated Willie. His feet tapped the floor.

I pointed out to him the few things I knew to watch for: the cowboys stretching and warming up behind the chutes; the two bullfighters; the judges; and the announcers standing beside the microphones.

"Where's Kayden?"

"He's behind the chutes. When his bull is loaded he'll start getting ready."

"Let me know if you see him." Willie settled down a bit and returned to watching the chutes intensely. "I've counted 18 riders so far. No Kayden."

"He'll be wearing a shirt the same blue as yours."

Willie's focus changed when the announcers began to warm up the crowd. The loudspeaker drowned out the crowd noise with a Garth Brooks song and the scoreboard lit up.

"It's time to meet the cowboys!" the first announcer screamed like Robin Williams in *Good Morning Vietnam.* Great film. Great acting.

The cowboys lined up across the arena, their leather chaps swinging as they walked. The announcer began with the lowest ranked riders. Kayden was in the middle. Willie was up, crazy cheering and dancing on the bleacher seat. "Kayden! Kayden! Kayden!"

The spotlight flashed onto him and he held his arms high, the white fringed sleeves of his glistening shirt spread out like a cowboy albatross. "Go Kayden!"

"Looks like our boy from Longview has brought his own cheering section," the second announcer drawled.

"Go Kayden!" the crowd shouted back when Willie pumped his wings.

"And if I'm not mistaken that's Kayden's Grandma Lillian and Grandpa John up there too. Owners of the Rockin' R. We heard they've got some tough bulls started. Gave the Jackson twins a rough go last weekend."

"Ron Atkins is the colour commentator tonight," Stevie whispered to me. "He has a quarter horse outfit north of here. We bought Sunshine from him."

The spotlight swung to the Jacksons who lifted their hats to the crowd and got a round of applause. Crowd favourites.

The riding began after a mother and daughter in sequined dresses sang *O Canada.*

Our seats were close enough to the chutes that we could watch the cowboys pulling their ropes on the bulls. I could hear Grandpa John explaining the getting ready rituals to Uncle Spencer. I tried to explain to Willie what was happening, but his focus on the chutes was so intense I don't think he heard me. He may have been memorizing the entire event.

The announcers gave the crowd a dramatic rundown on every rider. Any one of them could be the winner and every bull was one to watch out for. Grandma Lillian stood up and left the stands. She returned a minute later. "I got fifty bucks on Kayden making the top five tonight. Seven to one odds."

Uncle Spencer smiled. "Didn't know it was legal to bet here?"

"It isn't."

Kayden drew one of the last bulls, Black Bart, and that gave Grandpa John an opportunity to explain to Uncle Spencer how riders study each bull's bucking patterns. Bulls that spin away from a rider's hand. Bulls that spin into a rider's hands. Bulls with high kicks and twists. Bulls that try to hook a rider with their horns.

Ron Atkins built Black Bart up, saying he'd been featured at the Calgary Stampede last summer and bucked off four of five riders. In a confidential whisper, he let the crowd in on the whole story:

"This is a high kicking bull a cowboy could score high on. But we don't know much about this young Kayden fella. We heard he was a star quarterback last year and has given that up for bulls.

"He's an enigma on the circuit. He has two types of scores. Really high and bucked off. No middling scores. They tell me it's all or nothing with this young man. So far he's scored high at Pincher Creek and Lethbridge. Maybe he's going to be the upset winner tonight. I overheard the Jackson twins saying he's one to watch."

Stevie gave my hand a mechanic's squeeze.

Kayden nodded, the gate swung open and Black Bart reared out with a bellow. Kayden rode him all the way up. Back straight and chin tucked in. Then down and balanced for the high kick. His right arm swung up and he stayed dead centre on the bull.

And that's how he rode out the whole 8 seconds. Spurs jamming. In control. His right arm swinging high and free. Making music. Riding through the pasture.

We were all on our feet. Willie danced.

The scoreboard flashed Kayden's score 92.

"First place so far," the announcer drawled. "Let's give this young fella a cheer."

"Kayden! Kayden! Kayden!" The spotlight flashed back onto dancing Willie. A wind blown sky bird. Ecstatic.

Uncle Spencer caught my attention and nodded to me. He knew he had just seen 8 seconds of near perfect golf.

Only three other riders made 8 seconds. Dakota Tallboy, a slender Blackfoot rider from Montana, tied Kayden's 92. The Jackson twins scored 86 and 88.

Kayden found us during the intermission. Willie danced around him. "Thanks for the cheers," Kayden responded. "Great shirt."

Willie and his fringes would look good to a camera. An image that would be hard to forget.

"Who'd you draw for the final round?" Grandpa John asked.

"The one I didn't want. Knucklebuster. He'll spin into my hand. That's where I'm weakest."

"Ride him," Grandpa John said calmly. "Go for the ride, not the score."

Kayden smiled. "You know how I do it."

Kayden left when the announcer called the crowd back to the bleachers.

"We're gonna ride ten bulls soon so get back sitting down. We've got the four scored rides from the first round and we're giving the six riders who stayed on the longest a chance to make some go round money."

As the bulls loaded, Grandpa John explained to us why Kayden didn't like riding a bull that turned into his hand, to the left.

"It's just a damn scrap for a lot of riders," he said. "You've got to keep that free arm outside and high, and a little bit back through the whole spin. You can't let it cross your chest or you might never get it out. You have to keep pulling on the rope with your riding hand to drive your inside hip and shoulder forward into the spin. Spurring with your outside leg can be dangerous. It leaves you open to a fast change in direction.

"And it can be a wreck if the rider falls inside the spin – that's what they call The Well – and gets hung up."

Uncle Spencer turned to Grandma Lillian. "Going to make another bet?"

"Kayden's won me all the money I'll take home tonight. I'd bet on him if I thought he'd ride safe. That's not his way. He won't listen to reason, much less talk about it."

The scoreboard lit up with the order of the final ten. The first six would ride for go round money, then Jimmie with an 86 and Alex with an 88. Then the pair of 92s: Kayden and then Dakota.

The first of the extra six riders got bounced forward coming out of the chute and slammed his face between the bull's horns. The next buck threw him into the rails. The clown and bullfighters chased the bull into the alley as the paramedics ran in with a stretcher.

The rider tried to stand then crumpled, his face bloodied. The paramedics helped him onto the stretcher and carried him out. The other riders applauded him. Moments later the ambulance siren started.

Ron Atkins assured the crowd. "They'll check him over in the hospital. We'll let you know as soon as we get a report."

Only two of the first six riders made 8 seconds. Then the finalists rode. Jimmie scored 88, total 176. Alex bucked off, total 88.

Stevie grabbed my hand again as we watched the gate swing open for Kayden. He rode Knucklebuster through the forward rear and into the spin. You could see him struggling to keep his right arm high and outside. Then it crossed. He caught his balance again and pulled his arm back outside when Knucklebuster bucked forward. Kayden started to spur the bull hard.

He was in the air when the buzzer sounded. Knucklebuster turned on him and butted him once. A bullfighter sprinted past slapping the side of the bull's head as he went by. The bull forgot Kayden and chased the fighter to the rails.

Willie went wild, jumping into the air and shouting, "Did you see that guy run? Did you see him slap that bull? He saved Kayden."

Kayden stood and waved to the crowd. Ron Atkins sounded relieved: "He looks fine, folks. And how about a big hand for our bullfighters!"

"Bucked off again," Grandpa John said. "He could have scored if he hadn't kept spurring."

Dakota took his time adjusting his chaps and helmet.

"Now it's up to Dakota to claim first place with an 84 or better," Ron told the crowd as we waited for the final ride of the night. "He's got the experience and the reputation to take home the buckle tonight."

Dakota, slim and lithe, urged his helper to pull the rope tighter. He looked calm. Confident. As if this were one more Saturday night event. He pulled himself up against his riding hand and nodded.

The bull's first kick clanged high on the rails. Dakota rode as if every bull did that. He rode him tight, no big spurring, going for the buzzer. 8 seconds later he landed on his feet and raised his arm to the crowd.

The scoreboard flashed his score: 88.

The announcer pointed out that Dakota was eligible for a reride because the bull had kicked the rail. "We asked him what he wants to do and he says he'll go with his 88 and the win. Smart thinking!"

We said goodbye to Grandpa John and Grandma Lillian. She shook our hands. "Thank you for coming." She faced Uncle Spencer. "Thank you, too, for bringing these kids. They've got some potential."

Willie asked to be dropped off by the LRT station.

"I'm not dropping you off there at 11:30," Uncle Spencer told him. "I'll take you home. What's your address?"

Willie looked out the side window, "I was going to stay at the Shelter but it's already closed. And there's parties all weekend at the foster home. I'll call some friends."

"You can stay with me and Jean tonight. We'll drop off Nathan and Stevie first. I don't live far from them. Okay?" Uncle Spencer didn't sound as if he wanted to hear an argument.

"Okay, Mr. Uncle Spencer."

Stevie's house was dark. "My parents are out," she explained. "I have a key. Gerry will probably be home soon."

"Nathan," Uncle Spencer said, "walk her to the door and wait there until we see some lights inside."

Stevie leaned over the seat and kissed him on the cheek. "I don't see why anybody would say you're the mean uncle."

Outside my house Uncle Spencer asked me to call him the next day. "You've got something on your mind so we'd better discuss it." He waited for me to open the front door and turn on the lights.

I heard Mom and Dad come home an hour later. Mom cracked open my bedroom door to make sure I was asleep. I wasn't. I was acting.

"Goodnight, My Prince," she said softly and closed the door.

Superman Dad was already talking on his Blackberry. Probably threatening Lex Luther who was ordering a kryptonite brunch on a Toronto patio. 8:30 on a Sunday morning.

He pointed to a note for me on the fridge door.

"Nathan. Supper at 6. Love Mom." The Love Mom was circled with a heart.

"Is Mom still sleeping?" I asked when Dad hung up.

"She's having breakfast with a friend. She'll be back by 10. I've got a 9:30 tee time. Want me to drop you anywhere?"

"I'm going to stay home for a while. Maybe I'll go to the Glencoe after Mom gets back."

"I'll be in New York next week. If I close this deal we'll have a nice bonus cheque to spend. Maybe you and I could fly to Mexico for a few days, or even Australia. What would you say to that Superboy?"

We had a couple of sidekick names like that. Superman and Superboy. Batman and Robin. Mario and Luigi.

"Sounds like a lot of money," I said. "Let me decide this time. I want it to be legendary!"

"Done!"

I already knew where I wanted to go. The Canadian Finals Rodeo in Edmonton. Dad would love it just the way he loved taking me to the Stampede where we ate all the free pancake breakfasts we could and where his fastball arm won me stuffed toys from the carnies on the midway. His business contacts got us into the chuckwagon barns where he drank Coors and I drank Coke with the sponsored drivers after the races. He always finagled us seats right up beside the bucking chutes. The Stampede is that exciting childhood when I would have given all my bedroom treasures to be one of the boys in the chutes. Who wouldn't want to come home a hero with arena dirt pounded up his ass?

I phoned Uncle Spencer as soon as I had the house to myself.

"How's Willie this morning?" I asked.

"Gone. He had coffee with us and then said he was going to the group home. He wanted to walk. We offered to let him stay a few more nights. He said he didn't want to get accustomed to opulence."

"I'll see him at school tomorrow."

"Can you come over now?" he asked. "Jean is going to be near your house in half an hour or so. She can pick you up."

"That'd be good." We hung up.

Aunt Jean called a few minutes later. "I'll be outside your house in fifteen."

I liked my practical Aunt Jean. She'd been divorced before she married Uncle Spencer. Everybody says he must be difficult to live with. She says he's not. "I'm the one who's hard to live with." Always gets a laugh. They didn't have any kids.

We didn't talk much in the car. She said she'd heard about the bull riding. "Good for you having friends like Kayden and Stevie. Willie sounds ..." She paused.

"Willie doesn't have any family," I said.

"Well, he's got you as a friend. That makes it your responsibility to be sure he gets a good meal whenever you can. He's as thin as spaghetti." Anybody else would have worried about his dishevelled influence on me, as if I might turn homeless. Not Aunt Jean. She was worried that Willie was going hungry. People like Aunt Jean and Uncle Spencer don't understand how anybody can be an influence, good or bad. They are who they are all the time. They don't get blown around.

Uncle Spencer took me into his den. We sat across from each other.

"You're thinking about riding bulls like Kayden, aren't you?" One thing for sure about Uncle Spencer is that he doesn't waste any time.

"Sort of, I guess."

"What kind of answer is that? 'Sort of, I guess.' Yes or no?"

"Yes. I only want to make 8 seconds on one bull."

"One bull?"

"That's all. Just one to prove to myself I can do it. I've already been bucked off steers and survived. I'm going to keep trying until I'm good enough to ride a bull."

I was suddenly way more Chili Palmer confident than I thought I could be. "And I don't want Mom and Dad sticking their noses in it. This is all me. No Mom and Dad helping Nathan out. No making excuses for me. No hugs and saying 'Nice try' when I don't make the team."

Uncle Spencer marked my proposal hard. F. "You don't have a goddamn hope. You're not an athlete. You can try all you want and you'll never do it. You'll be killed. Pick something you have a chance at."

He was seeing if he could make me give up easily.

"This is what I'm going to do," I answered. "I've decided. And I want you to help me. If not, I'll do it on my own."

He leaned forward in his chair. "How can I help you? What do I know about bull riding? Last night I was as close to a bull as I'm willing to get. I don't know why you're asking me."

"Remember when I was ten and that neighbour kid was picking on me at my birthday party? You straightened him out and never said a word to anybody. You didn't make a conversation out of it. I remember that really well. That's what's happening to me now. Everybody's bossing me around, making plans for me. My parents. Reese. You're the only one I can ask for help to do something I want."

I think my calm determination made an impression on him. He leaned back in his chair. "Keep going."

I laid it all out. We'd drive to the Rockin' R every Saturday or Sunday. Kayden and Grandpa John could teach me. All I needed was a way to make sure my parents didn't interfere.

"If you're with me on the weekends, they won't ask a bunch of questions. They can't know what I am doing. Mom will do her best to stop me, or Dad will find some way to get involved. This has to be me. Just me."

He revised my mark to D, with reservations. "You know that if you get hurt, I'll be blamed."

"You're the mean uncle. You can take it."

"Apparently that's my reputation."

"But if I make 8 seconds on a bull, you'll have helped me prove I'm not a total screw up. You could claim that as your redeeming deed."

"I need to think about this. There are going to be conditions." I was now up to a C, with conditions.

We went back into the kitchen. Aunt Jean said, "You two boys look like Huckleberry Finn and Tom Sawyer formulating some scheme." She held up her hand when I started to answer.

"I'm not involved. I don't want to know."

Uncle Spencer offered to drive me home.

"Can you drop me at the Glencoe Club? I need to start working out. Did you see the size of Kayden's guns?"

Aunt Jean laughed. "Your cousin Aubrey did more than see them."

"She had a good look at Stevie, too. Said her eyes gave her impure thoughts."

Aunt Jean smiled. "In my day, I wouldn't have dared say anything if I was thinking that way. Good for Aubrey."

In the car, Uncle Spencer told me he'd have his conditions figured out in a day or two. "It has to be a signed deal, okay?"

Grandpa John had been right when he said: "What matters in life is knowing what you want to do and who can help you." Uncle Spencer was going to help me. I'd asked the right person.

I followed the weight lifting guide posted on the gym wall to find my starting level. Beginner. I met some friends later in the cafeteria and we spent the afternoon fooling around and gossiping about Reese's birthday.

I walked home working on an idea.

Dear Emily Arbutus

My name is Bull Rider (not my real one) and I've heard about your Film Studies class. I hear you're a good teacher and hope you can help me. I've been writing a screenplay but want to keep it to myself.

Here's my concept. Buck Off. (file attached) So far it's only a Synopsis. The characters are based on people I know so it's sort of autobiographical. Mostly autobiographical, to be honest, except none of it happened to me personally. I'm making up the action.

I have written a start of Act I with scenes 1 and 2. If you like the synopsis, maybe you'll read those scenes too.

Just tell me if you think I could make something out of this. I want to sell it to Hollywood.

Bull Rider

PS. Don't try to figure out who I am because I'm not the person you think I am. And this is a secret email address so don't try anything with it either.

PS PS. This is just the start. I've only written class papers before this, such as on prime ministers and other dead guys. So maybe my writing style isn't too studio ready, but I can learn that.

PS PS PS. I meant it about you being a good teacher. Willie agrees. You like real discussions.

PS PS PS PS. I'm not Willie and don't even know him that well. He's a nutcase. I overheard him in the cafeteria.

BUCK OFF

SYNOPSIS
WRITTEN BY BULL RIDER

THE PREMISE

Chet Jr. lives in the shadow of his legendary father, Chet Sr., the World Champion bull rider killed by a bull when Chet was a baby. Young Chet grows up in the family rodeo world, unaware that Keith Samson, the true killer of his father, has stolen Chet Sr.'s place as champion. Chet must overcome his insecurities by proving to himself that he is his father's equal in the rodeo arena, while bringing Keith Samson to justice. His overprotective mother, Marlena, thwarts his attempts to live up to the reputation of his heroic father.

The Main Story Line

The main story line is Chet's goal to ultimately win the Canadian Championship like his father did. He believes that if he can do this he will prove to himself his own self worth. We will follow the story of self-discovery, acceptance and the fulfillment of self-gratification.

The Challenges

As a boy, Chet is constantly bullied and embarrassed by his lack of self-worth. Only in a fit of shame will he address his own destiny.

He needs to prove to himself, to his mother and to the rest of the world that he is not a loser. If he can't, he will be a loser all his life.

One of Chet's challenges is overcoming his sense of worthlessness when Keith Samson and his son Max bully him. Keith is known to be a wife beater. His son is terrified by what he has seen.

Twist in Plot

Chet Jr.'s discovery that Keith is responsible for the death of his father will be a real turning point in the film. This is the knowledge that will strengthen Chet Jr.'s inner core and force him to Man Up.

THE LOCATIONS

The modern rodeo circuit takes the competitors to various rodeos around North America but a big part of the film takes place at the Canadian Finals Rodeo and the Calgary Stampede in Alberta. The ranches, rodeo camps, the midways and the arenas are the sets where we are introduced to the characters' lifestyles.

THE CHARACTERS

Chet Sr.: The Heroic, Fallen Father

The world of competitive bull riding is ruled by one man in the early 1980s and that one man is Chet Montgomery senior. He is the picture of a true cowboy. His handsome face is perfectly chiselled and unshaven. He looks like a model for Marlboro Man, rugged but clean. The intensity of his every move is mastered by his long lean athletic body that gives him the competitive edge to be a hero. He dominates every rodeo he enters, bringing home the daily cash and winning the National Finals.

Marlena: The Over-Protective Mother

Marlena grew up with little money. The day she stood in the stands and watched her husband die changed her forever.

Marlena is self-absorbed and can't control her need to keep her son from greatness and protect him from her own fears.

Chet Jr.: Determined to Prove Himself

Chet Jr. is the only child of Marlena. She has taken him on the rodeo circuit since he was a baby. They stay to themselves. Chet Jr. is tall but scrawny, so he appears somewhat weak. He is unpopular with the other young boys on the rodeo circuit. He is smarter and his mother does not let him associate with the rodeo "riff-raff." He often appears to be clumsy, uncoordinated and lacking in common sense.

He is our protagonist. He will be the driving force of the film. We will take him from an awkward young boy, weave him into the fabric of an underdog and an ultimate hero. His most important traits will evolve.

Chet's inner struggle for acceptance creates the urgency of the ultimate goal. He must prove himself against all odds to get the respect that he desires.

Chet will develop self worth, courage and backbone, three things he lacks at the beginning of the script.

His father, Chet Sr., is dead but very real in Chet Jr.'s life. The best bull rider in history. A legend and a hero. A constant reminder to Chet of how much of a failure he is.

Keith Samson, The Adult Antagonist

Keith has been winning on the rodeo circuit since Chet Montgomery's death. He is a stereotype bully. He is a role model for bad behaviour to his son Max. Keith and Max bully Chet Jr.

Keith dominates Chet's world. He rules the rodeo world with fear. Mean and morally defunct he takes what he wants. His desire to win creates embarrassment and anger when he loses. Because he is defined by winning, he believes in winning at any cost and retaliation when he doesn't. He often takes his frustration physically out on his son and wife.

Max Samson, The Young Antagonist

Max is Keith's son. When we first meet Max he is already a bully. He is terrified of his father but intensely craves his father's approval. This manifests itself into a mean young man with the same lack of moral fibre as his father Keith. He has the potential to be different.

Bobby Jo, The Love Interest

A barrel racer. Very competitive and successful. Determined and not easily distracted.

Jonah, The Sidekick

Chet's best friend. Extremely loyal. A dimwitted carney. He will add humour to the film.

Johnny Anderson, a Father Figure

Johnny (Marlena's brother-in-law) was the rodeo clown that witnessed the death of Chet Sr. He saw the pain it caused Marlena and felt somewhat responsible, deservedly.

Bruce, a Father Figure

Chet Sr.'s best friend and also his trainer and coach. Bruce is one of the good guys. Trusted and respected on the rodeo circuit. He is smart, athletic and has a strong desire to help his friend's son.

Chet Jr. looks up to Bruce; always wanting his approval.

ACT I SCENE 1
THE CANADIAN RODEO FINALS
MID-1980S

EXT. AN OUTDOOR RODEO ARENA - DAY

The movie opens behind the chutes of the big money day of the Canadian Rodeo Finals. The bulls are being brought into the holding pens. A gloved hand holding a syringe reaches through the steel rails and jabs the shoulder of a bull.

The bull riders are going through their preparation rituals nearby. A cowboy saunters nonchalantly by, face hidden, and squeezes a few drops from a small bottle into an open coffee cup. The owner of the cup doesn't notice, and a moment later takes a drink.

The scene switches to the arena where the announcer is extolling the record of Chet Montgomery, the favourite. His bull is Outlaw: the meanest and most repulsive bull anyone has ever seen. Today in the chutes he looks more agitated than usual. Chet Sr. will score some major points if he can stay on Outlaw. Normally cool, calm and collected, Chet Sr. looks worried today. In the chute, the excitement escalates as he has trouble pulling his rope tight on this crazy repugnant beast.

The scene is contrasted by the slow-motion scan of the crowd cheering.

Men in cowboy hats, western shirts, Wranglers and expensive boots. Women in colourful western attire. Everyone standing with a beer in their hand. The hairstyles of the men are typical 1980s: mullets and shags. The women have 'big' hair, crimped and teased.

THE CAMERA STOPS ON A BEAUTIFUL BLONDE COWGIRL.

She looks pure and organic. In her arms she holds her baby (Chet Jr.) dressed in a cowboy jumper that reads "Wanted." She stands and addresses her husband, "Good Luck Chet. We love you!" She blows her good luck signature kiss. The camera gets closer and we are able to see the fear in her eyes, the same fear she feels every time Chet Sr. rides.

THE CAMERA GOES BACK TO THE CHUTES

The chute gate opens and the bull and rider fly out.

THE CAMERA SWINGS TO THE CLOCK

The seconds are counted down in slow motion, it

seems like hours. The announcer's western twang, screaming into his mike can be barely heard.

THE CAMERA RETURNS TO THE BULL AND RIDER

Outlaw rips and roars as he bucks and spins. He is crazed, he wants this piece of shit off his back. Chet Sr. struggles.

Outlaw is usually more methodical in spinning right, then left, but today he is just wildly all over the place.

Chet is struggling, but he is somehow hanging on to his flat braided rope.

Then he is bucked off, high up in the air. His hand still above his head as he thunders to the ground. His violent struggle with the bull has come to an end. A loud collective gasp is the first sound we hear, and then Marlena's scream. The camera holds on to her image for a mere second. Now all eyes are on Johnny Anderson, the rodeo clown and bullfighter. He tears across the arena in his colourful costume, waving his red hat desperately. He gets the attention of Outlaw. Outlaw charges him. Johnny jumps onto the rails as Chet lifts his head.

The crowd screams: "Get up Chet! Get up Chet ..."

One arm seems frozen above his head. The other is holding his ribs. Outlaw wants blood and before Johnny can distract him again, Outlaw brutally gores and tramples Chet. The camera fades out.

ACT I SCENE 2
THE FUNERAL

EXT. AN OPEN AIR COUNTRY FUNERAL - AFTERNOON

Cowboys dressed in black suit jackets, brand new Wrangler jeans, white shirts and cowboy ties. Family and friends, drivers and farm hands.

The rodeo circuit family, the media, and the ranchers that live in the area. No one has yet accepted this reality. The livestock all stand still at the side of the road.

Cars and trucks line the highway into the Village of Longview as they slow down and turn into the community centre. One of the greats, gone far too soon.

We see Marlena and her family dressed in dark western clothing. She is holding her baby, Chet Jr. Her sister, Christina, and her brother-in-law Johnny Anderson are at her side. The audience's attention is on a podium.

BRUCE

I first meet Chet when his father George hired me to train him on rough stock. I was hesitant because he was young and I thought he was probably spoiled. I couldn't have been more wrong. Chet lived his life on his own terms. He was loyal and kind. I remember when he won the Canadian Championship. There wasn't a cowboy that didn't think he deserved to win. He put everything in it and became the rider to beat every year. He was a real family man and was so excited when Marlena and him had their first child.

As people line up to give Marlena their condolences, she sees Keith Samson, Chet's arch-rival. He looks at her, trying to get an idea of what she knows or suspects, if anything. Marlena senses he is evil.

KEITH

Marlena, what a terrible accident. I'm so sorry.

Anyone know exactly what happened?

MARLENA

I know exactly what happened. The one man you couldn't outride got killed.

She looks over at her brother-in law, Johnny, who is watching her as well. Keith walks over to Johnny and whispers something in his ear. Johnny looks like he has just seen a ghost. Marlena walks over to him.

MARLENA

What did Keith say? He knows something, I can tell.

JOHNNY

He said the usual stuff people say at funerals. Don't read too much into his rivalry with Chet. Chet broke his back when he fell. Marlena, I'm so sorry. Outlaw seemed crazier than usual, that's all I know.

MARLENA

Something else happened, Johnny. I can feel it in my bones.

I didn't hear back from Emily that night and went to school Monday figuring that she didn't think my idea was much good. I was regretting taking a chance at getting laughed at. Maybe I'd asked the wrong person for help.

Emily smiled at Kayden in class a couple of extra times. I suppose she thought he was Bull Rider. He certainly had chiselled hero looks. Maybe she'd looked up his record on the rodeo websites. If she looked me up she might find my computer award. She'd connect Bull Rider with Kayden, not with me. I considered warning Kayden then decided he could handle Emily's extra attention.

Willie had a gift for me after the class. "You could have written this," he said handing me a DVD. Instead of a title, he'd written 'For Nathan' with a felt pen.

I thought it might be porn so I was cautious in my thank you.

I waited until The Commotion were in bed before loading the DVD in my computer. It was a film from the year I was born, 1986. *Stand By Me.* I might have got a little teary that night over the four boys' Act III: Teddy went to jail; Chris got killed breaking up a fight; Vern got married and worked in a lumber yard; and Gordie became a writer. Could the stories be ours? Mine, Stevie's, Kayden's and Willie's? Were those our endings?

For a weirdo math whiz street kid, Willie had made a good guess at the type of film I'd like to write.

Uncle Spencer had his list of conditions ready the next day. First on the list was going to my doctor with him to make sure my health could take it. Then I had to keep to a workout schedule. Then I had to keep up my marks: good enough to get into university. Then I had to tell Kayden and his grandparents everything and ask them to help me. If they didn't want to, the deal was off.

That was it. We signed the list.

The only condition I was worried about was the doctor visit. If you've been in and out of doctors' offices and hospitals as much as I have, you don't see them as good places – you see them as going backward places where things get worse. More drugs, new inhalers, and less fun and more rules from The Commotion. I'd have to be desperate before I'd go voluntarily.

Doctor Sara was from Mumbai and had known me since elementary school – that is all my coughing life after I had been diagnosed with Kawasaki Disease. She always talked to me like an adult, even when my parents interrupted. I liked the way she was always straightforward. She had small fine boned fingers that touched you delicately.

I'd been in for a precautionary check up before school started so she had all the test results she needed. She listened to my lungs. Uncle Spencer and I sat opposite her desk.

I told her about my plans to ride a bull, how and why Uncle Spencer would be involved, about Kayden's family and how I hoped they would help me. I didn't hold anything back.

She listened to me as if Uncle Spencer weren't there, not even glancing at him until I finished.

"That's what Uncle Spencer and I agreed," I said to her. "That's our deal."

"And you want my opinion?" she asked.

"Yes," I answered. Uncle Spencer nodded in agreement.

"All right. Here it is. Bad idea. That's official. Nathan's definitely outgrown the Kawasaki issue. We did an echocardiogram three months ago and his heart and arteries are fine.

"His lungs are the problem. We've been seeing gradual fluid buildup. It comes and goes without ever getting completely better. We don't know why we're not seeing a long term improvement. It might be infection, or allergies, or asthma. We don't know. It could be pulmonary edema. I don't think it is. I suspect it is an after effect of the Kawasaki Disease. No test has been conclusive.

"What matters right now are the consequences. Think of it this way. The more fluid that builds up in his lungs, the less oxygen his brain gets. Too much fluid will slowly suffocate him. He won't feel it because his blood will be circulating carbon dioxide instead of oxygen. He'll get tired and fall asleep. Forever.

"That's why I say it's a bad idea. However, getting bucked off a bull won't cause more fluid to accumulate. I'd say stress is the bigger danger. He's putting himself into a life and death situation every time he rides, and that is going to stress every organ he has. I bet he almost pees his pants every time he gets ready to ride. That's stress."

"So what you're saying," Uncle Spencer said, "is that getting bucked off isn't the concern. It's whether or not his lungs can handle the stress."

Doctor Sara agreed. "That's right. What do you think, Nathan? Any questions?"

"Why did I get so sleepy after I got the wind knocked out of me last weekend?"

"Not enough oxygen. You're running close to empty most of the time and when you got the wind knocked out of you, carbon dioxide slipped into your bloodstream. It took all night for it to be eliminated.

"From now on you need to be prepared. You should have an oxygen mask and bottle nearby and have somebody ready to use it.

"You'll probably break a few bones same as any other rider. They'll heal. That's the situation. Bad idea, but you seem determined."

"I'm okay with this so far," Uncle Spencer said. "I was a downhill racer. I almost peed my pants a couple of times waiting for my start. I learned to handle the stress. Nathan will learn."

"I'm doing this," I said. "I'm going to ride a bull. It only takes 8 seconds. I'll always have enough air for that."

Doctor Sara laughed. "Of course you will. But if you end up in hospital afterwards tell the doctors to call me."

On our way out of the clinic Uncle Spencer told me to set up a round of golf at the Rockin' R. It took me a moment to get his humour.

At home I opened BullRider.rodeo@yahoo.com. One message.

Dear Bull Rider

I have to be cautious about encouraging you with your film script. Hundreds of thousands are written every year and only a few are made into films.

Considering this is your first attempt at a script, you already have a good hold on your characters, maybe because they're based on people in your own life. The dialogue and action need work. Too bad Chet's dad dies so early, although that's a common mythical device to introduce an impossible ideal for a young hero to live up to.

I think the big story will be in the film's Act III when grown up Chet confronts Keith Samson and he reconciles with his over-protective mother, Marlena. You'll find that difficult to write based on the way you have described Chet's weak character in the synopsis. (How autobiographical is this? What's your mother going to say?) Chet has a lot of ground to travel to get to the point where he can win a bull riding championship.

In my experience with new scriptwriters, I find being picky about typos, formatting and grammar slows them down. Keep writing, and don't worry about anything but story for now. You can always go back later and change anything. You will!

Buck Off to you,

Emily Arbutus

PS. I am pleased Willie likes my class.

Overall positive, I thought.

I called Stevie that night to tell her about my bull riding plan. "Don't get too excited," she warned. "Grandma Lillian might have something to say you don't want to hear."

I tried hard to stay focused in school that week without much success. Kayden sounded as cautious as Stevie about my plan although he agreed to invite Uncle Spencer to the ranch on Saturday. We didn't talk about it again. I wished he and Stevie showed more enthusiasm.

Dad was in New York and Mom had a sales seminar all week. She had a deli deliver my dinner two nights and I ate at the Glencoe once. I didn't see her until after dark. She always apologized for working late and promised me that she'd plan a special time for us to catch up when the seminar was over.

I did my homework and then wrote a few *Buck Off* scenes that sounded corny. I decided I would keep trying until I got a scene I liked enough to send to Emily.

On Saturday, when Uncle Spencer picked me up, Mom and I gave each other our love salute at the door. Right hand on our hearts and our left hands pointing toward each other.

Uncle Spencer was waiting impatiently in the car. He punched me lightly on the shoulder. "Are you sure you're old enough to do this? Don't you have to be out of elementary school?"

THE ROCKIN' R DEAL

Grandma Lillian and Grandpa John shook Uncle Spencer's hand at the door. Kayden and Stevie were on the couch and stood up when we came in.

"Coffee?" Grandpa John asked pointing to the table set with mugs and a plate of cheese and crackers.

"I'd like one," Uncle Spencer said. "We ran into weekend traffic on the highway."

Everybody sat at the table and helped themselves to the coffee pot being passed around. I put a lot of milk in mine. I didn't need caffeine.

"Kayden and Stevie filled us in on what you want," Grandpa John said. "But maybe you should tell us yourselves what you're thinking."

Uncle Spencer pointed to me. His big hands looked at home resting on the ranch table. There was power in them.

"Nathan's idea," he said. "Nathan should do the talking."

I told it the same way as I told it to Doctor Sara and added her concerns about my lungs. Nothing about peeing my pants.

"Getting bucked off won't hurt me any more than anybody else," I told them. "The only time that could be a problem is if I get the wind knocked out of me. Again." I smiled and they all nodded. They remembered me puking. "Then I might need extra oxygen."

"That's it?" Grandpa John asked.

"Tell them about peeing your pants," Uncle Spencer said.

Stevie and Kayden didn't laugh when I explained about how stress affects me.

"And everybody else," Kayden said. "You should see the puddles behind the chutes."

Silence.

Grandma Lillian made the table ring when she almost slammed her cup down.

"That's all well and good, us helping Nathan. It sounds like a lot of fun. But the truth is we can't afford to be babysitting anybody. We have to be practical. We're just hanging on here. Go ahead, Kayden tell them the jam we're in. Then we won't look too rude turning them down."

"Wait a minute," Grandpa John said. "Kayden doesn't have to explain anything."

"Then I'll do it," Grandma Lillian said. "When our son married Kayden's mother they took over the ranch from us. Seemed like the right thing to do. When Kayden came along they made up a will leaving it all to him – if he got through university. Good idea, except for two things.

"First, when his parents were killed we found out the ranch went under the control of a trustee, not us. We're just hired hands working for some bald accountant who doesn't know ranching and doesn't care. We're going under slowly and he's drawing his pay every month. We don't control the ranch chequebook. If the place gets sold, we're out of here with nothing. What's left of the money when the lawyers and accountants and realtors are done goes into trust for Kayden until he gets through university or turns 25.

"Second, he's in grade 12 now and he's repeating grade 11 math. With his marks he can't get into any kind of academic program at university. All those years of being a football hero made his teachers look the other way. They passed him through and now he's paying for it. We're all paying for it.

"That's the goddamn mess we're in. The trustee could sell us out and we'd get nothing. In the meantime we don't have enough money to run the ranch. We sold our herd to buy rodeo bulls. What's left is all the cash we have."

"You could contest the will," Uncle Spencer suggested. "Kayden's parents obviously didn't consider you outliving them."

"I won't contest it," Kayden spoke for the first time. "My parents wanted me to get an education before I got the ranch. If I can't get through high school with the marks I need for university, then I'm going to go along with what's in the will. I'm not going to sneak around it."
A lot of talking there, Kayden.

I turned to Uncle Spencer. "Can't you help sort this out? You fix things all the time."

"I don't know. I could look at the paperwork. Maybe you folks wouldn't want a stranger going through it. Maybe you've already decided to go along with whatever happens."

"Please, Lillian," Grandpa John said taking her hand. "I think Spencer can help. He knows what he's doing. We can't go on like this. Let's see what he can come up with."

"Can't pay him," she said.

"Teach Nathan to ride a bull," Uncle Spencer replied. "I'll do what I can for you in return. He may never ride one. You may end up with nothing. Who knows?"

Uncle Spencer never looked less mean.

"What about Kayden?" Grandma Lillian asked. "He's got to pass Math 30 this year. How's that going to happen?"

The answer bucked out of Stevie.

"Math whiz Willie will get him through."

Grandma Lillian dropped her forehead onto the table.

Uncle Spencer reached behind the table for a deck of cards. "Nathan says you play whist. Let's play a few hands and give ourselves a break."

Grandma Lillian sat up in surprise. "You want to play whist? Now?"

"Why not? You and I against Nathan and Grandpa John. For fun."

Grandma Lillian and Uncle Spencer showed us no mercy. "I watched you," she said afterwards to Uncle Spencer. "You could have helped Nathan out a couple of times. Gone easy on him. You didn't. You made him pay for his mistakes.

"That's the way John and I have always ranched. We expect to pay for our mistakes. That's why I've changed my mind. I'm agreeing with John now. I want you to have a look at our situation. Let's see what kind of ending you can come up with for us."

I lasted three bucks that afternoon. One on each steer. "You don't give up easy," Uncle Spencer said. "This could be fun to watch."

Afterwards, I walked out behind the arena where TwoBlackEyes snorted and charged the fence. I didn't back off this time.

"Get ready to meet me," I told him, "because I'm hunting you."

He knew I meant it. Shark eyes.

Dear Emily Arbutus

Act I Scene 3 is the setup of Chet Jr.'s journey, his conflict with Marlena, and his determination to be a perfect son for his father.

Bull Rider

PS. Maybe it reads too much like a book.

BUCK OFF

ACT I SCENE 3
THE ICE CREAM QUEEN
17 YEARS LATER

Chet (Jr.) is now almost 18 years old. Although his good looks of blue eyes, blonde hair and white teeth are beginning to bloom, he is immature, clumsy and self-loathing. He allows bullies to tease and belittle him. His lack of confidence and his inner struggles make him shy away from conflict.

Chet feels guilty, his mom has had to work so hard. She doesn't mean to but she constantly reminds him of this. He will never tell her that he hates working in the Ice Cream truck. Most of the boys his age work in the barns or on the midway. For the most part Chet and his mom are very close. People often tease him, call him a momma's boy. The fact is he loves his mom very much but he has to keep his dreams a secret. He wants to compete in the rodeo not dish out ice cream from a food truck at rodeos, or for that matter go to school to become a suit. He wants to be a cowboy but those conversations are off limits.

EXT. THE RODEO CAMP - MORNING

The rodeo camp beside the Stampede barns is a tangle of motorhomes, Ford trucks and long neck trailers, horse trailers, chuck-wagons, picnic tables and all kinds of rodeo equipment make up the maze of the impromptu village that surrounds the barns. Country music mumbles in the background. Mornings come with the dawn and are very busy. The horses have to be ridden and trained in the mornings, and these famous equine athletes are walked and fed. Cowboys training and ready to ride, wranglers, the unsung heroes of the rodeo, are wrangling. Little wanna-be cowboys are doing their chores, and always the sweet smell of bacon in the air. Everyone is getting ready for the big opening day of the 2004 Calgary Stampede.

THE CAMERA FOCUSES ON THE ALUMINUM DOOR OF A SMALL MOTOR HOME AGED BY THE SUN. THE CAMERA GRADUALLY MOVES INSIDE.

The green wide stripe is faded around the bottom half of the motor home.

Inside, a thick patch of blonde curly hair pops out of a quilted comforter. "I've Got Friends In Low Places" by Garth Brooks blasts from the static filled speaker on the old alarm clock, as it does every morning at 7 a.m. Chet reaches and slams down the button.

CHET

Awww shit.

Chet throws the covers aside and gets out of bed. The heat of the night is evident in his sweat soaked hair.

He is wearing his SpongeBob SquarePants pyjamas.

Chet looks out the small window, the sun is trying to creep through the dirty little window. Chet knows it's going to be a busy day. He makes his way to the small bathroom. The musty smell makes him cough. The bathroom has a fake marble sink that is part of an old plastic walnut cabinet, a toilet and a fiberglass shower with a plastic curtain, all worn. Chet looks in the mirror and then splashes water on his face.

He reaches for his worn Wranglers. He pulls the jeans up. He does up the belt. The belt buckle has a logo engraved in gold on a bronze oval. CFR 1984.

In the kitchen he takes a cast iron frying pan out of the plastic cupboard. He grabs four slices of bacon and two eggs from the small under-counter refrigerator. He cracks the eggs and scrambles them. He pops two slices of toast into the toaster. His motions seem automatic, like he has done this many times before.

He gets out two small plates from the upper cabinet. As he begins to serve up the plates, Marlena opens her bedroom door. At first sight she looks well put together, a short beaded denim mini skirt that she designed and fitted show a few extra pounds around the waist. The western shirt is tight and reveals some cleavage. Her thick blonde curly hair is the same hair as Chet inherited. Marlena's good looks from her younger days are still evident.

Chet looks over at his mom.

CHET

(cheerfully)

Morning Mom

Marlena kisses him on the cheek as she grabs the coffee pot and begins filling it with water. Both listen to a local radio station as they crowd around the small laminate table piled with tanned hides and cases of brightly coloured beads.

THE RADIO ANNOUNCER (V.O.)

Serious questions are being asked about the horrific accident that happened on a trail ride from a farm in Hanna to the Stampede grounds. 200 horses got spooked from the vibration caused by a train as they crossed the Bonnyville Bridge. Nine horses died as they plunged into the Bow River. The event was to replicate a Wild West historical cattle drive. The fatalities included some of the Stampede's finest athletes. The Vancouver Humane Society is expected to stage a large protest again this year. This will definitely start the Stampede off with a black cloud. There have been numerous animals hurt and killed, one man....

CHET

Did any of Grandfather's horses die?

Marlena stands up.

MARLENA

I don't know Chet, turn it off. I can't stand it. The media loves this shit. The truth is, as you well know, these horses are treated like a rancher's own children. The owners will be devastated. It's time to get to work.

Marlena hands Chet two crates filled with equipment and supplies. Chet turns and walks out the trailer door. The camera follows him from behind.

Chet walks towards an old truck/trailer. The side of the trailer has two doors bolted shut. It is brightly painted with colourful ice cream cones. A giant ice cream cone sits on top of the trailer. Chet walks to the front, unlocks the doors, walks in and flips on the generator switch. Music blares from the rusty speaker.

Chet opens the window doors from the inside of the trailer.

He leans on the counter and looks out. The sign to the left of the window has a blackboard with bright pink, perfectly square writing that reads "The Big Chill."

Marlena approaches the trailer.

CHET

(in sing song)

Gonna be a hot day on the midway, Momma

MARLENA

Excellent. I see money in my future, nothin' better than an ice cream cone on a hot day on the midway. (She laughs.) You're going to need some serious cash for school so get your butt in there and start pushin' the Smoothies.

Dear Bull Rider

This scene drags a bit, and doesn't seem to move the story ahead. Try to get some action going. For example, listening to the radio about the horses being killed doesn't do much to get the viewer involved in the Chet story. I think you should at least be hinting now through dialogue about the conflicts between Chet and his mother and Keith.

Emily Arbutus

ACT II

WILLIE

Willie, the foster home kid with math quirks, had danced into our lives the way he had danced into the crowd at the Claresholm bull riding. Skinny. Red hair. Salvation Army clothes. Card counter. We thought we knew everything about him. Then Mr. Uncle Creeley crept up our street in a chocolate brown Chevy van with blacked out windows and we knew we didn't know half of Willie's story.

Life was sweet for me after I signed my bull riding deal with Uncle Spencer. I had a destination. I had a reason to pump iron in the Glencoe gym. I'd have gone more often except Monday and Wednesday evenings had become Math Nights at our house. They started out as Willie and Kayden's tutoring sessions, then Stevie started coming by and The Jewel made everybody dinner and Dad liked having my friends around so much that Willie and Stevie began sleeping over. Kayden always went home to his aunt's.

I could have invited Reese but it would have got way too complicated: I don't think she and Stevie would have got along; Willie's brain would have confused her; and Kayden would have bored her.

So I limited the invitations to join Math Night. Kayden liked the way Willie helped him. They'd work on a problem until Willie could see where Kayden was going wrong.

"It's like you're trying to ride a bull with only one spur," I heard Willie say. He did a good impersonation of announcer Ron Atkins's Claresholm drawl: "We got to back you up a little bit and get your basic math equipment straightened out before we open the chute."

Kayden laughed. He'd probably never laughed about math.

"You're goin' to the Math Finals," Willie would encourage him. "You're goin' to be riding ten out of ten!"

Whenever Kayden got an answer wrong, Willie Atkins would laze into his rodeo microphone pen, "Bucked off!" When Kayden got one right, Willie Atkins would cheer, "You rode that son of a gun perfect!"

Willie had his own way of getting Kayden unstuck. "Every bull's got a pattern, cowboy. You've just got to figure it out. Then ride him. It's the same for math problems. Find the pattern. Find the way to ride 'em. Don't keep trying the wrong thing."

I think Dad was still a bit unsure about Willie. Dad can be like that, standing back awhile before accepting somebody as weird as Willie. He liked Stevie. Mom tolerated her.

Kayden got a 78 on his first Math 20 test. "Next semester you'll be in Math 30," Willie assured him. "There's some rank bulls in that course. We want you to be riding with two spurs buckled on."

When Dad heard Kayden's math mark he repeated his promise to help get him into business school. "That's the place for you," he said. "You're a leader. The country needs you."

"I'm going to run a ranch, Mr. Munro, not an oil company," Kayden replied. "If I get through university."

"You will. And call me Uncle Rick."

"Yes, sir."

Mom decorated a cake with cowboys and a 78% and invited the Aunts and Uncles and Cousins over. And Willie and Stevie.

In the family, a 78 math mark isn't a celebration. The family expects 90s, but they were happy for Kayden. I suspect in their hearts they didn't expect better from a bull rider. Uncle Spencer didn't act as if he knew more about Kayden's life than anybody else, only telling him that the 78 proved he'd made the right decision not to sign up for high school sports.

Stevie backed Aubrey off from Kayden twice when she decided Aubrey's congratulations were getting too personal. Aubrey didn't like it. Kayden didn't notice. I stepped in, being the third party conciliator who never gets the girl.

"Hey, Stevie," I said to her, "The Jewel needs help bringing out Kayden's cake. Want to be the one carrying it?"

"What's this? A kid's birthday party? Jesus." She almost headed back to Aubrey when I pulled her into the kitchen.

"You can't win if you start something now," I told her. "You've got to let Kayden figure it out for himself. He and Aubrey are going different places in life. She's not going to want to get long term involved with a rancher. Let him find that out on his own. Just keep showing him who you are and where you're going."

Stevie took a deep breath. "Give me the fucking cake!"

Willie wore his blue satin shirt with the fringes to the party. As Stevie brought in the cake, he jumped onto a chair and began his arm waving dance. "Kayden! Kayden! Kayden!"

From the huge smile on my dad's face, I could tell that Willie's spontaneity had won him over.

Stevie cut the cake and handed the corner with the most icing to Aubrey. "You're going to need to keep up your strength!"

I knew I was going to have to warn my cousin about Stevie's tendency to get physical. But ... Aubrey was a soccer player. Could be interesting.

Dad and Uncle Spencer were in a corner looking serious. I thought I'd better investigate, not because I didn't trust Uncle Spencer. I only wanted to make sure we had our stories straight.

"Uncle Spencer says you've asked him for a little mentoring to get your life organized," Dad said to me. "I must admit I've seen an improvement lately. Working out at the gym. Studying. You're more focussed than I've ever seen you."

"I'm learning to listen to other people's advice, but making up my own mind about things I want to do." That sounded very adult. Thanks Uncle Spencer who is almost smiling.

"I'm all for whatever gets you into the accounting program," Dad said.

"Good marks are part of our agreement," Uncle Spencer said.

Dad looked over to where Willie, Mom and Stevie were talking. "Your friends have turned our house upside down," he laughed. "It was getting quiet around here last summer. Not any more. That Willie – he's different. Doesn't talk to me much. Where's he heading after grade 12? A vocational school?"

I hesitated. Uncle Spencer nodded slightly to me, encouraging me to answer.

"He's probably going to Harvard next year on a computer sciences or math scholarship."

Dad gave me a WTF look.

"That's right. Makes my computer award last year look not all that exciting."

"That was a good award. But Harvard!" He looked back toward Willie. "I thought Elbow Park had cornered most of the talent. Guess I was wrong. Looks like there's some on the other side of town."

Now it was my turn. WTF. Dad might be wrong?

On Friday night we went to the Rockin' R where Grandma Lillian was so pleased with the 78 she kissed Willie on the cheek. "Thanks for proving that Kayden can do more than ride bulls and throw footballs."

"That's nothing compared to what Mr. Uncle Spencer has taken on for your family," he replied. "If anybody can straighten out that situation, it's him. You can trust him."

Before we loaded the chutes for the Saturday afternoon practice, Stevie swore the Jackson twins to secrecy about my plan to ride a bull.

"You'll be sorry if you open your big mouths," she warned them.

"What the hell kind of idea is this?" Alex said. "Nathan's got a serious lack of natural talent. All he's got is an unnatural willingness to get bucked off."

"Here's the deal," Stevie answered back as quick as usual. "We all help each other or we practice somewhere else."

"Fine by me," Jimmie grinned. "Can I be in charge of helping you with anything?"

"You bet cowpoke. You can be in charge of making sure I don't beat the hell out of you for thinking any girl's gonna put up with you for more than 8 seconds."

"It's been known to happen."

I envied his self confidence.

Uncle Spencer had driven down that morning bringing the oxygen cylinder. He, Willie and Grandma Lillian watched from the plank walkway.

"Okay. Same as last time," Grandpa John announced. "Three bulls or three steers each. Draw for order. Except this time Grandma Lillian has an electronic timer. She'll sound the 8 seconds."

Grandma Lillian pushed a button on the timer letting loose a blast that woke the bulls. "No more complaining about a late buzzer," she told us.

Grandpa John called to Willie, "How fast can you run?"

"No cop's caught me yet," Willie replied. He might have been joking.

"Good. Let's see if you can outrun a bull. You're our bullfighter today. Get in here."

Willie raised his arms. "Speed of Light."

Grandpa John gave him a white towel to distract the bulls from the riders. "Stay close to the rails and if any bull turns towards you start running and climbing."

"Speed of Light. 186,000 miles per second. Up the rails and over the moon."

After every ride, Grandpa John made suggestions to the rider. Stay forward on your hand. Back straighter. Slow your free hand down. Take some chances. Expose yourself. Spur.

Alex and Jimmie coached Stevie and me. "If you're ever gonna ride a bull," Alex told me, "you can't ride like a sissy. One hand from now on."

I started to argue. "But I can't …"

Alex stopped me. "That's fine. We'll get you the broom." He ran to the door and brought back the broom used for sweeping the concrete. "Put this between your legs and hang on with both hands. When you can ride it, we'll get you a calf. You should be ready for a bull in five or six years."

I grabbed the broom and threw it over the rails.

Stevie went first and rode her steer one handed until the horn sounded.

I climbed into the chute with my steer. Kayden was spotting me. "You can do this Nathan," he said. "Believe it. We'll take our time getting you set up and out of the chute. Take some deep breaths and settle onto the steer's back. Jimmie will pull your rope."

I breathed as deeply as I could and felt my back relaxing. "Good," Kayden said. "Now here's how you'll do it. Tuck your chin in and look straight down at the steer's neck. Follow it and you'll keep up with his turns. Left arm bent and shoulder height." He patted me on the back. "You can do it."

Jimmie pulled the rope tight and Kayden wound it over my glove. "Pull yourself forward. We'll wait for you. Take deep breaths until you feel calm."

I took a few slow breaths.

"Is Jack Sparrow ready?" Kayden asked.

"That's *Captain* Jack Sparrow," I answered. I bit down on my mouth guard and nodded.

Everything went into slow motion. I wasn't thinking any more about falling off. I was thinking about riding. The gate swung open and I rode the first jump no problem. I followed the steer's neck to the right. My left hand swung forward and I slipped a little. I did what I had to do. I loosened my legs for an instant and then jammed my spurs into his sides. Suddenly the horn sounded. I let go.

It happened so slowly I thought I might land on my feet. Almost. I landed on my hands and knees. Willie sprinted by waving his towel at the steer.

Stevie ran up to me shouting, "You spurred that bastard. You spurred him! Holy Christ!"

That was my first 8 second ride. On Sunday I made another. But I wasn't Sunday's main event.

Willie had begun sprinting across the arena in front of the slower bulls on Saturday. On Sunday afternoon he began taunting them with his white towel. It was harmless fun.

The afternoon looked to be routine until Jimmie drew a Brahman that Grandpa John warned him about. "He'll use his horns if he gets you down. You don't have to take him. This is just a practice."

"I'll take him."

Grandpa John called Willie over to where we could all hear his instructions. "This could go bad. If Jimmie is on the ground and can't get to the rails, that bull might go for him. We'll have to be ready to draw the bull away. You okay with that?"

"Speed of Light," Willie answered.

"Fast and careful!" Grandpa John.

"Got it. Fast and careful."

Stevie pulled the gate. The Brahman's first high kick flipped Jimmie forward. The next jump bounced him backward and off. He landed on his face. Not moving.

The bull spun onto him, head down.

Alex was almost over the rails to help his brother when Willie ran full speed toward the bull. His arms pumping. The towel a white blur.

As he passed the bull he smacked its face with the towel and didn't stop running until he was on the top rail with the bull snorting up at him. It was the same bull slap run we'd seen the fighter make at Claresholm.

Kayden caught Willie from below just as he crumpled off the rail, white faced.

Alex helped Jimmie to his feet.

We all got bucked off our last rides of the day.

Grandma Lillian had burgers and beer for us again. The riders and Willie sat on the porch and discussed ways to score. The Great Bull Hunters telling their stories.

Grandpa John, Grandma Lillian and Uncle Spencer sat on the couches, knowing their day had passed.

Alex and Jimmie got excited about the Canadian Finals in Edmonton late that fall. "Jimmie and I have already qualified," Alex told Kayden. "We're going."

Stevie gave Kayden's shoulder a rub. "You'll qualify next year." You could tell by the tightness around his mouth how badly he wanted to be going this year. A reveal.

"Why don't we all go?" I suggested. "My dad has promised me a trip anywhere I want this fall. England, Australia. Anywhere. I could save him some money by going to Edmonton and bringing some friends."

"Don't go to Europe," Alex answered. "They got no bulls to ride there."

I didn't tell them I knew Dad would want to see the Finals, especially if we knew some of the riders. And I didn't say my birthday was right around that weekend and going to the rodeo would be my special day so the Aunts and Uncles and Cousins would come. I didn't say anything about my birthday. It would sound like I was 10 years old.

"If Willie went, he'd see some of the best bullfighters at work," Kayden said. "It'd be exciting for him."

"And for you, too," I said making Kayden smile. "You might see the riders you'll beat next year!"

That started a new back and forth about bull riders – especially the Brazilians who were making a name for themselves on the Professional Bull Riders circuit.

"I saw Adriano Moraes on TV win the 2001 Professional Bull Riding," Kayden said. "That guy really spurred. Like Nathan today."

Big laugh.

"I looked him up," Willie said. "Adriano, not Nathan. Two PBR titles. Rides left handed. Started when he was 15."

The twins stared at Willie.

"Got to know your subject," Willie said. "Alex, you're ranked eighth as of last Monday. $11,232. 1765 points. Jimmie's next with $10,566. But more points. 2170. Next rider has 1490.

"You both stay healthy and you're gonna win some real cash this fall."

He turned to Kayden. "I did the math on you, too. You could qualify. There's enough time left."

"How do you figure that?"

"Simple. I counted the events left before the Finals, and added up all the possible scores you could get. If you rode eleven out of twelve before then, you'd be in. You'd just have to get scores above 75 each ride. Nothing spectacular."

Alex shook his head. "That's not Kayden's style. He wouldn't be satisfied. It's 90s or bucked off for him."

"He could do it. He could ride eleven in a row," Stevie argued. "Then he could go for a perfect ride on one of the best bulls at Edmonton. That's your quest, isn't it Kayden?"

"I'll ride 'em all," Kayden said. "I'll make the Finals." Bull riders don't lack confidence.

Alex rubbed Willie's bristly head. "We owe you. And thanks for saving Jimmie's butt today. That Brahman had him lined up."

"I got something for you," Jimmie said. "By way of appreciation." He opened the welding rig door and pulled out a grey duffle bag. "Couple of years ago, I tried out for bullfighter school. I didn't like it. I liked seeing those cowboys get bucked off too much. I was always sympathizing for the bulls. But I ended up with this outfit. Might fit you."

He unzipped the bag and dumped out a protective vest, padded shorts, shin guards, and a pair of football cleats. "You'll have to get yourself some tights and underwear. Mine got ripped up!"

Alex shook his head. "They didn't get ripped up. They got messed up."

Jimmie handed the bag and gear to Willie. "They're yours if you want them."

No aurochs would catch Speed of Light wearing blue tights and football cleats.

Uncle Spencer, Willie and I left as the twins loaded their gear into the welding rig. Kayden and Stevie were going to change the oil and antifreeze in the tractor. I liked to see them working together. The Kayden and Aubrey romance would naturally wear itself out. The Kayden and Stevie friendship would survive bulls, broken down machinery and trustees.

I fell asleep in the back seat and didn't wake up until we got caught in the weekend traffic on Deerfoot Trail heading into Calgary.

Willie didn't want to spend the night at Uncle Spencer's. "My foster parents are getting suspicious. They want to know where I'm spending so much time on weekends."

"What do you tell them?" Uncle Spencer asked.

"That I'm working nights at a restaurant and then sleeping at a friend's. I can't keep it up much longer. They want a piece of my wages. I think I'm going to have to get fired." He laughed, his red hair bobbing up and down above the BMW's leather seats.

"All right. I'll take you home."

"You can't. Just drop me by a bus stop on 17th Avenue."

"Don't you want a ride?"

"Nope. They're suspicious. If they see me get out of this car, they'll think you're a dealer. They'll get your plate and find you. They'll threaten to turn you over to the drug squad if you don't pay up. I'm not 18 until Christmas. You and I'd be in a lot of hell."

Uncle Spencer shrugged. "Great life you got going there."

We dropped Willie off on 17th Avenue. "See you in Movie Club, Nathan," he said as I got into the front seat.

Uncle Spencer drove me home and parked in the driveway. "You did well this weekend," he said to me as I was getting out of the car. "Keep it up." I was expecting more enthusiasm.

Mom and Dad waved to us from the front door. Uncle Spencer waved back and drove away.

"Why did you come home with Uncle Spencer?" Mom asked as if it were her business. "Is everything all right?"

"Everything's fine. He came to the ranch to see me work the cattle." To work the cattle? A useful invention that was my business. I continued. "You know how Uncle Spencer is. Once he gets involved in a project, he's relentless. I'm his project until I graduate."

"Your father and I like to stay involved."

"You love me too much. Uncle Spencer doesn't give anybody a second chance when they screw up. Not even if he loves them."

There was no family dinner that Sunday so I showered and put on sweatpants and a hoodie to eat with Mom and Dad. As usual, it was Jewel's Restaurant, the best place to eat in Calgary.

"With all the exercise you're getting lately, I thought you should have extra protein," she said serving me a huge T bone. I couldn't tell her I'd eaten two of Grandma Lillian's No Buck Burgers.

"Your 18th birthday's coming up," Dad said with that bad boy look of his. "The Jewel and I have got some suggestions that are going to surprise you!"

I was dreading this. Elbow Park parents and their party plans.

"So do I," I said, surprising them.

"Tell us," Dad said. "We're listening."

"I want to take everybody – all the Aunts and Uncles and Cousins – to Edmonton for the Canadian Finals Rodeo. They'll love it. And it won't cost as much as a birthday party like Reese's."

"What about your friends?" Mom asked. "Don't you want to celebrate with them?"

"They want to come. Kayden and his grandparents, Willie, and Stevie. Jimmie and Alex Jackson – they're a couple of bull riders we're friends with – will be competing. We could buy a whole section of tickets or even a box."

I don't think I ever loved The Commotion more than when they didn't hesitate. I knew those weren't the friends they were thinking of.

"If that's what you want," Mom said, "we'll buy the tickets." There wasn't a trace of disappointment in her voice.

"I bet Dad's got a guy," I said making them smile. "Just like he always has a guy for the Stampede tickets."

I wished then that I could have told them about my plans to ride a bull, but all I could tell them was about watching Kayden, Jimmie and Alex. And Stevie riding steers one handed. And Willie the bullfighter.

"It doesn't sound safe at all," Mom said. "Any one of them could be injured or even killed."

"Sounds like fun," Dad said. "I might have tried it myself a few years ago. I'm surprised you're not tempted."

"I pull the chute gates sometimes. And I'm the announcer." I don't know where that invention came from.

"Grandma Lillian says I'm pretty good at announcing. I have natural charisma."

Mom nodded. "I agree. You've got stage presence from your drama classes. It makes you a great model. Which you should be doing more of, by the way."

I didn't correct that assumption. Models don't get their black and blue butts bucked off every weekend. I felt guilty about my inventions.

Emily Arbutus had her *Deep Throat* DVD ready to go that week. We settled in our desks and watched Linda Lovelace perform. Emily leaned back in her teacher chair, legs crossed. She had healthy calf muscles. After fifteen minutes, we were all restless and bored. Emily, sensing the mood, stopped the DVD and suggested we take a discussion break. She walked slowly amongst us.

"What do you think so far?" she asked.

No hands up.

"Stevie?" she asked. "You introduced the film, so tell us what you're thinking."

Stevie leaned back. "To be honest, I'm disappointed by my choice. I thought it would be better than this. Once you've watched a couple of sex scenes, it's kind of repetitive."

Willie raised his hand. "I agree. The sex scenes aren't enough to keep us interested. This is not 1970. We can watch better porn on the Internet."

"That's a good comment, Willie. Does anybody know what's missing, what would make the film work?"

"It needs more story," I said. "I agree with Willie, once the sex loses its appeal, there's no reason to keep watching. You don't really care about what happens to the characters."

"That's right," Kayden said. "I lost interest after ten minutes. It was boring."

Emily nodded in agreement. "That's what I thought too. Films need to be page turners. They have to keep the audience wanting to know what's going to happen next. That's one of the most important ways they hold our attention." She ejected the DVD. "Let's talk about plots in films – what makes a good one? What types of stories appeal to you?"

Willie raised his hand. Again. "I have one. It's about people our age. Not me, but somebody else. I like math and I'm going to go to university and study math and then work for a computer company. That's not an interesting story. No plot.

"But suppose, just supposing here and not talking about anybody in particular, suppose there was somebody and that somebody was told he had to be a doctor like his parents but he – or she – didn't want to. He – or she – maybe wanted to be something unexpected like a fashion designer. I'm only using that as an example. Nobody here but Emily looks too fashionable. Well, maybe Nathan who is wearing a $200 Hugo Boss shirt.

"Anyways, maybe this somebody – call him the main character – can't tell anybody about his fashion designer idea. And he ends up being a doctor in a hospital and gets sucked into this Stephen Hawking black hole until only his arms and head are showing. But he won't call out for help. He just gets sucked in deeper and deeper – I'm not making a *Deep Throat* joke here – and all his famous friends are standing around him with their arms out and ready to pull him free. Maybe cowboy type Matt Dillon is there and Gillian Anderson who sort of looks like Emily, and a couple of other marquee names like Kate Winslett except with Stevie's calloused hands and grip. Anyways, the point is our main character won't reach back.

"That would be a good start to a film I'd like to see."

Emily looked from Willie to the rest of us. "Any of you have a way to move Willie's plot forward? Kayden?"

"I don't think the black hole idea works," he answered. "Too science sounding. I think the main character needs to be trapped inside himself. Metaphorically. He needs to be caught in some sort of lie that he has told himself."

"Metaphorically?" Emily raised her eyebrows. "I'm impressed Kayden. Keep going."

"Well, he might not admit to himself that he wants to be a fashion designer – personally a bad choice if you want an action film – but he doesn't want to disappoint his family and friends. So the lie he tells himself is that he can't be a doctor because he has chosen an even more impossible career."

"What kind of impossible career could he pick?" Emily asked.

Stevie laughed. "He could choose to be a bull rider like Kayden."

"Are you a bull rider, Kayden?" Emily asked. No hint of anything there. No suspicion that he might be Bull Rider.

"I'm going to be a rancher. I ride bulls but I won't do that all my life. I'm like Willie. I know where I'm going."

"All right," Emily said. "Let's say we have this main character who wants to be a fashion designer but doesn't want to disappoint his family's dream of him being a doctor. So he traps himself in something metaphorically impossible – bull riding."

Willie raised his hand again. "Kayden's idea is better than mine. He sees the way we fool ourselves. Deception by others or by ourselves always moves a plot forward. That's what a rodeo bullfighter does to bulls."

Emily shook her head in disbelief. "And I suppose you're a bullfighter."

"You bet. When a bull gets a cowboy down, I jump in fast as light waving a towel. Distract that mean machine from the cowboy he wants to kick the shit out of."

Willie leapt to his feet, skinny elbows and knees pumping as he ran on the spot. "Look at me, Mr. Bull! Forget the cowboy. Run. I'm Speed of Light fast." He circled the classroom and leapt onto his chair. "Speed of Light."

Emily turned to Stevie. "And you?"

"Steer rider and mechanic."

Then me.

"Announcer."

Willie slapped his desk. "Bucked off! Wrong answer! You ride. Go on. You rode one handed last week. 8 seconds."

"I'm not very good. Only steers so far. Everybody's better than me."

Emily looked intrigued, giving me an all strawberry blonde interested in me smile. "Well, isn't this a class of four surprises. I'm guessing one of you doesn't want to be the doctor Willie talked about, the one with the arranged destiny."

"It's not me," we all said at once.

"Of course not," she answered. "We've still got a few minutes left. I think the discussion today showed us something about how films work. We started off with a classic porn film and now we're talking about ourselves and how we see our lives. And we're finding out that often we are not who we appear to be. That's the real life version of exposing the persona in films that Nathan told us about last week.

"Willie is the best example. He didn't talk in the first few classes. Just gave us facts. Then we let him and Stevie show *Deep Throat.* Now he's Speed of Light talking. Why the change Willie?"

He didn't hesitate. "This is the only class where anybody ever cared what I had to say."

"You just made my career, Willie." Emily's blue eyes lit Willie up.

The others could tell I wasn't happy as we walked to Kayden's truck.

"What are you pouting for?" Stevie asked.

"You guys were talking about me in there."

"Only metaphorically," Kayden said. "You don't want to be a doctor, do you?"

"Or a fashion designer," Willie added. "You just want to wear the clothes."

Stevie told me what she thought of my mood in the only way she knew. She jumped me from behind and put me in a headlock until my ears burned.

"Give up!" she demanded. "Admit you want to be a Pretty Boy Fashion Designer."

"I want to be left alone."

She released me and I turned to walk home alone.

"See you Friday back in Movie Club," Willie shouted to me as they loaded into the pickup.

They passed me on the street. Stevie waved, leaning out of the truck window.

"Assholes!" I yelled. They thought that was funny. It was hard to stay mad at them.

I figured I had at least two hours alone before The Commotion got home. I had a physics assignment to do which was a total waste of time for me. You need physics, Nathan. How often had I heard that? Had anybody ever asked if I wanted physics?

I decided to stretch out on the couch for a while and enjoy the quiet. That was impossible. You live with The Commotion long enough and sooner or later you're going to see that lying on the couch opens the guilt door. Get busy. Accomplish something. I couldn't fight it. Homework seemed like giving in to an ambition that I didn't feel connected to. I decided to do something selfish. Just for myself. For a change. That's what Chet Jr. should do.

Dear Emily Arbutus

Thanks for your email last week. And suggestions. So here's some more for you to read. I agree, way too much backstory. I'm trying hard to introduce action.

You're making me a believer in myself. Thanks.

Bull Rider

PS. Have you thought of 'Good Will Hunting' for your Film Studies class? I overheard Willie say he would like to discuss that one.

PS PS. Willie's definitely not a friend of mine. Too weird. He mentioned the film in cafeteria while he was eating somebody else's fries.

PS PS PS. No, I haven't said anything to my family about Buck Off. I want this to be mine.

BUCK OFF

ACT I SCENE 4
THE MANBULL

EXT. THE ICE CREAM TRUCK - LATE MORNING

CHET

Mom, it's time for my break, I'll see ya later.

WIDE LENS OF FAIRGROUNDS

Chet hurries along the rows of carnival games, food kiosks, consisting of the regular carnival menu; corn dogs, hamburgers, pizza, mini donuts and frozen lemonade. Young kids selling tickets to the midway rides. The big ride this year is the "Drop of Doom."

A mosaic of people line up to try their hands at various games of chance. Periodically "We have a winner," is shouted to the crowd.

THE CAMERA NARROWS IN ON A POPULAR MIDWAY SKILL GAME

Jonah, a 17-year-old carnie-raised smart aleck is taunting a 10-year-old boy who is trying to knock three pins down with a ball. The odds are obviously against this young boy. He throws and he misses by a mile.

JONAH

Ohhhh, so close, yet so far off.

Ha, you suck kid. You can't hit the broad side of a barn, ha ha ha.

When the kid starts to cry, Jonah becomes incorrigible.

JONAH

Oh boo hoo you little creep. You want a free throw?

Jonah hands the kid the ball, the kid stops crying, he isn't sure what to do, he finally goes for it. He throws the ball. Jonah jumps up and intercepts the ball out of mid air. He fires it back at the kid.

JONAH

(yelling)

Hey kid ... think twice!

The little kid runs away frightened and bawling.

JONAH

(chants)

Oh ya baby. In-your-face.

Denied, rejected, stuffed like a Thanksgiving turkey.

Get your little garbage can of a self out of here.

Go cry to mommy!

Chet rushes over.

CHET

Jonah, you're an asshole.

JONAH

Did you see that little pansy step into my shit?

CHET

Ya Jonah, I did. I don't understand it.

You rig the game, and you still want to taunt and bully anyone who plays that is smaller than you.

JONAH

It's called repeat business. That little shit wants a piece of me now! I bet he's back today and every day till he beats the odds ... which is never ... ha ha.

CHET

Whatever, Jonah, I'm headed over to catch the opening of the rodeo. Wanna come?

JONAH

Oh yeah, look at the time. The barrel racing is starting. Bobbi Jo should be showing up soon. You better run!

Chet can't hide his red face, he looks embarrassed.

CHET

Shut up Jonah. I like the rodeo and I'm on a break. Come or not, I don't give a shit.

JONAH

Oh yeah, you piece of crap liar, your mommy forbids you to go to the rodeo. Ha ha. You have a giant crush on that smokin' hot barrel racer and everyone knows it.

Jonah turns to the carnie that works for him.

JONAH

You watch the station. I've counted all my stuffed shit, so I'll know if you try anything funny and I'll kill ya if anything's missin'."

Jonah looks at Chet.

JONAH

Well, what do ya know? I'm on a break too.

Chet and Jonah walk towards the outdoor stadium grandstand.

They walk through the tunnel and past the chutes to the alley entrance where the barrel racers wait their turn. Nobody asks them for credentials, everyone knows them.

JONAH

So I'm your friend right? But when it comes to chicks, I don't care if you're hot on a girl, I can still hit on her! It's a contest and may the best man win. Ya got that Chet?

Chet isn't interested, he hardly hears Jonah. His eyes are on the centre aisle of the arena. The barrel racing has begun. A beautiful blonde girl in a shiny cowgirl outfit confidently rides her horse to the starting line.

CHET

(whispering)

There she is ...

ANNOUNCER

These amazing athletes are a crowd favourite, being right here from Alberta. Bobbi Jo's mother was the barrel racing champ in 1992. She has passed the reins to her daughter who is now her own name at the Calgary Stampede.

Both Chet and Jonah are speechless as Bobbi Jo and her horse Rain, an 11-year-old quarter horse palomino mare, enter the arena. Both she and Rain have beautiful blonde manes that shine as they gallop past the electronic eye to start the timer. The duo circles the first barrel with perfection, Rain nicks the second barrel but calmly Bobbi Jo reaches down and steadies the barrel with her hand. The 17,000 fans are on their feet in the grandstand.

Bobbi Jo and Rain flash past the electric eye finish line.

ANNOUNCER

17:48 The best time of the day.

Bobbi Jo and Rain wait quietly on the side of the centre aisle for two more barrel racers to finish. Bobbi Jo spots Chet and waves. Chet makes his way over to Bobbi Jo and Rain.

BOBBI JO

(whispers)

Well if it isn't my biggest fan? Hello there Chet. Thanks for coming.

She winks. Chet as usual is awestruck by her beauty and can barely talk. He is crimson.

CHET

Hey Bobbi Jo, great ride! You were awesome!

She smiles.

After a moment of awkward silence Chet struggles to make conversation. When he means to say you can ride with me anytime (weak) he somehow blurts out, "You can ride me anytime?"

Thank God this doesn't really register with

Bobbi Jo.

Chet is now mentally coaching himself to speak. Say something!

CHET

Umm

BOBBI JO

Not that I don't love it when you come to watch me but what about your ice cream fans? You better get back to work so I can come and get one of my favourite double dips. How's your mom? I can't wait to see her. She made this shirt. She's the best.

Chet realizes how long he's been gone. His mom will be pissed.

CHET

Good bye, catch ya later. Jonah, you gonna hang for a bit?

JONAH

Ya, I'm going to hang for a bit.

Jonah gives Chet a silly grin, indicating he'll be making his move.

Chet runs off leaving Jonah with Bobbi Jo. Bobbi Jo is nice to everyone but she finds it hard to be nice to Jonah who she finds "just too weird."

Jonah seizes the moment.

JONAH

Hey cowgirl, you from Tennessee?

Bobbi Jo gives Jonah a confused look.

JONAH

Cause you're the only 10, I see.

BOBBI JO

Really. That's all you got, Jonah?

The announcer, Bob calls her name.

ANNOUNCER

And here they are folks, today's barrel racing leader. Miss Bobbi Jo Williamson from Ponoka, Alberta, on her horse Rain.

They gallop into the wild clapping of the crowd; she turns and waves to the crowd. They circle the arena for a well-deserved victory lap.

Chet returns to the ice cream truck. He sees his mom working the long line. He apologizes.

CHET

Mom, sorry. Why don't you and Auntie Chris go grab a coffee, I got this.

Out the back Chet hears some laughing, then hears the freezer door open and close. Did he forget to lock it? He walks to the back of the truck and sees Max Samson and some of his friends. They have stolen a bucket of ice cream from the freezer.

CHET

(yelling)

Max, you guys drop it now!

Marlena walks around the back.

MARLENA

Oh just ignore it Chet and next time make sure you lock it up.

Chet yells again.

CHET

Drop it Max!

They drop the bucket and it explodes when it hits the ground making a huge mess. Chet makes a fist.

MARLENA

Stop Chet. It's only one bucket.

CHET

Mom, no. They're rude. They tease and bully everyone. They have taunted us for so long now. It's a game to them. They steal more than they could ever eat. We need to end this crap.

MARLENA

Chet! Ignore them.

Chet is indignant ... he feels terrible for his mom but he also wants his own revenge.

MARLENA

Chet, please.

Chet goes to walk away and then notices Bobbi Jo. She has seen Max and his hooligan friends steal the container.

BOBBI JO

(shouts)

Hey Max, what do you think you're doing?

Chet is now forced to do something. He must show his manhood.

CHET

Max get back here, you have to pay for that.

Max keeps running.

In a way Chet feels sorry for Max. With a dad like Keith Samson, Max has never stood a chance to be a decent guy.

Max turns around and walks back.

MAX

Yah, what's it to ya, ya dairy serving dork?

CHET

Come on Max, you know you can't steal ice cream from my mom.

MAX

I never stole nothin', you popsicle pushin' pansy.

CHET

I'm done Max ... pay for the ice cream or I'll kick your ass.

Max laughs and starts to run away again, looking back he yells.

MAX

Ya right, go tell your mommy!

A larger line is beginning to form in the front of the truck. The customers have heard the commotion and curiously are looking to the back of the ice cream truck. Marlena is getting anxious. She needs Chet to back down. She has never seen this kind of aggression from him. She knows nothing good can come of a conflict with the Samsons.

Chet runs after Max, mumbling under his breath. The sun blinds his eyes.

CHET

I'll get that little shit.

Chet runs right into the stone hard chest of a massive cowboy, Keith Samson. The force sends Chet backward on his ass. He looks up, still blinded by the sunlight and sees the outline of the huge man.

KEITH

Well hello there. If it isn't the Ice Cream Queen himself? You in a hurry?

Chet jumps to his feet and dusts himself off. His head is spinning. He can hear Keith's gaggle of cowboy goons laughing. The roaring laughter echoes in Chet's head. The goons also fear Keith. Most of the time they are drunk or high.

CHET

Your son owes my mom for a bucket of ice cream that he stole. He dropped it running away and left this mess.

Chet points to the ice cream that is melting all over the ground. Keith approaches looking Chet right in the eye.

KEITH

Whoa. Slow down, you little Ben and Jerry fairy. My boy don't owe ya shit. Anyone see him steal ice cream?

Keith looks at the goons, they shake their heads.

CHET

Oh come on, Keith.

KEITH

No, you come on. I'm the number one rider on this circuit. I bring in all the fans and all the money. You don't mess with me, or my kid. Is that understood? My boy is the best junior rider. We don't pay for shit ... ya got that? And if I ever hear you picking on my kid again I'll see that you don't sell another one of your precious little ice cream cones.

CHET

I'm sorry Keith but we can't afford to overlook this.

As Chet turns to walk back into the truck. He mumbles under his breath.

CHET

You beefcake piece of crap.

Keith lunges towards Chet.

KEITH

What was that boy?

Chet sees Marlena at the door. She looks frightened. The midway is busy and we now have a crowd watching.

CHET

It's not right Keith ... we'll forget it this time but Max can't be stealing from people. He needs to learn right from wrong.

KEITH

Well ya don't say and ain't that mighty hospitable of ya boy. Now show me some real manners and get your ass back in the truck and get me a chocolate waffle cone with two scoops of fruit. On the house.

Chet growls. Stops. Looks at his mother, freezes for a second and then puts his head down and slowly walks to the door.

Keith notices the crowd. Right behind him the goons are waiting for what is going to happen next. Keith's constant need for attention overcomes him. He sticks his long leg behind Chet's and trips him from behind.

Chet falls into a puddle of the ice cream that has collected at the back of the truck. He now has mud and melted ice cream all over him.

The goons have broken out into a fit of laughter; the crowd dissipates as Chet gets up. Anger, embarrassment, and rage fire from his sky blue eyes. But he knows he is defeated as he looks at the small group left standing.

His eyes turn to Bobbi Jo. Chet can't read what

she is thinking; probably what a loser he is.

Chet's head falls to his chest. He wants to disappear. The situation has escalated out of his control.

KEITH

Ok now boy, get my cone, you sissy.

Chet slinks back inside.

INT. THE MOTOR HOME - MORNING.

MARLENA

Chet, it's just not worth it. Why do you have to engage?

CHET

We should report them.

MARLENA

To who? You have no proof. Are you going to make Bobbi Jo a witness?

CHET

I just don't think it's right.

MARLENA

Leave it alone Chet.

EXT. THE SAMSON BARN - MORNING

MAX

(quietly to his father)

Why do we hate the Montgomerys?

KEITH

Cause they think they're better than us. That bitch Marlena walks around like she's above it all. Her husband was the same and now she's got that goody-two-shoes kid that thinks his shit don't stink.

Keith puts his hand in the air and does a little flap of the wrist.

KEITH

The Montgomerys would rather have a spot of tea than have a beerski with the rest of us. I tell ya, I'd like to get rid of them all.

MAX

I think the mom seems nice.

KEITH

Well she ain't. Women like her pretend they're all nicey nicey, but that one is dangerous. We gotta watch her. (He pounds a fist into his other hand threateningly.) We got to teach her that the Samsons run the show.

INT. THE MOTOR HOME - LATER THAT MORNING.

Chet and Jonah are sitting around the table. In front of them sits a giant bowl of ice cream topped with chocolate and fruit. They each have a long ice cream spoon that they use to take turns diving into the bowl, pulling it to either side as they talk and eat.

Chet's elbows never leave the table. His bright blue eyes have become raven, taken on a sense of darkness. His smile has all but disappeared, turned upside down.

JONAH

Man that Keith is a fuckin' asshole. If I was there! Man, I would've messed that bitch's ass up.

CHET

Whatever Jonah, let's just leave it alone.

JONAH

No! Why are you such a pansy ass? Really, are you kidding me, you need to stick up for yourself! Chet, seriously ...

Chet looks up in a moment of clarity.

CHET

You know what Jonah ... you're ABSOLUTELY right. I need to go tell that half-evolved barnyard SOB what's what.

JONAH

Ya boy, that's what I'm talkin' bout.

CHET

What the hell. I'm doin' it!

Chet shoves the ice cream over to Jonah with authority and storms out slamming the trailer door behind him.

Jonah forms a fist in the air and hammers his arm down with force. He stops; he clearly pictures the dangerous explosion he has ignited.

JONAH

(yelling)

DUDE! DUDE! get back here!

INT. THE SAMSON BARN - MORNING

Keith stands tall in the barn. His massive bull-like body demands the respect and adoration of the simple-minded goons.

KEITH

What does an ice cream cone and Marlena Montgomery have in common?

The goons try to look interested. They've heard most of Keith's jokes many times.

KEITH

They are both sweet but too frigid.

The goons slapping their thighs and laughing,

over animated. Chet barges in, throws his arm up and points his finger at Keith. In unison the goons say oh oh ... they look first at Chet and then slowly turn their heads to Keith. Chet opens his mouth but nothing comes out.

KEITH

All right now, you slow down, you hear me, you banana split bitch, you don't just come barging into my barn.

CHET

No Keith, you got it wrong. No more free ice cream, and you'll keep your rude comments to yourself.

Chet has a moment of self satisfaction before the goons followed by Keith burst into laughter.

KEITH

Well looky here boys; Smoothie Susie wants to be a man now.

Keith slowly moves toward Chet. A tank ready for combat.

KEITH (CONT'D)

Look boy, you don't want to get into this, so you turn your sorry ass around and get the hell out of my barn before I get pissed off.

Keith has put the same fright back into Chet. Chet reverts back to his cowardly behaviour. His head hits his chest. He shuffles off. From the corner of his eye he sees Bobbi Jo again. That same crushing look on her face.

Chet slowly turns around. His shoulders move up and back. He stands tall.

CHET

No Keith, you've bullied me and others for a long time now. I've had enough. It's over.

Keith shoves his chest toward Chet. His strong breath upon him.

KEITH

Now listen here boy ... just cause people been tellin' you your daddy is some kinda hero don't give you the courage you never had. Right boy?

Keith shoves Chet. Chet stumbles backward.

CHET

Let's take this out on the field Keith? Where real men show their strength.

Jonah has walked in. His mouth drops open as he hears the conflict. What the hell is Chet thinking? Chet also can't believe the challenge he has just made. His body language contradicts his words.

KEITH

Don't make me laugh. You wouldn't know a steer from a bull, you little numb nuts. You couldn't even beat my kid.

Keith looks over at Max who has run over to his father's side.

KEITH

Right Maxie?

Keith rubs the top of Max's head.

CHET

Oh yeah, I can and I will. So here's the bet, Keith. If I win, you lay off me and start paying for your ice cream.

KEITH

Ok, but if Max wins, you'll shovel the barn shit for a week all by yourself.

He laughs and walks off. The goons follow.

Let's go get the sheep boys.

CHET YELLING

You gotta deal! Wait, what sheep?

He looks over to Jonah.

JONAH

Jesus Chet, what just happened?

CHET

I think I might've just screwed up.

JONAH

Let's go find your Uncle Johnny and get you some gear.

An hour later Jonah is giving Chet a pump-up massage.

CHET

So what is this sheep thing again, what do I do?

JONAH

I don't really know, I think ya just hold on like hell.

Bobbi Jo enters the barn and looks at Chet.

BOBBI JO

You know Chet, I really want you to win. Everyone hates Keith. I wish I could help. It's not that easy. You ride on the back of the sheep as long as you can. The one who stays on the longest wins. But you'll have to try and keep your legs up, you're way too tall for this. Did ya not do this as a kid?

CHET

This is ridiculous.

BOBBI JO

It should be entertaining, if nothing else.

Chet looks into her beautiful eyes and loses his thought.

JONAH

Chet, you there?

Chet snaps back into it.

CHET

Well Bobbi Jo. I'm tired of the jerk and I have to stand up to him.

BOBBI JO

Ya, he's a jerk, but a children's rodeo event seems crazy, do you know what you're doing?

CHET LAUGHS

Mom never let me try anything like this. But it's too late now.

EXT. A PRACTICE ARENA - AFTERNOON

Keith and Max are in the background. Keith is getting Max ready for the contest. They push and shove, do a chest bump and a high five. Max turns to look over to Chet.

MAX

You ready for 31 flavours of pain?

Chet turns red. His boiling point is rising.

JONAH

Want me to just take the little bastard out?

Chet is wearing a white safety helmet, a Wrangler shirt and jeans that look too tight. He also looks petrified and ridiculous.

Max is wearing a black helmet. He looks meaner than any kid should. He continues to taunt Chet.

Chet knows this game and ignores him.

A small crowd has gathered. Keith blows the horn. The gate swings open. Max comes out of the gate, solidly riding the sheep. The sheep zigzags across the arena as fast as a pup chasing a rabbit. Max jumps off the sheep and lets out a giant yahoo!

The horn sounds again! Chet comes out of the centre chute, running after the sheep, he grabs the rope and tries to gain on the sheep but his foot gets tangled in the slack and the sheep drags him around the field. The goons go crazy. They are laughing hysterically, so hard they can hardly stand, slapping each other. Keith is laughing and shaking his head. Chet's uncle, Johnny Anderson, is in Keith's crowd, trying hard not to laugh.

Chet finally releases himself and is walking off the field, feeling like a fool.

KEITH

8 am tomorrow. The shit will be waitin' for ya, Miss Milkshake!

Chet leaves the field, kicking the dirt as he walks. Jonah is running after him.

CHET

How could I be so goddamn stupid? Mom's gonna kill me. Who will work in the truck tomorrow? Bobbi Jo probably thinks I'm a loser and she's not wrong.

Jonah's trying hard not to laugh.

JONAH

Why wasn't you on the sheep ever? Why was ya chasin' the sheep from the start? Ya looked like an idiot.

CHET

Close it! Jonah

JONAH

I'm just sayin'.

CHET

I'll keep my word, not that he would understand that, but I'll shovel the bastard's shit. But if he thinks this is over, he is sadly mistaken.

JONAH

Your mom is going to be pissed.

CHET

Who cares? At least I did something.

Emily replied two hours later.

Dear Bull Rider

I don't know if you did this intentionally, but you have returned your character to his childhood: 'Mutton Busting' is a children's event. Does Chet (or Bull Rider) still view himself as a child, especially around Marlena?

You're doing better at writing the action and dialogue, and that's where films make an important connection with an audience.

We see Chet Jr. in a world of bullies and the bullied. Jonah the carnie is bullying the small boy who wants to win a prize, and Keith and his goons are bullying Chet. And he's afraid of his Mom.

Let's go back to the original premise you sent me:

Chet must overcome his insecurities by proving to himself that he is his father's equal in the rodeo arena, while bringing Keith Samson to justice. His overprotective mother, Marlena, thwarts his attempts to live up to the reputation of his heroic father.

I think this is an important writing intersection for you. Maybe it is time to see if you need to work out your own story first before you write it. There's nothing wrong with taking a break here and thinking about it. Every writer needs to take a break from a story.

Emily Arbutus

PS. I'll ask if the class would like to discuss 'Good Will Hunting.'

PS PS. I'm a bull riding fan – Adriano Moraes and anybody else who can make 8 seconds.

Adriano Moraes. Emily!

I went downstairs when I heard the front door open and Mom call out: "Nathan. Are you home?"

She'd turned off her I Love You smile.

"I just saw Stevie hanging out the window of Kayden's truck on Elbow Drive, waving at some boys."

I shrugged. "That's not so bad."

"It's wild behaviour. And dangerous." Like steer riding?

"She's your friend. You should talk to her." And get another headlock. No thanks.

"Are you studying?"

"I'm working on a Drama Department project."

"Is that the class you're in with Stevie? Does she ever study?"

"She's passing everything. She's smart, you know."

"No. I don't know. She certainly didn't look smart on Elbow Drive."

Mom didn't want to like Stevie. She wanted to see Reese around the house more often. Reese's intentions weren't hard to understand. She was the manager, and I was the project she'd be taking over from Mom. Great plan. Simple. With a happy ever after ending.

I suppose.

"Stevie's ok," I said. "Not everybody can be like you."

"Obviously, but she's going to be a mechanic. That's not where you're …"

I stopped her. When she gets to the 'but' part of a conversation I know that what's coming next is going to be her version of what's right.

"Stevie's fun to hang around with." A hunter.

"You should be thinking about your future. You need to start building relationships that will last."

"With Reese?"

Mom changed the topic, sort of. "How's physics going?"

"Willie said he would tutor me. He's in the advanced class. Probably teaching it."

"You need a proper tutor. One with a degree. Reese's mother told me about a nice young man with a science and a business degree. I think he would be perfect for you. A life coach. A friend for you. I called him and he's going to come over next week to meet you."

"Willie will help me. And Uncle Spencer is mentoring me."

"Willie won't be around after this year and then who will tutor you at university? And, yes, Uncle Spencer is involved in your life more than ever. But he has ideas that we think don't suit you."

"Like what?"

"We raised you to be less judgmental. He's critical. And he pushes too hard."

"I'm learning to handle it."

My phone rang. Bad coincidence. It was my too judgmental uncle.

"Listen," he said. No hello or how are you? Straight into it. "I've got all the paperwork together on the Rockin' R. This would be a good opportunity for you to look at an actual accounting situation. I'll pick you up in five minutes."

I turned to Mom. "It's Uncle Spencer. He's got some accounting project he's going to let me help with. He's on his way to pick me up. It will be a learning experience for me. Ok?"

"All right," she said without any positive reinforcement.

I told Uncle Spencer I'd be waiting outside.

"Total involvement," I said to Mom as I hung up. "That's Uncle Spencer. Mr. 100 Percent Commitment."

I think I impressed him a little bit by how fast I caught on to what he was showing me. First, he walked me through the ranch income and expenses. I got that right away. Then he gave me a problem to solve.

"Look at those numbers again and tell me if anything doesn't look right. A little too high or too low. Or if something seems hard to explain."

I went through the numbers again. "I'm not sure what some of these should be," I said. "I don't know what hay costs, or how much fuel the ranch uses."

"Don't worry about that, just look at the types of entries."

I tried again and saw it sharp as an aurochs' horns. "What are Administrative Fees?"

"That's what the trustee is charging to manage the ranch for Kayden."

"Don't Grandpa John and Grandma Lillian manage the ranch? How are they getting paid?"

"They're not. You asked the right question. That's one of the questions we're going to ask. Here's another." He handed me a sheet listing the ranch's assets and liabilities. "This is what they own and what they owe. Now, look at it the same way you did the income and expenses."

The ranch was worth a lot of money. Kayden would be rich one day – if he got through university.

"I'm not sure how to tell if the figures are right. It looks like the land is the most valuable part of the ranch."

"Good so far. Now what doesn't make sense to you? What would you question?"

I went through the lists again. "Boy, Kayden has a big university fund. Good to see he's got that."

"Keep going." Uncle Spencer was patient.

"And the ranch has a big reserve fund."

"You've got accounting instincts, Nathan. You spotted the dubious items right away. Well done. Now tell me why you think those funds could be a problem."

"I don't know. It's just money, isn't it?"

"No. Those funds could be anything the trustee invests in. Stocks, real estate. Term deposits. We don't know. That's what we're going to ask about."

"We?"

"Yes. We. I'll talk to Kayden's grandparents this weekend and get the authorization for us to twist that trustee's tail – if we have to."

"Us?"

"Yes. Us. You're my student."

I agreed. I wanted to see Uncle Spencer twist some tail.

Dad was pulling into the driveway as Uncle Spencer was dropping me off.

"Hey, Spence," Dad said to him. "What are you teaching Nathan now? Bridge or golf?"

"Forensic accounting. He passed my first exam. He found the cheat first time."

"Your clients don't cheat."

"This cheater's not a client. It's a trustee we've caught with his hand in the family's cookie jar."

"Well, I hope Nathan gets paid for his detective work. Rule number one for accountants." They both laughed.

"The only pay he gets is my goodwill," Uncle Spencer said when they got over that joke. "Want to buy some for yourself?" Wow. Accounting humour. Sure to get a standing ovation around the commerce campfire.

"Seriously," Uncle Spencer said to Dad. "I've underestimated Nathan. He's got guts. And brains. He's a Munro."

Dad was grinning. His son getting praise from Uncle Spencer. Unheard of. I know Dad had been worrying about my career goals. This boost from Uncle Spencer settled his concerns. For now.

"Time for dinner," Mom called. Uncle Spencer waved to her and left.

Chicken Parmesan and a half glass of Chardonnay for dinner tonight. I don't know how Mom expects me to get married as long as Jewel's Restaurant stays open. Mom would have to promise the happy couple that we could stop by anytime without a reservation.

After dinner we played crib. No studying. Dad told Mom I was on my way to becoming Canada's leading forensic accountant. Fabulous!

When Stevie called, Mom grabbed my phone and asked her to come over and play cards. I think Mom had had a little more than her share of the Chardonnay.

"Stand back, I'm spending a couple of nights," Stevie said as she threw her suitcase and a sleeping bag through the doorway. "It's an emotional Chernobyl at my house."

"A glass of wine, perhaps," Mom asked. "Chardonnay is very settling."

"No thanks. Wine makes me want to fight. I don't want to hurt Nathan."

Mom told me to carry Stevie's suitcase and sleeping bag to the spare bedroom.

Mom put her arm over Stevie's shoulder. "Now you just tell The Jewel what happened and we'll sort it out."

"My mom kicked me out. Somebody told her I was waving out of Kayden's pickup on Elbow Drive."

"Were you?"

"Of course. I spotted a couple of cute boys and tried to get Kayden to stop. He wouldn't so I could only wave. It was funny."

She smiled at me. "You should have seen me, Pretty Boy. High School Cheerleader out of control."

Mom interrupted. "And that's what your mother is upset about."

"Well, I might have yelled a few things too. Kayden laughed so they must have been good."

Mom frowned. "No wonder your mother is upset."

Dad interrupted. "Let's not go into that now. Let's have a quiet evening. What do you say, Stevie? Want to play bridge with us? We need a fourth."

Stevie surprised me by agreeing. Then she surprised all of us by turning into a card counting, finessing machine as she and Dad whipped Mom and me. Whipped us badly.

Dad didn't make any comment that night about scratches. I think he was in awe of Stevie. Maybe scared.

I found Willie in the cafeteria the next day and bought him lunch. "I need to talk to you," I said.

We sat at a quiet table eating burgers and fries. Willie was so hungry I bought him a second order.

"I don't get breakfast at the home," he told me. "And I was up late at the public library. It'd be easier if I had a computer at the home but it would get sold. Only one more year and I'll be at university. I tested the computers at the U of C. Way better than the library."

I stopped him before he got into telling me the specs on all the public computers in Calgary. "You remember how you said you'd help me with physics?"

"No problem."

"Actually the problem is my mom has hired a tutor for me. She didn't tell me and ..."

"Still no problem. Any physics you'll be doing is just applied math. You're okay at math. Anybody can help you with physics if you want to learn it, unless you're going to be like Einstein and mostly do thought experiments and then figure out the math later. Curved space. The quantum mystery of randomness. You planning on studying any of that at university?"

"Nope. I just need Physics 30."

"Take the tutor offer. Is it a girl?"

"A man. A grown up."

"Too bad. Physics chicks can be hot. I sat in on a class at the U of C for fun. One of the girls smiled at me. Those physics dudes act like they got their heads up a black hole. Stevie could beat up any of them."

He finished his second burger and wrapped the rest of his fries in a napkin and shoved it in his pocket. "See you later for Math Night," he said as he left, his red hair sticking out in tufts from the back of his head. Probably the place he couldn't see to cut it.

He had the fries out of his pocket before he left the cafeteria and was eating them while doing his dancing walk.

Mom had a surprise announcement for us at the dinner table. We were all there: Kayden, Willie, Stevie, Dad and me.

"Kayden's grandfather has invited us to the ranch Sunday afternoon to watch the bull riding and have a picnic on the Munro homestead."

Stevie's hazel eyes flickered at me as if to say, "Your Mom invited herself."

"It must be a beautiful ranch," Mom continued. "I'm looking forward to meeting Kayden's grandparents."

"We'll be seeing the family place at last," Dad said. "Too good to be true!"

"We'll meet you there Sunday," I said to The Commotion. "We're going Friday after school."

"I could draw you a map," Kayden offered. "It's about a 90 minute drive."

"Uncle Spencer has already done that. But thank you."

"You'll need old clothes," I suggested. "The arena is ..."

"Oh, don't worry," Mom reassured me. "Uncle Spencer has already filled us in on what to wear. I'll pick up a new outfit this afternoon."

We met as usual on Friday afternoon in Emily's class. Willie had a bag of fries open on his desk. "Want one?" he asked as I sat in the next desk. "I saved them from my breakfast."

"Where'd you get breakfast?"

"One of the food trucks. You make The Goddess smile and she

gives you extra fries. Lunch to go!"

"What do you say to her?"

"I ask her if she'll go out with me. She smiles and says no, but gives me extra fries. That's our deal, every Friday, corner of 17th and 3rd."

I had eaten a cheese omelette and fruit smoothie at Jewel's Restaurant that morning so I wasn't hungry. I offered Willie my lunch.

"Want a ham sandwich? Mom made it with Dijon mustard. I'm not hungry."

"You bet. I love Dijon. And all your Mom's cooking. You don't see her creativity at the trucks."

Emily came in, talking with Kayden.

"Hey, Emily," Stevie said. "I heard we're watching *Good Will Hunting* today. I guess we've given up on the course curriculum."

"I'll deal with the curriculum requirements later," Emily said. "I don't think there's much chance of getting this class to watch the 1940s classics."

"This is a class for taking personal risks," Willie said swallowing his last French fry. "We're all growing as viewers here. We're reaching into ourselves for illumination of life's greater context. Opening up and blossoming spiritually and with love, all through the wonder of Hollywood."

"Nobody's growing around here Willie," Stevie replied. "What are we, potatoes?"

I stepped in. "But isn't that what films are meant to show, how characters grow? Become better people."

"Do you think people blossom?" Stevie asked back.

"People change," I replied.

"That doesn't make them better. Their behaviour changes, but they're still the same person. We are always the same person. An asshole character can grow all a writer wants, but in real life he's always going to be an asshole. That doesn't change."

"Let's watch the movie," Kayden said. "Then we'll decide if anybody's blossoming."

"Or just changing their behaviour," Stevie said as the film began.

Emily made us watch right to the end, including the credits. Matt Damon. Ben Affleck.

"There's nothing authentic about that story," Willie said as the

DVD ejected. "That's victim glorification. Poor misunderstood Will Hunting. Can't love anybody. Child abuse. He's a genius but he can't figure out anything without beating people up and smashing old buildings. Oooh, he needs mandatory counselling. Give him some enabling. He's feeling like a loser."

"It won two Academy Awards. Maybe you could be more specific in describing what you didn't like, Willie?" Emily asked.

"It's Oprah Winfrey crap. The film panders to our desire to blame others for our problems. What a tearjerker plot. All they needed was to write in a puppy and then drive over it and everybody would find a way to be sympathetic."

We all stood up and clapped.

"Wait a minute," Emily said. "Let's look at some other parts of the film. What moved the story along for you?"

Willie had made me feel brave. "The dialogue and the action told the story," I said. "We got enough of the backstory in the dialogue and action so that we didn't have to listen to actors explaining stuff. We just absorbed it as the film moved along. That was good."

"Your turn, Stevie."

"I agree with Willie. It wasn't real life. It all worked out too well. Nobody ever gets exactly what they want. Will Hunting got everything – the perfect girl, true love and happiness. The final sunset scene is Walt Disney Cinderella and Prince Charming shoot yourself before it happens to you or you'll throw up in your pink lunch bucket and the director will make the audience eat it."

"Very graphic, Stevie. Your turn, Kayden."

"I think Chuckie is the real hero, telling his friend Will to get a better life. Chuckie already knew his own destiny as a construction labourer. He told Will to go find his. That was good writing. I agree that the rest is unrealistic."

Emily gave Willie's bristly red hair a pat. "Lucky you're not voting on the Awards. You're deadly! I think the world might hear a lot more from you in the future."

"What about you?" he asked. "What's your opinion on the film."

"Platitudes written for the Hollywood market. The same old furniture rearranged."

She definitely had an Uncle Spencer side. You could trust her.

In the parking lot, Kayden told Willie and me that we would have to sit on the narrow back seat of his pickup going to the ranch.

"Nathan's cousin Aubrey is coming with us."

"She can't have the window," Stevie said. "She has to ride the stick."

"Right," Kayden said. "You need the window in case you want to yell at some boys!"

"Come on, Stevie," I said. "Show us how you do that! Tell us what you yelled."

"Fuck off and get in the truck," she answered. "And don't ask any dumb questions Willie or you'll get some trouble. Aubrey better behave or she'll be getting some too."

We stopped by Aubrey's house in Elbow Park. She was dressed for the ranch in jeans, hiking boots and a denim jacket. She looked good although I didn't say that when I stopped her on the sidewalk.

"You can't come unless you promise not to say anything to anybody about what you see," I told her.

"Tell me what the secret is first. And then I'll tell you if I'll promise."

"I'm learning to ride bulls. Mom will kill me if she finds out."

"That's it? Jesus, Nathan. I promise. I'm not going to tattle tale to your mom. Grow up. You're almost 18. You can be such a baby."

She looked toward the truck. "Where am I sitting?"

"In the middle between Stevie and Kayden. On the stick shift."

"Could be fun."

Aubrey didn't know she'd changed the dynamics of our hunter group. She's not the world's most sensitive person. A little self centred, actually. She stays with us when her parents are out of town. She leaves her dishes and leftovers on the counter. The Commotion lectures her on thinking about other people more, but consideration is not her nature. She makes up for it by being cheerful and always ready to try something new. Hard not to love her.

Anyways, she's sitting between Kayden and Stevie and not noticing that they're not talking while she's yakking away nonstop about the school soccer team and trying out for a provincial team and maybe a national team. Happy as can be. The rest of us have bulls on our minds and we're about to do something that might kill us.

I lean against the door. I'm considering a theme for a film: To kill like a hunter you have to be willing to die like a hunter. What would you do to save a friend? A good start.

The Great Bull Hunters are travelling. TwoBlackEyes' bellow echoes in my silence. I focus, tracking his hot breath scent drifting across the ancient steppes of my mind. The Land of Ground Thunder Running. The chutes clang. Total commitment. Forget about The Commotion. Forget about grade 12. Forget about accounting. TwoBlackEyes is my genetic obsession. I won't count my 8 seconds on just any bull. It has to be TwoBlackEyes. I have my bull rope, bell and spurs. He has all the buck in hell. The braided rope will bind my hand to his thick hide. I will take every risk. I will endure. I have no back up plan. Ultimately it will be me, a bull and the ending. Nothing more.

I think we all follow Palaeolithic rituals to learn how much pain we can endure. Red paint on a cave wall. Stevie, rejected by the parents who chose her, tests herself against the pain of being unloved. The sadness is she doesn't know we all love her.

Speed of Light Willie is foot dancing a complex rhythm on the pickup floor. The wild eyed one who taunts the Great Bull, draws him in for the kill. Running through the bush. Screaming and yelling. Fearless. The huge one gains speed. Willie sprints around a steep corner. The narrow path closes. A dead end. The bull slap. The spears are waiting.

And the hunters travel through millennium, destinies entwined, across the river and into the arena.

Aubrey wouldn't know any of this as we turn off the highway to the Rockin' R. Is she thinking the same as I did the first time I bumped along this potholed gravel road? The rundown ranch. Tired. Not too impressive. But that's not what I see today. I see Grandma Lillian and Grandpa John holding it together for Kayden. I see could be popular Kayden quitting football to ride bulls and pass Math 30. I see the Jackson twins as complete bull riders: nothing more and nothing less. I see Stevie finding shiner calm in this sanctuary. It is the story of life experienced in blood and broken bones, as old as all of life's beginnings.

I see the film I will write one day. I will write that we don't have to be afraid of our bull. We don't have to puke if we draw TwoBlackEyes. We don't have to back down from his snot and arrogance.

The rhythm of the Rockin' R found me that Saturday. Even Aubrey's presence, like a stranger who doesn't speak the language, became part of the ritual. The whist game Friday night, the hurried breakfast, saddling

Fatso to drive the young bulls into the corral, eating canned tomato soup and crackers for lunch, the Jackson twins' rig in the yard, loading the bulls in the chutes, and then the understanding.

Kayden had drawn his first bull of the afternoon: the little black one that Alex said damn near tore him apart.

Kayden prepared, first talking to Alex about the bull's pattern, and then settling himself on the bull's back. Absolutely no hesitation in his eyes. He was thinking about that perfect score. He wasn't concerned with staying on board. I guess he was leaving that for the bulls he needed to qualify on for Edmonton.

Kayden runs his choices through his mind, the way a gambler decides whether or not to take another card.

Chest out, back straight, chin down, free arm under control.

Make a bet: spur the black ace every chance you get.

Kayden nods and there it is. The right arm directing the orchestra.

The little black spins away from Kayden's hand. His outside spur pounds the bull's side with every twisting buck.

Then I saw the risk: Kayden purposefully swung his spur out further than normal, a flashy high scoring move. Exposed to danger. The bull reads Kayden's bet and changes direction. Kayden loses his grip, smiles and is bucked off.

The Jacksons ran over to him cheering. "Beautiful, Kayden!"

And if I hadn't seen that smile I never would have known that they cheered the risk that didn't pay off. That was how they lived. Take the risk.

Kayden only knew commitment. Choose your moment. Brace against the aurochs' rush. Time the thrust of your spear. And not be killed yourself.

I watched closely after that, looking for the risks, looking for a rider's determination to stay on top of the bull, to be in control and spur.

On my first steer I could feel my right bicep flex against my sleeve. Pulling me tight onto my rope. I'd use my balance to sit straight, position myself.

Afterwards, nobody said anything more than a quiet "Nice ride." I knew they were disappointed. They wanted to see me spurring the way I'd let loose last week. I didn't care. I had a plan.

I rode the second steer the same way. 8 seconds. Another nice ride. On my third ride, I did everything I had seen Kayden do that afternoon.

I sat straight. My free hand balancing me. The steer circled to the left away from my riding hand. And my spur began to pump. Bang. Bang. Bang.

I found his rhythm. And then … I let my spur swing out like Kayden's. Pop him a good one Nathan!

Busted.

One more somersault over a steer's head and smack down on my back.

Winded.

Stevie had the oxygen mask over my face when I woke up.

They cheered as Kayden pulled me up.

Aubrey was sobbing. "I don't know if I'm crying because you scared me or because I'm proud of you. You're really doing this!" Very insightful, Aubrey.

We ate our burgers on the deck. Grandpa John made a little speech.

"I've been thinking about this. Nathan damn near got three rode this afternoon. We all know his first two were kind of gutless, hanging on rides, but the third was glorious.

"So I'm saying if the day comes when he can ride 8 seconds like that on any steer, he's going to graduate to bulls. But we're in this together. So what does everybody else say?"

Alex answered. "Pretty Boy's got no chance of doing that again. The bulls are safe."

Laughter all around.

"I'd like to see him do to a bull what he did to his last steer today," Jimmie added. "So I'm all for him gettin' a chance. And if anybody disagrees with me they have to fight Stevie."

More laughter.

Kayden was serious. "I think Nathan's bull riding could have a surprise ending. If he keeps spurring."

Grandma Lillian brought the oxygen into the trailer that night and made me sleep on the couch. She sat up all night in an armchair as I coughed.

I felt bad because Aubrey was still crying when she said goodnight. "If I don't tell your mother about this, she'll murder me," she whispered. "But if I do tell her, your friends will murder me. And they're scarier than she is. You're lucky to have friends like them. I never knew who you were."

Her crying had a smile in it. I thanked her.

UNCLE SPENCER

Uncle Spencer doesn't leave anything to chance. He arrived early on Sunday morning, making sure we would have time to talk to Kayden and his grandparents before The Commotion arrived.

We sat in the kitchen as he told the Montgomerys how I had identified the accounts that needed to be examined.

"Maybe I underestimated your nephew," Grandma Lillian said.

"Maybe he underestimates himself," Uncle Spencer says.

"For sure," Kayden said giving me an elbow nudge. "He's got some unused bull riding talent. Almost scored some points yesterday before he got bucked off."

Uncle Spencer didn't let the conversation get deflected by Kayden's compliment. Could anybody deflect Uncle Spencer?

"Here's what I think we should do, if you agree," he said.

"I'll make an appointment for Nathan and me to meet with the trustee. We'll need to catch him off guard, so I won't tell him what it's about until we're in his office. Then I'll show him my authorization. If he balks, I'll get you on the phone. Then we'll get things sorted out. He won't like it."

Grandpa John nodded. "Good plan. We'll sign that authorization and back you up all the way." He turned to Kayden and Grandma Lillian. "Agreed?"

They did. Kayden nudged me again. "I bet your Uncle Spencer can be one rank bull coming out of the chutes."

Uncle Spencer's loose wristed hands sat as still as ever on the table. This was business, they said.

"If we get the accounting sorted out, I'd like to have a look at the will. No point in just doing half a job."

Kayden said he would get a copy for him.

The phone rang. It was Julia, saying they were turning off the highway at Longview.

"They're bringing a picnic lunch to eat at the old Munro Homestead," I told Uncle Spencer. "Grandpa John thinks he found the site. Not for sure, but most likely. Some of us will ride horses, and the rest can ride in the pickups."

"I'll go in a pickup," he replied.

"We will too," Grandma Lillian said. "Let the kids ride the horses."

Grandpa John shrugged. "Good thinking. If I let Stevie ride my horse, Nathan can ride Sunshine and Willie can ride Fatso. If Aubrey wants to ride, she can ride Fatso back from the homestead."

Aubrey shook her head. "After what I saw yesterday I don't want to ride anything."

Uncle Spencer gave her his mean uncle look and I knew he would pry yesterday's bull riding details out of her. Resistance is futile. Little Red Riding Aubrey.

The thought of getting on Sunshine made me nervous. Riding a horse through the brush is seriously different than one handing a steer in an arena for 8 seconds. I had just begun to feel comfortable on Fatso. Sunshine might not be so lazy. Maybe it wasn't a good idea. Maybe Willie wouldn't want to ride. Maybe I could get out of this. Maybe I should shut up.

Willie wasn't nervous. You'd think all the worst things in life had already happened to him.

I was tightening Sunshine's cinch when The Commotion arrived.

Reese was in the back seat waving to me as if I had been expecting her. That confused me, but not as much as seeing Willie lift his foot into the stirrup and swing onto Fatso the way Kayden and Stevie swung onto their horses.

"Summer camp," he said to me. "Disadvantaged kids get sent to summer camps if they can find a sponsor. I chose a horse camp. Five summers of buckaroos. Lots of food."

He trotted Fatso between Stevie and Kayden. "Saddle up, Nathan," he shouted over his shoulder. "We're burning daylight!"

I was caught between riding with them and waiting for Reese who was giving me her come over here look from the corral rails. I led

Sunshine over.

"The Jewel invited me. I love her. This place is soooo cowboy. I hope they have clean bathrooms."

"They do. We're all going to the homestead for lunch. Some of us are riding. You can come with the others in the pickups. I'll introduce you to everybody out there."

Grandpa John saved my life. "You'd better let me hold onto Sunshine," he said putting his hand on the reins. "She can be snorty first thing."

Mom grabbed Dad's arm and whispered.

Dad shook his head. "He'll be fine."

Grandpa John boosted me on Sunshine and I adjusted my reins. I turned her towards the others and she trotted up to them.

Thank you, Grandpa John, I said with an over my shoulder salute. Looking completely at ease. The four of us rode for an hour like old time buffalo hunters through the pasture toward the scrub brush where Grandpa John had said the homestead might be.

"There should be a spring around here," Kayden said when we got to the edge of the brush. "Look for signs of water, any place that's wet."

Stevie found the spring by riding straight into the brush. "It's over here. My horse is up to his hocks in muck. I'm coming out."

We gathered on the edge of the brush again. "Now we need to find the straight lines of the old caragana hedge around the foundations," Kayden said. "It won't be far from the spring."

We could hear the pickup trucks coming over the rise to the south. Aubrey was standing in the box of Kayden's truck, her arms braced against the cab. She looked beautiful with the wind blowing her ponytail.

"Hey, Nathan," she said as she jumped from the truck. "Glad to see you made it all the way out here without getting your face scratched again. You must be learning to ride better. Horses, that is."

Stevie thought that was funny.

I introduced Kayden, Stevie, and Willie to Reese. She gave Kayden a second look but ignored Stevie and Willie. I knew they weren't her type. Not well dressed. Not much money. Not Elbow Park material.

She told me to let my horse go and stand with her.

"If I let Sunshine go I'll have to walk home," I explained. "We'll hobble all the horses in a minute and then I'll help Mom get the lunch out."

Reese frowned then turned to Aubrey. "Imagine that. I'm playing second fiddle to a horse! And it smells. And my phone doesn't work. What kind of world is this?"

"You're on a ranch," Aubrey said. "Things are different here. You'll have to get used to it if you want to manage Nathan."

Reese wrinkled her nose. "He's in his cowboy phase. He'll outgrow it."

After we hobbled the horses, Grandpa John led us into the brush where he'd seen the old caragana hedges. Reese hung onto me as if wild animals were lurking in the caragana shadows.

"This is it," Grandpa John said standing in the corner where two hedges met. "The house was probably right in front of us, facing south. The brush would have been cleared." He showed us the ruts of an old road. "I'm surprised I never connected these tracks with the road we drive the cattle along."

Mom and Dad hugged each other and pulled Reese and me in. "This is our roots," Dad said. "The Munro Homestead."

I saw Aubrey say something to Stevie who grinned and nodded in agreement. I felt sorry for Reese. All she had were amazing looks, honour roll brains and ambition.

The Jewel must have worked overtime in her restaurant last night. She'd packed the perfect picnic. Sandwiches, cold chicken, individual tubs of salads, bottled water, coffee, tea, cakes, cookies and, to make the celebration memorable, a bottle of wine.

She uncorked the bottle and held it up. "To mark this occasion!"

We all looked at her. What were we supposed to say?

Willie saw that the ranch folks, including him and Stevie, weren't expecting to be served wine.

"That looks drinkable," he said. "I don't mind going first." He tugged the bottle from Jewel and held it high above his head.

"As my namesake Willie Nelson sings:

"'Mommas don't let your babies grow up to be cowboys …'"

He swigged back a mouthful, his eyes closed. "Don't tell me. Let me guess." He swirled the wine in his mouth then swallowed. "Yes. As I suspected. French. Likely the Morey St Denis region. I'd guess a 1990."

Without a glance at the label, he handed the bottle to Dad. "Drink up Mr. Uncle Rick."

Dad glanced at the label. "Amazing."

We all took a swallow. It was memorable.

As we were packing up the picnic, Aubrey caught me from behind in a bear hug. She breathed into my neck. "I love you, Nathan. And I know why you're here. It will work for you. Don't let anyone talk you out of it."

Then she was gone.

We asked Willie about the wine as we rode back to the barn.

"Two guesses. Either I'm a speed reader and I read the label while The Jewel was talking, or I'm a busboy in a fancy restaurant and squeeze the last drops from the bottles."

"Speed reader," Stevie guessed.

The Jackson twins were very Ma'am and Sir with my parents. Like Kayden always was.

"You should see some fine bull riding this afternoon," Alex told them. "The Montgomerys are raising high quality bulls. They've been giving us a rough time all fall. It's good practice for the Canadian Finals."

"Nathan's told us you and Jimmie will be riding in Edmonton," Dad said.

"Too bad we can't get Nathan on a bull or two," Alex replied.

Mom shook her head. "Our son's got another future and bull riding isn't in his cards."

Alex gave me a Jackson grin. "I figure Nathan's life would make a great movie. Lots of future. I hope I don't get stomped by a bull and killed. I'd like to see the ending. It would be worth hanging around for."

Goddamn. That sounded too much like Kayden talking.

Mom quietly explained to me that Reese's parents were considering divorce. "They're arguing again. She needs some time away from them and who better than us? We're family to her. Better than those older sisters of hers who don't give a darn now they've got careers. Reese needs our support. Right?"

What choice did I have?

Willie had rigged up an old stereo with speakers and a microphone in the arena so I could pretend to be an announcer. All my instincts told me I should be in the chutes pulling myself tight against my rope and staying focussed on scoring.

Up in the stands I felt like an actor. I made the best of it.

"Good afternoon folks," I word stretched into the microphone. "And welcome to bull riding at the Rockin' R. We're loading the first bulls into the chutes and I don't mind telling you there's not a more dangerous place to be today in all of Alberta than on top of one of these rank Montgomery bulls.

"And this afternoon these bulls are facing off against three of the most reckless and handsome and downright irresponsible cowboys on the circuit. So, ladies and gentlemen, I want you to stand and give our heroes a round of applause because your appreciation is going to be the only reward they'll take home today."

The Montgomerys, Mom, Dad, Uncle Spencer, Aubrey, and Stevie stood and cheered. Willie, in his blue tights, ran crazily around the arena waving his albatross wings. I glanced at Reese and she shook her head in disgust. She mouthed a response. "Never again!"

Kayden, Alex and Jimmie were laughing as they saluted the crowd.

Alex drew the little black bull. I knew a stage opportunity when I saw it.

"First up is Alex Jackson, the good looking identical twin. (Only Dad laughed.) He and Jimmie hail from Turner Valley and right now they're both heading to the Canadian Finals next month. I don't think Alex will mind me telling you this, but he knows he's got a tough ride on this black one. He's bucked everybody off in the practice rounds.

"So let me introduce this feisty twister. He's not your big bucking Brahman type. He's got a touch of Mexican fighting bull in him. He's fast. He can change direction in mid air and – as Kayden and Alex know – just when you think you're scoring high he pulls out his trick move and – bucked off!

"Now, folks, I'll let you in on a little secret about the Rockin' R. Their bulls don't get named until they've proven they have a future in the arena. So far this year, only two bulls have earned names. This little black one and a bone cracking Brahman named TwoBlackEyes. You'll meet him later.

"Grandpa John allowed me to name this one because he reminds me of someone who is just as ornery and just as tricky and just as challenging – yes, folks, there is only one man you don't want to tangle with unless you're ready for a real scrap.

"That's right folks. You guessed it. This bull's name is Uncle Spencer!"

Well, they went wild. Aubrey fell over the rail holding onto her sides with laughter. Uncle Spencer raised his arms and accepted the cheers.

Goddamnit … I was good!

Alex made the 8 seconds.

"Now folks, wasn't that a wonder to see?" I drawled. "Good to know that every bull and every uncle has a weakness."

Things were going smoothly, I thought, even though I wished with all my heart that Stevie and I could be riding steers and being part of the action rather than being spectators. I wanted Mom and Dad to see me taking my chances on a steer, risking it all one handed. Living my life. I wished I could tell them the truth without hurting them. Without disappointing them.

My inventions ate away at my heart.

To make things worse, I was sandwiched between Reese and Mom – sandwiched between whole grain concerns.

"Oh, it looks so dangerous," Reese said hugging me from one side. And from the other side of the Nathan sandwich, Mom added, "I'm glad our boy's safe up here."

I smell a Palaeolithic campfire while Grandpa John and Willie load the second round of bulls into the chute. We are butchering a kill. We, the weak ones who stay behind. We, the ones who chop the lifeless chunks with blood red hands, and dry the flesh thin over fires and stretch skins for winter clothes.

Behind me is a stranger, a visitor to our camp. Fair haired with a straight smile learning language from a slope eyed woman hunter. The visitor is from the grassland where they hunt the fast antelope and horses. She says their hunters fear the Great Bulls. Our slant eyed woman shrugs. The fair haired one is only staying a few nights. They talk about the hunters as chutes clang and bulls bellow. Which man is yours? The silent one? Is he the leader? The stranger gives her new friend a necklace ringed with wolf teeth. To keep her hunter safe.

She has guessed right. Kayden is the silent leader of our camp. His ways have brought us together. Me, gathered from Elbow Park. Stevie, gathered from loneliness. Willie, gathered from the streets. The Jackson twins, gathered from the rodeos.

We are Kayden's hunters. Except me. Today. I should be riding but am a sandwich talking into a microphone.

I picked up my pace for the third round. "Now folks, we're heading into the last bulls of the afternoon. It's been an even fight so far. Three rides. Three bucked off. Let's see how the last round goes."

Kayden rode his Brahman. Alex bucked off a Charolais cross.

TwoBlackEyes is being loaded and I am nervous talking. "This is it," I whispered dramatically into the microphone. "The deciding match up. One bull, the soon to be legendary TwoBlackEyes versus that dictionary of intellectual razzmatazz. Mothers – lock up your daughters – the slick talking Jimmie Jackson is climbing on board."

As Jimmie waved to me, I gave the crowd the inside info on TwoBlackEyes, drawing on my fear of his cold rage.

"Now you've seen smart and fast bulls this afternoon. Like Uncle Spencer. Quick and tricky. Lightning punchers. But nothing like TwoBlackEyes. Look at the size of him. And it's all muscle.

"He's a toe to toe bruiser with the mentality of an eye gouging ball kicking alley fighter. He wants to hurt you bad. Bam. Bam. You're done. Bucked off and looking down the road for the truck that ran you over.

"He's the great hope for the Rockin' R – a heavyweight champion worth millions."

Willie warmed up, sprinting back and forth across the arena waving his white towel. Stevie climbed over the rails to pull the gate. Grandpa John readied his hand on the latch.

Jimmie settled himself on the bull's back. Kayden and Alex both pulled his rope. TwoBlackEyes grunted. Jimmie yanked himself hard into his handhold. He tugged his helmet down and nodded to Grandpa John.

He swung the gate open.

TwoBlackEyes powered out of the chute with a high rear that Jimmie rode straight up. Down the bull came, jarring Jimmie and sending him back up again with a high kick. In two jumps, Jimmie had gone from almost pounding his head on the bull's horns to smashing backward into the bull's almost vertical back.

TwoBlackEyes slammed down with another jolt that almost broke Jimmie's grip. The bull's gracelessness and his back cracking landings added octane to his power. He pounded Jimmie relentlessly and Jimmie had to shut down the pain. It was a jailhouse brawl. TwoBlackEyes began to spin and Jimmie had a chance to spur him, taking a chance by swinging his leg high, exposing himself to danger. The bull sensed Jimmie's weakness and turned back without warning. Faster than I thought he could.

As Jimmie lost his balance, the bull kicked up and flipped Jimmie forward and to the right. He landed face down on the dirt.

TwoBlackEyes turned on him. Willie was already sprinting between Jimmie and the bull, waving his towel. The bull turned on Willie while Jimmie pulled himself to his feet.

TwoBlackEyes kicked backward, clipping Jimmie's arm. It looked intentional.

Jimmie walked slowly to the rail, holding his arm tight to his chest.

"Thanks," Jimmie said to Willie. "He had me down for a second. It could have been worse."

"You rode him good," Willie answered handing him his rope and bell.

I replayed Jimmie's ride over and over in my imagination, looking for a way to counter TwoBlackEyes' quick turn back that had thrown Kayden off balance and now Jimmie. There had to be a way to ride this reincarnated aurochs.

Grandpa John and Willie drove the bulls back into their pens while the rest of us went to the house for burgers and beer, as usual.

Grandma Lillian made a makeshift sling from a scarf for Jimmie. "Lucky it's not your riding arm," she said as she knotted it. "You might have to work for a living this summer."

Mom hovered. "I'm worried about him. We should take him straight to the hospital," she urged while Grandma Lillian fitted the sling around Jimmie's neck. Willie helped him pack his gear and throw it in the pickup.

"Don't worry, Ma'am," Jimmie said when he saw mom's concern. "If it's broke now, it'll still be broke in a couple of hours. If not, then I would have missed the beer and Grandma Lillian's No Buck Burgers for nothing."

"Jimmie's been a grown up all his life," Grandma Lillian said to Mom. "He'll go to the hospital when he wants."

Mom shook her head. "Not if his mother were here."

As Grandpa John handed her a plate with a hamburger, she asked, "Why are these called No Buck Burgers."

"Simple. A couple of months ago that burger was a bull. We send the ones that don't buck to the meat packers. All they're good for is burgers."

Reese set her plate down and looked about to vomit.

I think everything about the ranch scared Reese, even the Jacksons. Normally she'd flirt with any attractive man; harmlessly, of course. She was good at sending boys like the school football players a taunting, I dare you to try, look. They usually responded, and were always disappointed.

She wasn't trying it on the Jacksons or Kayden. Instead she was hanging on my arm, maybe for protection. She ignored Willie when he offered her a can of beer.

The Jacksons, Kayden and Grandpa John invited Dad to join them leaning against the porch rail. Alex handed him a can. "Did you enjoy our show?"

Dad gave him his mischievous boy smile. "I've been going to the Stampede for years and I thought I knew something about bull riding. But being this close to it makes it real. I guess I never knew how goddamn dangerous it was and how brave you sonofabitches are. I loved it."

He took a long pull on his beer. "Got to admit that I'm surprised Nathan and Stevie are sitting on the sidelines. It looks tempting."

Mom overheard that remark.

"Don't even talk like that! One boy's got a broken arm. And I don't know how long that ragged Willie is going to survive, running in front of bulls like that."

"He's fast," Grandma Lillian said.

The porch leaners glanced my way. I ran my finger across my mouth, zipping my lips tight. Conspirators.

Uncle Spencer made the right move, saying he was planning to leave for Calgary in a few minutes.

"Nathan, Willie, and Stevie get your things loaded in my trunk. We'll head back to town before the weekend rush hits the Deerfoot."

Mom interrupted. "Why don't Nathan and Stevie come with us? It would be more convenient."

"Won't work," Stevie said. "Nathan gets mentorating in the car from Uncle Spencer. We're the muscle in case the young fella gets argumentative."

"Mentorating isn't a word," Reese pointed out.

"It's new," Stevie said. "It's a group term originating in the social deconstruction contextual analysis labs of the University of Illinois. It's a landmark peer reviewed study."

"I read the paper," Willie added, "so I can save you the bother of looking it up. Basically, they took the older style mentoring program with a mature counsellor, such as Mr. Uncle Spencer, and introduced two student colleagues who bring relevant experiential understandings to the new process dynamics. Thus, one on one mentoring has become group mentorating. Very post graduate."

"Yes. That's what we're doing," Uncle Spencer agreed. "It's our routine. Mentorating."

"I'm going with Kayden to the hospital to see if Jimmie's arm is broken," Aubrey said. She gave Stevie a nudge. "Just friends. No mentorating."

Mom looked suspiciously at us, as if she sensed a plan she wasn't part of.

"Let's go, Jewel," Dad said. "This is these kids' world. We're just spectators."

He opened her car door. Reese got in the back, not looking happy.

"Don't forget Reese is spending a few days with us," Mom said. "We'll see you at dinner."

"Nothing more satisfying than a good mentorating," Willie said as The Commotion's car climbed the hill.

I wanted to say something grateful and meaningful to all the faces looking at me. All that came out was, "Nice riding everybody." I guess that was all I needed to say. There were a few see you next weekends, and then we were gone, leaving Aubrey and Kayden beside Grandpa John and Grandma Lillian waving from the porch.

"I heard you hit the ground pretty hard on Saturday," Uncle Spencer said as we turned onto the highway.

"Who told you? Aubrey?"

"We've got no secrets on this. Are you okay?"

"I might have bruised my ribs a little. I'm sore, but I don't feel out of breath."

"Should we see Dr. Sara?"

"No."

He passed a semi trailer. "How's everybody's marks? Everybody keeping up?"

"Yes," I said for everybody.

"Anything else?"

Stevie grabbed my right arm. "Check out Nathan's guns! I do believe The Chosen One is getting some manhood going."

"Never mind me," I said. "I noticed you were actually friendly with Aubrey."

"I've got an understanding with her."

"I think she wants to try kissing you. Experimentally. She wonders."

"Wrong. And don't change the subject. We have a deal that if you don't quit being so fucking compliant, one of us is going to send you back to your supposed girlfriend with your underwear pulled over your head."

"I'm trying to help."

"Try helping yourself. You don't need a manager. You need someone who's interested in who you are now, not who you can be turned into."

"Her name's Reese and she's having problems at home. Her parents are fighting. I have to be supportive."

"Yea," Willie agreed from the front seat. "Nathan's a nice guy. He never wants to hurt anybody's feelings. He thinks he'll be happy if he makes everybody around him happy."

"Forget the group support crap Willie," Stevie said. "How do you make up bullshit so fast? What I want to know is why none of us has met Kayden's aunt? The one he lives with. Does she have a name?"

Nobody could answer.

"If he wanted us to know, he'd tell us," Willie said.

"Right," I said. "Kayden doesn't tell you anything unless you ask him."

"And that reminds me, what's your last name Willie?" Stevie asked. "What's the big secret there? And don't give us any of that Willie Nelson stuff. Very funny by the way. Don't let your babies grow up to be cowboys. The Jewel was getting ready to kick you in the balls."

Uncle Spencer's shoulders shook as he stifled a laugh.

"I'm undercover," Willie answered. "I can't disclose my true identity. I'm in a witness protection program."

"Always got an answer, don't you Willie?" Stevie replied. "I can see you really fitting in at Harvard. I hear they're recruiting bullfighters."

"Speed of Light. It would look good on my C.V."

"So would your blue tights."

I fell asleep after that and didn't wake up until we pulled into Stevie's drive. "Good to see you're living at home again," Uncle Spencer said to her. "Willie will walk you to the door."

Willie jumped out and opened Stevie's door with a low bow. "Hurry Sweetie, the coach will be a pumpkin before you know it. Don't look back."

She leaned over and kissed Uncle Spencer's cheek.

"Nothing for you, Mister I'm Just Being Supportive," she said to me. "Willie gets double at the door."

Willie danced Stevie up the walkway and rang the doorbell. Stevie pulled him over – too eagerly I thought – for his kiss. He was halfway there when the door slammed open.

"You little bitch!" her mother screamed. Gerry stood behind her, his hands raised in caution to Stevie.

Willie knew exactly what was coming. He must have seen the signs hundreds of times before: the roundhouse punch from behind Stevie's mother's back.

Willie jumped forward and caught it on his left eye.

Gerry pulled his mother back into the house.

"Go," he ordered Stevie. "Call me later."

Uncle Spencer and I were already running up the sidewalk. "Get me out of here!" Stevie shouted, pushing us back to the car.

Uncle Spencer dropped Stevie and me off at my house, stopping long enough to describe Willie's gallantry to The Commotion. Stevie didn't want to talk and closed the bedroom door.

Mom knocked.

"Nothing to share," Stevie replied.

Mom was still worried about Jimmie's wreck and kept calling Aubrey for an update. No answer. Finally, Kayden called our house and told her that Jimmie's arm was broken, not seriously, and he'd be able to ride in the Finals. "He's a fool," Mom said as if she were Jimmie's mother. "He only thinks about himself." Once she'd dragged everything she could out of Kayden, she told him about Willie and Stevie.

"Kayden says he'll see you at the lunch break tomorrow," she said to me when she hung up. "He's driving Aubrey home now."

The doorbell rang. It was Gerry. "Stevie texted me to bring her some clothes for school. How's Willie?"

"Nathan's uncle drove him home," Mom said. "I'm sure he's fine."

After everybody went to bed, Reese came into my room, definitely not in a snuggly mood and I didn't feel like being compliant.

"What a horrific day! I used half a bottle of shampoo trying to get the smell out of my hair. The only good thing that happened was Stevie getting a reminder about her behaviour. Can you imagine her poor mother opening the door and seeing her kissing that awful boy?"

I sent her back to her room.

I didn't sleep much that night. We'd come back to camp with two injured hunters: one broken arm and one black eye. And Stevie feeling unloved. By Kayden. By her mother.

Dear Emily Arbutus

I agree with your comment, "You have returned your character to his childhood: 'Mutton Busting' is a children's event. Does Chet still view himself as a child, especially around Marlena?"

This scene illustrates what's wrong. Instead of writing about the young man emerging I'm writing about the young man as if he were still a boy being bullied and overprotected by his mother

Personally, I want to move into a man's world, and the way I'm writing this script is holding me back.

But I'm not going to give up on Buck Off. I think what I'm learning about myself will help me make the script everything I hope it will be.

One of my writing problems is I have spent too much time writing detailed scenes. You have made me see they will need serious revision. Instead of going backward, I'm going to try something new going ahead and see if that helps. I'm going to write plot summaries for the scenes and then only write pieces of script that will help me develop the characters and action and see how I can develop them later when I have an ending.

What do you think?

Bull Rider

Stevie, Willie and I met for lunch in the cafeteria. Willie's eye was swollen shut. He looked rough, as if he had slept in his clothes. He needed a shower. Only his smile was Willie bright.

"Let's get out of here," he said. "There's a food truck on 6th Street. We need nature's restoratives. I know the owner." I texted Kayden to meet us there.

Willie bounced up to the serving window of the Lovely Golden Fries truck. "Hello, Miss Goddess!" he said to the back of a dark haired girl cutting the raw fries.

"Hello, Willie," she replied without turning around. "What do ya got for me today – money or a compliment?"

"I got better than that, Marie. I got hungry friends and they're dying to buy your splendiferous delights."

She turned. She was splendiferous. Black hair tied back. Green eyes. Did girls go for Willie?

Her hand swept up to cover her mouth as she gasped when she saw Willie's eye. "If that was your moronic uncle, my cousins are going to beat the hell out of him."

"Nope. I caught a roundhouse from an upset mother. I brought her precious darling home a bit late."

"You need to go out with a better class of girl."

"Like you?"

She laughed and smiled at Stevie. "Like that babe beside you. She go to your school?"

Willie introduced us to Marie who said our lunch was on her. "Willie makes sure I don't have any competition around here," she explained. "Brings in a few of his wino friends who pass out in front of any food truck that parks too close to me."

Willie ordered for all of us: Marie's largest bags of fries and coffees with two sugars and cream.

As we walked to the picnic table beside the truck, I told Willie I had brought a lunch. "Mom makes me healthy choices."

"Let's see what you got."

"This isn't your lunch," he said when I showed him my cheese sandwich and sliced apple. "This is my dinner." He shoved them into his jacket pocket.

"We had a night to forget," he said. "We need lots of fat, sugar, and starch. That's North American cultural food. Gets you over any emotional upheaval."

"But Mom …" I began.

"Mrs. Momma Julia is not here. Brush your teeth before you get home. She won't smell fries on your breath."

I picked up my fries and coffee. They were good.

Kayden and Gerry showed up a few minutes later.

"Hi, you guys," Gerry said. "Can I join you? I'd like to talk."

"First, get some fries and coffee," Willie said.

Kayden sat down while Gerry waited at the truck window.

"Jimmie's arm's not broke too bad," Kayden told us. "The doctor says if he gets it x rayed before the Finals and it looks okay, he'll leave the cast off, tape it and Jimmie can ride in the Finals."

"Jimmie will cut it off himself if the doctor doesn't," Stevie said.

Kayden smiled at Willie's eye. "I heard Stevie's mom swung pretty fast. Did Speed of Light Willie forget to duck?"

Gerry slid Kayden's bag of fries and coffee onto the table. "Willie took Five in the Eye for my sister," he said.

"Eat your fries," Willie replied.

Gerry ate a few. "I have to say something. I got you guys all wrong. I don't think any of my friends would have stepped up the way Willie did. And I'm embarrassed. I hesitated too long."

He turned to Stevie. "I should have been looking out for you. I've got no excuse."

"Eat your fries," she said.

"No," Gerry said. "Not until I'm finished talking. I know you and Kayden don't talk much. I don't know about Nathan, but if he's your friend, then what I have to say is for him too. And Willie."

"Wait a minute," Kayden interrupted. "I told you nobody's mad at you. Nobody's blaming you for anything. Listen, we all get a beating now and again. Bulls, parents, teachers, accountants, gangs. That's life, Gerry. It never stops."

"Kayden's right, Gerry," Stevie said. "Don't turn this into an Oprah episode."

"I am! I should have been a better brother. A friend, too. I'm going to be that from now on. I've learned my lesson. After last night, I don't want you to be alone with Mom. I don't want you going home without me being there. If I have to miss football practice or a party, I'll miss it to make sure nothing happens to you. Phone me, text me. I'll drop what I'm doing. I promise."

He turned to Kayden. "And I apologize to you. It's not up to you whether or not I get a football scholarship. I was being an asshole."

"You'll get the scholarship," Willie said. "Even with a lousy quarterback you're catching a lot of passes. And scoring touchdowns. You're getting the scholarship. I asked the principal."

What didn't Willie know?

We thanked Marie for the fries and coffee and walked back to school. I liked seeing Kayden, Stevie and Gerry being friends. I liked being Willie's friend. I was looking forward to going to Edmonton and seeing Alex and Jimmie ride in the Finals. What's a broken arm or a black eye? We had forever days of hunting ahead.

We were going through the school entrance when Stevie jumped me and put me in a headlock. "Check him out, Gerry. Check out his guns. This little fart has been working out."

Gerry rolled my bicep in his hand. "Sonofabitch. Good for you Nathan."

Stevie let me go.

"Psycho," I said to her.

"Watch it!" Gerry growled back. "She's got a brother backing her up now."

"Cool. Now I have two psychos to watch out for."

Uncle Spencer called me after school. "We've got an appointment tomorrow afternoon with the ranch trustee. I'll pick you up at school. 12:30 sharp."

"But I have physics in the afternoon."

"Skip it. This is more important."

"Mom and Dad will find out."

"You want to ride bulls … and you're worried about your parents finding out you've skipped a few classes?"

"Sort of."

"You can't be everything to everybody. Make a decision: help Kayden's family, or avoid trouble with your parents. I'll be there at 12:30." He hung up. Some mentorator!

I decided to skip class and take my chances. If I told The Commotion about going to the trustee's office, Uncle Spencer would get a phone call. Knowing him, there would be an exchange. So, what the hell? Besides, I'd rather meet this accountant who was screwing over the Montgomerys. More fun to see Uncle Spencer twist his tail than sitting in physics class discussing the conservation of momentum when objects interact in an isolated system. I already know what happens when the momentum of my face interacts with arena dirt.

That reminded me. Paul, my new tutor, would be coming over after dinner to meet The Commotion and me. Willie and Kayden would have to hold Math Night somewhere else. Maybe they could meet at Kayden's mystery aunt's house. Maybe Willie would eat my ham and cheese there and be cavalier about his black eye. "A roundhouse from a girl's mother when I brought her daughter home a bit late."

Gerry and Stevie came by with a suitcase of clothes. She was going to stay with us until things settled down at her home. Julia's Shelter For Girls Fighting With Their Mothers. First Reese. Now Stevie.

Nobody would pick Stevie and Gerry as brother and sister. Gerry, fair skinned, the tall and narrow wide receiver. You could imagine him hanging high in the air, hands outstretched to catch a long pass. Running for the career goalposts. Stevie, soft slanted eyes, dark hair, the mechanic. You could imagine her under the garage hoist, pulling a wrench.

Adoption: acceptance, not expectations.

"I can pay," Gerry said to Mom. "You figure out what Stevie's room and board comes to, and I'll pay cash. I'm hoping it won't be more than a few weeks, but I don't care how much it costs. Stevie has to be safe. And when she comes home, she'll never be alone. I'll always be there. I screwed up once but not again. That's my promise to Stevie."

Julia loves bonding scenes. "She's very fortunate to have a brother like you. And don't even think about paying us."

"Thank you, Mrs. Munro, but I'll pay. Here's $100 to start. I'm going to talk to the principal tomorrow with Stevie. We'll explain the situation, just so there's no mix up."

"Good for you. School's very important. We know that Stevie struggles to keep up her grades, so we'll do our best to make sure she has a good desk and computer. We've been meaning to buy a new one and this is a good excuse."

She leaned forward. "Do you mind if I give you a hug? I think you are a wonderful young man."

He didn't mind. And he didn't mind lying to my mom: he and Stevie weren't going to talk to the principal and get teachers and counsellors involved in their lives.

Stevie didn't talk during dinner. As if what happened was her fault. Mom and Dad asked me questions about the ranch. They had loved seeing the homestead and the bull riding. Except when Jimmie got hurt. Dad had seen his friends injured worse than that when they were racing on the Provincial Ski Team. Broken legs. Concussions. "Part of the thrill," he told Mom.

"Nonsense." As if mothers should control everything.

Jimmie's broken arm wasn't enough nonsense, though, to change her mind about going to the Finals in Edmonton. I knew there was no holding her back from making a big splash for my 18th birthday as part of going to the rodeo. My most serious worry was that I might see my name flashing on the scoreboard at intermission and hear the crowd singing happy birthday to me.

She didn't waste any time booking and paying for the Montgomery's and Jacksons' hotel rooms, and had given all the Aunts, Uncles and Cousins the details to book their own rooms.

"Reese is coming, too," she told me. "And she's inviting her friends from your old school. Some of them are coming on the weekend for the final rounds."

Dad spread his arms out, expansively. "Guess what? I've ordered a block of tickets for the entire rodeo, and a box suite. It's going to be unforgettable! Legendary!"

"What about school?" I asked. "And your work? The rodeo starts on Wednesday and lasts until Sunday."

Dad grinned. "Got it covered. I've chartered a King Air 200 to fly us back and forth every evening. We'll stay overnight on Saturday for your birthday party and then watch the Championship round Sunday afternoon. The plane holds nine."

I counted on my fingers. "You, Mom, me, Stevie, Willie, Aubrey, and Reese. Two extra seats."

"We'll fill them," Dad said. "No problem."

"Maybe your brother would like to come," I said to Stevie. "He'd like the Jackson twins. They'd take him down to the chutes if he wanted."

"That would be fun for him. He told me he thinks bull riders are cool. Never thought I'd hear him say that about anybody who didn't play football."

Stevie and I did the dinner dishes. She rinsed them and I loaded the dishwasher. "Don't worry," she said handing me a plate. "I don't care if your manager comes to Edmonton. I won't say anything if she bosses you around. I'll just hang out with Willie."

Mom came into the kitchen before I could say anything. "Hurry up! Your tutor will be here any minute. You should have your books out to show him where you're having problems."

Speaking of bossing people around.

The doorbell rang before I had my books ready. I wasn't going to make a good impression. Mom and Dad covered up for me by quizzing Paul on his background. He was academically perfect. Science major and working on his MBA. He looked soft, like leftover mashed potatoes. I wanted to like him, but it was hard to pretend to be interested in physics and commerce, subjects he loved.

"Why do you think you're having trouble with physics?" he asked. Mom and Dad waited for my answer.

"I'm not personally interested in it. I don't know why I'm taking it."

I could imagine Willie laughing: "Bucked off! Wrong answer."

"You need a science for university entrance," Paul pointed out. "And if you have an aptitude for math, physics is your best choice."

"That's right," Dad said. "I felt the same way as you. What did I need a science for? I was going to be an accountant." Compelling argument, for sure.

"I understand. I'm only trying to say why I don't do well in physics compared to my other courses." Such as being a Great Bull Hunter.

That led to another invention. Paul wanted to know the rest of my curriculum. Movie Club? I lied. Drama. Things were getting complicated for me. The Rockin' R. Skipping school. Eating fries and drinking coffee. Giving away my healthy choice cheese delight and apple. I was disappointing my parents big time.

Paul asked Mom and Dad to leave us while he looked through my physics assignments. We worked for two hours. After that, if I had wanted to, I could have calculated the personal velocity needed to overcome academic inertia. He did a good job of earning $75.

Emily replied to my email that night.

Dear Bull Rider

I'm pleased that you have seen that Buck Off and Bull Rider need to mature. You've learned something important about not falling so in love with a script that you can't see its shortcomings or how you can overcome them.

I believe in Buck Off and you. I think your idea of writing plot summaries and illustrative scenes will help you introduce bigger ideas that will intrigue viewers.

Be patient.

Emily Arbutus

In the morning I told Kayden I was going with Uncle Spencer to interrogate the accountant and wouldn't be in Movie Club. "We'll miss your sincerity," he said. "It elevates us." Kayden jocularity. "I'll say hi to Emily for you."

The accountant had a rundown office on the second floor of a strip mall in southwest Calgary. The sign taped to the door read "Robert T. Scalbanski, C.A., Trustee." His receptionist said he was expecting us.

We could hear him talking on the phone in his office about a condo he was selling.

When he came out he looked very cartoony accountantish. Glasses resting on a beaklike nose, a scrawny chicken neck, thin shoulders and almost bald. I could put him in a headlock. Easy.

He introduced himself and shook hands with us while studying Uncle Spencer's business card. Spencer Munro, C.A.

"You've paid for an hour of my time," he said as we sat in front of his desk. "What can I do for you?"

"We're here to talk about the Rockin' R accounts," Uncle Spencer said. Very calm.

"You might have wasted your hour," Scalbanski replied. "That's confidential information. I'd have to have the Montgomery's permission."

Uncle Spencer drew an envelope out of his suit jacket. "You've got it," he said handing the envelope across the desk.

Scalbanski's hand trembled as he read it. "What's this all about? What's your interest in this?"

"That's confidential information," Uncle Spencer replied with a slight smile.

Scalbanski shook his head. "I'll have to verify this letter."

"Mr. Montgomery should be calling you any minute now. We'll wait. Part of the hour we paid for." Two minutes later the phone rang at the receptionist's desk. She answered and then knocked on Scalbanski's door. "Mr. Montgomery is on line two. He said you're expecting his call."

Scalbanski looked pale as he lifted his receiver. He looked a lot more pale when he hung up. "I'll have my girl get the files."

"Have her make an extra copy of the most recent balance sheet and income statement," Uncle Spencer said. "We're in no hurry." His loose hands rested on the desk. Scalbanski kept looking at them as if they might suddenly jump across the desk and strangle his chicken neck. Maybe he thought Uncle Spencer was a rancher's hit man.

The receptionist gave me a second look as she handed the paperwork to Scalbanski. She wasn't much older than me. I think the look said it would be worth my while to say hello on the way out.

Uncle Spencer focussed on the balance sheet, acting like he'd never seen it before. "Valuable ranch," he commented without looking up. "When was the land last appraised?"

"Three years ago. Land prices haven't changed much. Things are slow. I don't follow agricultural land too closely but it usually tracks the Calgary market. House prices have begun to move up a little – thanks to oil heading up from $40 a barrel. A new appraisal on the ranch might show a slight improvement."

"You like real estate, don't you?" Uncle Spencer commented.

"It's always been a core long term investment for me." He sounded confident about that.

"Is that what the ranch is holding in the Reserve and the University accounts?

"Yes sir. Real estate."

"Let's take a closer look. Could you get me those files?"

Scalbanski's eyes met Uncle Spencer's. "Now," Uncle Spencer said.

Scalbanski returned almost immediately with the files. "I can explain," he said as he handed them to Uncle Spencer.

"Let me review everything first." It only took a minute, then he handed them to me to review. I pretended to know what I was looking at while Uncle Spencer made another request.

"Now, we'll have a look at the income statement."

He read it the way he had the balance sheet. Once, thoroughly.

"Here's the deal, Mr. Scalbanski," he said his hands draped over the armrests of his chair. "You've made a few transactions that are definitely questionable, that would open you to scrutiny from the Chartered Professional Accountants' organization. That review could be embarrassing for you and might not be in the Montgomerys' best interest.

"Reporting those transactions to the CPA would be one way of handling this. The other way would be for you to straighten up the accounts on your own so nobody but me and you will know what happened."

Scalbanski took a deep breath. "Can you be more specific?"

"Sure. Suppose, to start, you took a look at the administrative fees you've been charging and realized that in view of what valuable clients the Montgomerys are, they might deserve a bit of a refund."

"How much deserving do you think would be appropriate?"

"That's up to you. I know the CPA has fee guidelines you could go by. But speaking personally, I'd say if you had a realization by mid December, before year end, and it came with a chequebook so they could begin running the ranch accounts on their own, I'd say I probably wouldn't remember this visit. Yes, if I was happy, then I'd probably not even recognize you when we met at the next CPA luncheon."

"That's it?"

"Sorry. No. As an investment strategist, I'd say the Reserve and University accounts are over invested in real estate, especially property managed by the Scalbanski Development Corporation. I assume that's run by relations of yours. In any case I think you might suggest that they consider buying back some of the investments they sold the ranch."

Scalbanski held up his hand as if asking permission to comment.

"Don't worry," Uncle Spencer continued, ignoring Scalbanski's hand. "It doesn't have to be done today. I agree with what you said about land prices climbing a bit. Maybe the corporation could take their time. I think we can afford to be patient on that."

"I could talk to the corporation," Scalbanski said. "I could see what they would be willing to do."

"That would be helpful. Just make sure you include all the paperwork in the next statements. Mr. Montgomery is taking more interest in the accounting now."

Uncle Spencer glanced at his watch. "Well, look at that. We've only been here half an hour and we're done. Imagine that. We paid for a whole hour. That's a credit to you Mr. Scalbanski. Your cooperative nature has skunked us out of half an hour of your time. Congratulations. It isn't too often somebody gets the better of me."

I stopped to talk to the receptionist on the way out. I wasn't planning anything, but I figured I would feel good if she flirted with me a bit.

"Are you connected to the ranch?" she asked. "Do you know Kayden? Do you think you could get me his phone number in Calgary?"

In the car, I thought I'd make Uncle Spencer laugh. "You weren't as mean as I thought you'd be. You were tough, that's all."

"I'm not mean, and I'm not tough. I'm right."

He offered to take me back to Western for the last class of the day. I said I'd rather be dropped at the Glencoe. "I need to work out."

On the way he told me it wouldn't be a good idea to tell anybody what happened at Scalbanski's. "If we say a cheque is on the way and it doesn't show up, the Montgomerys will be disappointed. We'll let them wait for the ending. In the meantime, I'll look into the will, see what I can do there."

I lifted weights for an hour. I'd moved up another level and was almost strong enough to practice on the bucking barrel with Grandpa John after the Finals when the riding went on hold until January. He said it would be a good transition from the steers to the bulls. It would help my balance.

And, most important, he could use it to demonstrate how to get out of tough spots such as getting my hand hung up in an inside spin. That didn't scare me as much as going to university next fall. Odd, isn't it? I had misgivings about university, and a good feeling about riding bulls. Guess which one was most likely to kill me? Doesn't make sense, does it?

Emily Arbutus, looking lovely I thought in a navy blue cotton dress belted at the waist, began the Wednesday class discussion by asking us why novels and films were structured differently. I hadn't realized before how much I liked navy blue. She smiled at me and I looked away, knowing that if Kayden had been close enough he would have elbowed me. Girlfriend!

Did I mention that it was pretty obvious that underneath that dress I could tell there was a lot of experience happening?

"What do you think Kayden?" she continued. "What's different about how novels and films are written?"

"Novels are more complicated. More characters. More plots. Films are simple, only a couple of main characters and one story."

"That's good. Why are films simpler Stevie?"

"Because they're written for ten year old brains. Short attention spans. Two hours is the max they can stay in their seats."

"Generally, yes," Emily agreed. "Novels can pick up and drop several storylines and not connect them again until the end. That makes them complicated and require focus. Film viewers can't carry many stories in their heads. They lose interest, or forget."

"Or have short attention spans," Stevie pointed out again.

Emily turned to Willie. "What do you think, Mr. OneEyeShut? Care to tell us the plot of your shiner?" She was treating Willie's black eye differently than Stevie's, probably because he had returned her first glance with a hero's smile.

"Easy to do," Willie answered. "It's a remake of *Casablanca.* The hero, that's me, has to make a chivalrous gesture for the heroine he loves. An unrequited love.

"Humphrey Bogart, me playing a tough guy with a marshmallow lining, gives up his plane ticket to safety so his hot pants sweetheart – Ingrid Bergman – can escape the Nazis with her lover. Bogart knows he's going to pay the price for his symbolic gesture when the Gestapo show up. In my case, the price was a front door roundhouse punch."

"Quit being perfidious, Willie," Stevie interrupted. "That's not at all what happened. There's no hot pants Ingrid. There's no unrequited love. There's nothing like that."

"No perfidy intended," Willie replied calmly, as if he were at a film production meeting. "We're still sketching out the characters. Besides that, you're missing the quintessential point. I'm planning to show that as we live we are writing the scripts of our own lives. We never stop living through the cycle of Acts I, II and III.

"We may have more than one quest in our lifetime. We could accomplish one, have a short Act III and start another."

"Very profound Willie!" Stevie said. "But your dictionary words don't fool me. You'd better start running when the class gets out. When I catch you, you'll be yanking a few pseudo intellectual *bon mots* out from where the sun don't shine."

Emily interrupted. "Willie has a good point about how we live ongoing versions of the Three Acts.

"Nathan. You're the expert on the Three Acts. What do you think? Do we sometimes have to postpone a quest while we take on a more immediate one?"

Like deciding for yourself what's important.

"Yes," I answered. "It might be that we aren't ready for a quest, that we have to accomplish another one as preparation."

Emily gave me her blue eyes and we were together.

"Can you believe Nathan has finally said something that isn't film festival cheese and wine conversation?" Stevie responded, ending that togetherness. "Sounds like you're learning from personal experience."

She turned to Emily. "Do us a favour, will you? Willie says he's in the witness protection program. What's it say in the class register?"

"Off topic," Emily replied. "Back to the original discussion. Nathan, what's different about how novels and films are written?"

I frowned. "I don't know."

"Yes you do. You just did it."

"What?"

"I asked you a question. You answered by frowning, and that told me you didn't like the question. Your face told me what you were thinking. Now, if you were a writer, would you use that face in a book … or a film?"

"A film. The director would tell the actor to reveal his thoughts through that frown."

"Right. And what would you do in a novel?"

"I'd write what the character was thinking as he frowned. About his relationship with whoever asked the question."

"The deeper meaning of a frown," Stevie said.

"Bucked off!" Willie almost shouted. "Wrong answer. The deeper meaning doesn't come in until Act III. We're still in Act II."

"You're both bucked off," Kayden said. "The true relationship and the deeper meaning aren't revealed until the last scene. Anything can happen right up to then."

We all looked at Kayden. He leaned back in his chair. "It's like bull riding. You don't have a relationship with a bull until after the buzzer sounds. After that, you won, or he did. There's no time for thinking about relationships in 8 seconds. That's how you get through life. Do the best you can and wait for the ending. Then you can decide what happened. You might be dead."

"Are you saying there's no deeper meaning to bull riding?" Emily asked.

"Not until the buzzer sounds."

"John Donne," Willie said. "'Never send to know for whom the buzzer tolls; it tolls for thee.'"

"Right," Kayden agreed. "Hearing the buzzer means you took the risks and you're still alive. There's your deeper meaning. No point in dragging it out with a lot of discussion and review. I like a short Act III. The score. Then it's over."

Emily stood beside my desk. "Back to your frown. What were you thinking? Were you thinking about our relationship, or about my question?"

Our relationship?

"Neither," I said. "I was thinking about how lucky we are that people can't read our thoughts."

Kayden smiled at me.

"That's why films are trite," Stevie said. "An actor frowns and we're supposed to believe he's resolving something serious in the scene. In real life, he's probably frowning because he wants to scratch his balls. Who the hell wants to know what anybody else is thinking? We've got enough of our own crap flying around in our heads."

"Very Cartesian," Willie noted. "*Cogito, ergo sum.* I think therefore I am."

"I'm in the air," Kayden concluded. "Therefore I'm bucked off. No deeper meaning."

The class buzzer goes and our profound discussion comes to an end.

I had to catch a bus right after school for a modeling audition. I offered Stevie my house key.

"Thanks, but I'll hang out with Willie," she said. "We'll come together for Math Night."

I'd worked for the modeling agency since elementary school. The owners, a pair of elegant women in their late 30s, absolutely loved my blonde hair and boyish smile. They liked my Mom's blonde hair too.

They wasted no time in taking my shirt off – no modesty in modeling – and getting me to try on some shirts for the upscale store they represented. The shirts didn't fit too well.

"You've matured," Kerry said.

"Yes," Liz added. "You've lost the sweet vulnerable look our client wanted. Women love buying for that look. Needy is very appealing to certain women. Your shoulders are wider. More of an athlete. You're a take charge man now."

"I agree," Kerry said undoing the sample shirt. "Our client sells to power women buying for their men. You look like a truck driver compared to them. How'd you fill out so quickly?"

I showed them some photos on my phone of the bull riding.

"Could you get Kayden and those hunky twins to come in?" Kerry asked, raising one razor sharp eyebrow. "We could sell them a hundred times in Calgary. We know what gets the local hormones boiling. We'll pay you a commission if you bring them in."

I said I'd ask if any of them were interested. No chance.

I thanked them for the audition.

"Maybe we could do a macho thing with you and your friends," Kerry said, seriously. "We've got a client pushing a line of outdoor clothing."

"Hunters?"

She nodded. "Maybe. Something primal."

"Palaeolithic," I suggested.

"Yes."

Liz whispered in my ear as we hugged goodbye. "And bring that Stevie." How wrong could she be about Stevie?

Math Night began with dinner at Jewel's Restaurant, love being the main course. Maybe that's what I liked best about having friends around. Jewel's intensity got spread out. It was a thinner love then, easier to carry.

Stevie and I volunteered to do the dishes while Kayden and Willie rode the math books.

A vehicle door slammed on the street. "It looks like one of those molester vans with blacked out windows," Mom said. "Holy hell! He's coming to our door. He's dressed like a biker!"

Willie stared out the window. "Tell him I'm not here!"

Too late, Dad had already opened the door.

Willie slipped back into the hallway, shaking his head. "I'm not here. I'm not here."

I moved to his side and whispered, "Who is it?"

"Uncle Creeley."

Dad was in the doorway, looking small in front of beer belly Uncle Creeley wearing a black leather vest with steel studs, saggy ass jeans and heavy black boots.

"I'm here for Wilfred Mercury," he barked. Good job on revealing aggression, Emily would say. Great script so far.

"Wrong house, sorry," Dad answered. "I don't know a Wilfred

Mercury." Good job on revealing don't care.

"I saw the little weasel sneaking in here after school. I followed him. I know he's here. Skinny. Red hair."

"Oh, Willie. Yes, he's here. But he's busy tutoring math students. Can I take a message?"

Dad's politeness made a nice contrast to the barking.

"You tell him his Uncle Creeley is here. That slippery bastard owes me money and I want it now."

"Willie doesn't have any money. He barely has enough for food."

"That's what you think. He owes me 25 grand."

"I don't believe Willie has that kind of money."

"Tell the foster home that. They say he's hanging out with rich folks like you. Drivin' around in a fancy BMW. Going to Edmonton for a rodeo – in a private plane! First class hotel. The whole shiteroo. He's got to be blowing a couple of grand for that."

"He's going as our guest."

"What about this famous scholarship he's getting to go to Harbour University next year? He's got to pay me before he's running around acting like a big spender."

"Do you have an IOU of some sort? Any proof at all? I'd like to see verification of your claim."

Dad … a smart aleck!

Uncle Creeley sneered. "The little know it all son of a bitch stole my money."

"Stay beside me," Kayden said as he moved toward the entrance. We stopped about three feet behind Dad, where Uncle Creeley could see us. Mom kept waving us back into the living room.

We ignored her.

Dad spoke louder, revealing his not backing off polite determination. "You're not getting a dime out of Willie. Nothing. You're getting behind the wheel of your van and leaving."

Creeley leaned forward, threateningly. "I want my money."

"Get in your van. Now."

"I'm not leaving with nothin'."

"Yes you are." Dad stepped forward. Creeley backed up. Dad stepped forward again. He didn't see Kayden and me stepping forward in time with him.

"Get going!"

"Gonna make me? I'm gonna stomp your Elbow Park butt if I don't get my money."

Dad's volume edged up. You could probably hear him halfway down the block now. "When I'm through telling you how much trouble you're already in, you're going to be running to get out of here.

"First, child abuse. Willie's not 18 yet and you're extorting his money. And Willie has a fresh black eye. I suspect you might have given it to him. We'll let the police sort those charges out. And, if I don't see your van heading down the street in 30 seconds, I'm pressing charges personally for threatening violence against me. You'll go back to jail."

Good scripting Dad, slipping in that extempore back to jail line. It worked.

Creeley sneered as he turned toward his van. "This ain't over. Not by a long shot. I'm comin' back with reinforcements."

"Don't bother. You've been on our surveillance cameras the whole time. We've got every word recorded. We've got your photo. And we'll have your license plate. Don't come back. And stay away from Willie."

Creeley opened his van door and yelled: "Wilfred Mercury. You lying little thief. I want my 25 grand! Pay up or else!"

Creeley's van rumbled down the street into the dusk, one taillight burned out.

Mom had her arms around Dad before he got through the door. Like some sort of teenage groupie kissing his neck and almost wrapping her legs around him.

He unwound her and gave her a kiss on the cheek.

Kayden, Willie, Stevie and I swarmed him. Kayden lifted him onto Willie and my shoulders.

"Legend! Legend!" Willie chanted as we paraded him around the living room.

"What was all that about you owing Creeley money?" Dad asked Willie.

"Uncle Creeley tells everybody that. He thinks I've got money hidden away. If I did, I'd be better dressed. It's all crapola."

"Where exactly is that Harbour University you're going to?" Stevie asked. "And can I borrow a couple of grand from you?"

We didn't do any homework that night. Dad phoned Uncle Spencer and Aunt Jean who came to take Willie home.

"Don't worry," Willie said, "I'll call my social worker in the morning. She'll find me a new place right way."

"We're not worried," Jean replied.

The groupie and Mr. Legend went to bed early. Stevie and I talked awhile.

"Willie can make up stories faster than anybody I know," Stevie said. "That's how he survives on the streets. This is the best one yet."

"Tonight looked real."

"It was."

"Should I ask The Commotion to help him? Or Uncle Spencer?"

"Willie makes his own choices. He's got his own life. Wilfred Mercury. Get it? Freddy Mercury. Lead singer of Queen."

I looked it up on the Internet. "He could also be Mercury, the god with winged sandals. The guide of souls to the underworld. Maybe he's leading us there."

I didn't expect everything to go smoothly for those five days of rodeo in Edmonton. I could see complications: Reese, especially. She'd expect me to be at her side the whole time. None of her private school friends wanted to come to a rodeo. She'd be lonely and nervous until she figured out how to play the cowboys the way she played the high school boys. It wouldn't take long.

Mr. Legend and The Jewel were perfect rodeo hosts. Mom scheduled the bleacher and box suite seating so everybody got to feel special.

Aunt Jean took Willie to her hair stylist and bought him new clothes. "Maybe Uncle Creeley won't recognize you," I said when I saw the transformation. "Very Harbour."

"He'll know me. But he won't catch me. Took him three months to find me this time. If I'd been on the lookout, I would have been flash out the back door. Gone. Won't corner me like that again."

Then there was Kayden. In his closed mouth no persona way he'd not bothered to tell us he'd qualified for the Finals, riding eleven out of twelve. Nothing to talk about, apparently.

As well as I had prepared myself for the week, a major upset that I hadn't anticipated opened the door of our box on the first night – Jimmie and Alex with a blue eyed cowgirl on their arm. Miss Emily Arbutus of the once glimpsed ivory thighs.

She was wearing tight jeans, a sequined shirt with the top button open, and a felt hat pushed back slightly over her long, strawberry blonde hair. She was very curvy. As I had suspected. Breathlessly.

"This here sweetheart is our Aunt Emily," Jimmie said introducing her to The Commotion.

"I'm Nathan's teacher," she said as she shook hands with everybody. "I'm with the drama department." The Legend was grinning like a crazy person. "You're a teacher. Wow. I want back in school!"

Everybody but Mom and Reese laughed.

"I bet you're Kayden's mystery aunt, the one he lives with," Stevie said.

"I'm not really his aunt. He was in elementary school in Longview while I was in high school. I learned to rope calves on the Rockin' R working for Grandpa John and Grandma Lillian. They asked me to look after him in the big city!"

She took Willie's arm and rubbed his hair gently. "What happened to your do it yourself haircut? Would you like to meet the bullfighters? Kayden's been telling them about you."

For a moment her eyes caught mine. For a moment. Then she turned and left with Willie and the Jackson twins.

That moment of eyes touching is what it would be like if somebody picked you up by your feet and shook you upside down until your eyes crossed and brains poured out your ears.

Uncle Spencer, Grandpa John and Grandma Lillian were congratulating each other.

"How's it going Mr. Buck Off film? Finally outgrown that tall tale?" Grandma Lillian laughed.

How could they know about my unfinished script? Who could have told them? Emily Arbutus? Who else knew? Probably every fucking body. Pick me up and shake me again.

Emily Arbutus. Who the hell are you?

Mom's lips were tight and thin. She wasn't happy. "Why didn't you tell us your drama teacher dressed like that – and Kayden lived with her – and she was the Jackson twins' aunt?"

"A rodeo femme fatale!" Aunt Jean added. "I bet she's hogtied her share of cowboys."

"Honest Mom, I didn't know. I promise."

"Well, she's an unsuitable role model. She's not setting a very good example."

"Who cares?" Dad interjected. "Too bad she doesn't teach physics. Then he'd be paying attention!"

Hilarious laughter.

I left.

Kayden found me at the concessions. "How's it going?" he asked. "I hear you met Aunt Emily."

"Not funny, Kayden. I suppose everybody knows about my *Buck Off* script."

"Not everybody – only Movie Club and my grandparents."

"And Uncle Spencer, and the Jacksons!"

"Same people who know about your bull riding. Don't worry. Wait for the ending."

I shook my head. "Why do you always say that?"

"Because you need to let your story work itself out. Who knows what's coming your way next. You're the one who's always yakking about Three Act stories. Do you want yours to end here, with you pissed off because you got surprised by your secret girlfriend, Emily Arbutus?"

"She's not my secret girlfriend."

"Whatever you say. But why not let the cameras roll. You're at a rodeo. Enjoy your movie."

When I got back to the box suite, Uncle Spencer told me he'd been talking to the announcer, Ron Atkins, and had arranged for me to sit with him in his booth.

"I told him about the job you did last week at the Rockin' R. He said he'd like to meet you."

I remembered Ron Atkins from the Claresholm bull riding. He turned out to be as smooth in person as he was on the microphone.

"Pleased to meet you," he said shaking my hand.

He showed me around the booth, letting me look over his background sheets for the competitors, the bucking horses and the bulls. That explained how he had been so glib in Claresholm introducing the riders and bulls.

I got a little carried away when he asked me to describe the practice rides at the Rockin' R, and gave him a real dramatic introduction to the bulls, Stevie, how Willie had become our bullfighter, and how Grandpa John and Grandma Lillian were making men of us – except Stevie.

"Nobody can make anything of her."

"That would make good filler for one of the breaks," he said. "There's always some downtime when they're loading the bulls. A human interest piece like that would keep the crowd's attention."

He measured me up and down. "How would you like to give it a try tomorrow night? I'd hand the mike over to you and let you run with your story. Your uncle said you had a style all your own."

Kayden was right. I should try to have some rodeo fun, so I told Ron I'd come to the booth before the bull riding started.

I planned to keep this to myself.

Sitting in the bleachers later, I paid close attention to Ron's chatter as the crew started to load the bulls for the final event of the evening. He used his Oklahoma drawl to introduce the riders, and, I noticed, he kept his introduction of Kayden and the Jackson twins to a minimum. No personal background and no mention of the Rockin' R. That meant he was leaving it up to me tomorrow.

"Look at the far end of the chutes," Grandpa John said to me. "Willie's in there with the bullfighters! We all put in a good word for him this afternoon. The bullfighters listened mostly to Emily. Willie challenged them to a race. A standing start from one set of rails and up and over the opposite side. They couldn't catch him. Speed of Light."

Emily was at ground level, talking through the rails to the bullfighters as Ron finished his introductions.

"Looks like we've got an apprentice bullfighter tonight, a young fella named Speed of Light Willie. I'll have to find out more about him and get back to you folks."

The bulls won the first night, bucking off seven of the twelve cowboys. Jimmie, Alex and Kayden all scored. Mom hustled us out of the arena and to the limo where we waited for Willie. He brought Emily.

"Could I get a ride back in your plane?" she asked Mom. "I've got classes tomorrow."

"Of course."

Mom gives everybody at least one chance to improve themselves in her esteem.

I had trouble concentrating in school the next day. I'd written myself a Rockin' R spiel for Ron and kept rehearsing it mentally.

Emily waited with us in the school parking lot for the limo to take us to the airport. As we settled into our seats on the plane, I relished the thought of the surprise everybody would get that night: they'd all be sitting in the box suite and suddenly they'd hear Ron Atkins handing me the mike.

When the crews started running the bulls into the chutes that night, Ron did it. No warning. "It's all yours Nathan," he said. "Let's see how you do. You have to fill at least five minutes."

I belted out my opening. "You got someone new in your ears folks. Nathan Munro. You're probably wondering how a darn high school kid got hold of this mike. Well, Ron forgot to turn it off when he snuck out for a bathroom break. Of course, he's the trusting type and, to tell you the truth, I'm hoping right now that the speakers aren't working where he's sitting.

"I'm here on a mission. An assignment I call The Shameless Promotion of the Rockin' R Bull Ridin' And Growin' Up School.

"It's run out of Longview by a couple of experienced hands, John and Lillian Montgomery. That's them up there in Box 54. Swing the lights up boys so we can all get a look at what healthy living does for you.

"Besides raising their grandson Kayden Montgomery – yes, that's the good looking young man competing in tonight's event – John and Lillian have built themselves an arena and packed their pens with bulls as cold eyed as Clint Eastwood in *Dirty Harry.* For all you kids texting on your cellphones – that's one of the great baby boomer films.

"Back to the Rockin' R bulls. Hang on, Ron's banging on the door. I'd better move along quick and just talk about the meanest bull they've got. TwoBlackEyes. He's a gangsta'. A thug. A toe to toe back alley bully who can take all the punches you care to give him. He's gonna snap your neck. He's gonna jam your back. He's got no style. No rhythm. He's only got hard and harder.

"He's bucked Kayden off. He's bucked the Jackson twins off. If you look over at the chutes you'll see Jimmie Jackson's left arm taped up – courtesy of TwoBlackEyes.

"In fact, the only Rockin' R man that's got the best of this bruising giant is Willie 'Speed of Light' Mercury. He's that red haired fighter on the rails. He's given TwoBlackEyes his trademark insult – the Bull Slap – twice and each time he's been over the rails inches ahead of sure death. Show us your stuff, Willie!"

Willie dashed across the arena waving his white towel and slapped one of the judges on the back and scampered over the rails before the judge caught him.

"And of course, with all that testosterone flowing down at the Rockin' R we've got to counteract it with a healthy dose of girl power. And that's Sweet Stevie, whose headlock is as crushing as her one handed grip on the steers she rides. And we've brought the gorgeous Emily Arbutus, our breakaway calf ropin' inspirational high school teacher. That's her by the rails. Raise your hat Emily!

"There you have it folks. The Rockin' R bunch. We'll be back next year to introduce you to TwoBlackEyes. And if you need some personal straightening out in life, go talk to Grandma Lillian. If she can keep the Jackson twins in line, you know she can handle any trouble you got.

"Yikes! Ron's broken down the door and is beating me with his hat to get the microphone back, so I'd better hand it over ..." and that's when I let loose with what I hoped would become my signature sign off:

"Let 'em grow up to be cowboys!"

Ron took over the microphone with a big grin. "How's that for a natural first time talent? Nathan Munro. And speaking of talent, that Rockin' R is loaded with it. We should be seeing some champions coming out of there.

"Right now it looks like the bulls are finally seeing the wisdom of getting loaded and the riding will start any moment. So I'll take this chance to ask Nathan a question.

"Can you tell us a bit more about Willie? Are we seeing the beginning of a bullfighting career for him?"

"I hate to disappoint you, Ron. Willie is retiring next spring. He's heading to Harvard on a math scholarship. The talk is Microsoft and Apple are mighty nervous – they've heard about his Bull Slap!"

Jimmie's bull fought him in the chute, refusing to settle long enough for Alex to pull Jimmie's rope. The chute crew jammed a wooden beam between the rails to hold the bull's head down.

Jimmie nodded, the beam slid back, the gate swung open and the bull reared out. He kicked high and swung right, into Jimmie's riding hand. Jimmie lost control of his broken arm as it swung forward. He fought hard and stayed on. It wasn't a pretty ride ... he bucked off with the buzzer and landed hard, protecting his broken arm. The bull turned on him, his head lowered to toss him with his horns.

Willie was there instantly. Sprinting like mad, jumping over Jimmie's outstretched legs, and smacking the bull's face with his white towel.

The bull chased him to the rails as Jimmie got to his feet. As the fighters lured the bull from the arena, Jimmie limped over to Willie and raised Willie's arm in a salute to the crowd.

Ron pounded me on the back as he announced: "You called it, Nathan! Willie's Bull Slap."

The video screen pulsed "Willie! Willie!"

We celebrated my birthday after the Saturday afternoon performance. Alex and Kayden had made the top five with a good chance at the championship. Jimmie squeaked in at number ten, with not much hope at the championship, but a possibility of go round money.

The Commotion booked a dining room and buffet for the night. The hotel had decorated my birthday cake with cowgirls.

The open bar got well used by the Aunts and Uncles and Cousins. I didn't drink because none of the Rockin' R bunch did. All night the other finalists stopped by to eat and relax, and show off their sort of girlfriends. Reese scowled at the girls in their tight jeans and button breaking shirts.

Reese made sure everybody knew I was with her. I didn't like the way she referred to my interest in the rodeo and my announcing as a hobby. "Little boys!" she said after Ron Atkins and I gave the party an impromptu rodeo routine that had everybody laughing. "Nathan will grow out of this phase."

I wished I could tell Ron about my plan to ride a bull before spring. He's a genuine guy and I felt bad about not treating him straight. Then again, most of the week had been an invention one way or another. But, like Kayden said, wait for the ending. Still in Act II, the adventure.

Emily had a birthday card for me. Inside was a handwritten note to her from the Cannes Film Festival.

"Emily – Keep us in mind if you find a script you believe has potential, Love"

I couldn't read the scrawled signature.

"How would you like to take *Buck Off* to Cannes?" she asked after I read the card. She meant it.

I had to smile, imagining rope swinging Emily in her rodeo clothes at Cannes.

"What's your smile telling me?" she asked.

"I'll never say," I invented.

She kissed me on the cheek. "Mister 18 Years Old."

Maybe one day ... that was a confusing thought. I worked on understanding it later and felt foolish. I'd been yakking my mouth off in class about personas and never seen the smoky and mysterious one in front of me. Emily Arbutus. Movie Club Teacher. Aunt. Calf Roper. Cannes Film Festival.

She believed in *Buck Off.* She believed in me.

I watched Kayden go for the win on Sunday afternoon. Ron Atkins built him up while Alex and Jimmie helped him in the chute.

"This young cowboy is full of surprises. When I first met him at Claresholm, he had talent but no consistency. He'd scored a few 90s up to then and a lot of zeroes. Then something happened. He went from riding 25 percent of his bulls to riding 92 percent. That's right. 92 percent. He rode 11 out of 12 to move himself into the Finals. Last night he did it again, making it 12 out of 13. Can he make it 13 out of 14 tonight?"

Kayden played his goin' for perfect music and bucked off. No deeper meaning.

Jimmie must have eaten a handful of painkillers because he scored the high ride of the day and moved into fifth place. Alex moved up to third.

On the plane ride to Calgary, Mom and Reese wanted to see Emily's birthday card. They suspected it contained something more personal than Happy Birthday. I said I had lost it. Hard to prove.

Two weeks later we were all back at the Rockin' R. The bulls and steers got a break as the rodeo season ended for the year. We'd start riding again after New Year's. Until then I would get slammed around on the bucking barrel and learn to roll my hand over if I got hung up.

Grandpa John and Grandma Lillian got their Christmas present early, a chequebook and a bank statement showing $100,000 had been deposited in the ranch operating account. Uncle Spencer hadn't mentioned any progress on his investigation into Kayden's parents' will.

The ranch chewed off a big chunk of the trustee's cheque by ordering a liner load of bred heifers. We spent the weekends feeding them and the bulls. When the weather was good we checked the heifers on horseback, making sure they were settled in the snow drifted pastures. Grandpa

John enjoyed riding out and seeing his own herd grazing.

Grandma Lillian and I were unbeatable at whist, unless Uncle Spencer stayed after dinner and partnered with Stevie.

Ron Atkins helped me pick Christmas presents for everybody at the ranch. We spent a Saturday afternoon in western shops. In the end, I chose rugged winter jackets.

"We're working people," he had said when I wanted to buy more fashionable shirts and jackets. "They'll thank you every time they feed in a blizzard."

Reese helped me pick out presents for The Commotion. We bought Mom gold, bull rider earrings that Reese didn't like. To make up for that, I let her choose Dad's present: a five pack, gift box of scotch. I wrapped a Superman cape around the package. Maybe he would wear it if Uncle Creeley returned.

I bought Uncle Spencer a book of card tricks. What else?

I bought Willie the best MP3 I could find and a $100 Lovely Golden Fries gift card; Stevie a scarf and cowboy hat; Aubrey a fart cushion and a photo taken of her at the Rodeo Finals looking cowgirl sexy; Kayden a Dale Carnegie book on public speaking and a gift card for a handmade bull rope; and Emily a shiny ceramic apple.

I bought Reese a relaxation spa treatment. She needed it.

I was teary on Christmas Eve with Mom and Dad, traditionally our sacred time alone. I would be leaving home next fall. Into a university residence most likely. This would be our last Christmas in Camelot: The King, the Queen and the Little Prince. Part of me could hardly wait to get away, to be on my own and make my own decisions. And part of me wanted to stay forever wrapped in their love, and be their Peter Pan who never grew up. And the biggest part of me wanted to confess my inventions, to tell them about TwoBlackEyes, and Bull Rider's script and maybe going to Cannes with Emily Arbutus.

It felt as if we were all hanging onto yesterday as hard as we could, pretending that tomorrow was so far away it wasn't real.

Wait for the ending, as Kayden said. But if I could have, I would have stopped the camera on that Christmas Eve.

Instead of the usual Empire State Building of packages under the tree, this year there was only a knee deep pile.

Jewel's Restaurant served a spectacular dinner for three, and we laughed and told stories about Christmas excitement in the old days when I believed in Santa Claus. Then we started talking about our favourite family memories.

"Try to guess my favourite family movie," I said. They couldn't. Dad said it had to be the 1978 *Superman* starring Christopher Reeves and Dad in his speaking role – with a credit!

"That's your movie," I said. "What's our movie?"

They couldn't guess. I relented and told them: *City Slickers*.

Mom and Dad laughed at that because the movie was the way we had joked about Dad's midlife crisis eleven years ago. He'd been working for Big Blue – IBM – and wanted to make a change but had a wife (Julia) and a son (me). He bought a new Sony Betamax, and we bought him *City Slickers*.

"Remember how you got so excited at the first scene, when Mitch and his pals ran with the bulls at Pamplona?

"And you jumped up and said, 'I want to do that!'"

Mom and Dad snuggled on the couch when I reminded them of that day, and the nine years later day when he and I really did it. They were surprised I remembered the details of that trip so well. How could I forget?

"Don't you remember taking me to the topless beach in Spain?"

No comment.

"Do you remember going to the bullfight where we saw the crowd bringing in buckets of sangria and fruit? And Mom was wearing a new, white Chanel shirt. Remember how mad she was when the sangria soaked oranges and lemons started flying? And how we started throwing everything we could back, and Mom pasted a teenage boy with a lemon?

"And then we saw the dead bulls outside and Mom barfed.

"So then Dad and I had to buy more white clothes and red neckerchiefs – just like Mitch had in *City Slickers* – so we could be part of the running of the bulls.

"And Dad didn't want me to run and tried to keep me outside. The rules said you had to be 18 and I was only 15. But then I saw you running by and I slipped under the fence and ran with you.

"And you got knocked down by another runner and claimed it was a bull. I had to help you up. Our hearts were going a million miles an hour. Then we found Mom and she let us try again the next day.

"We made it all the way into the stadium!"

Mom and Dad just stared at me from the couch.

"That was the best movie I was ever in," I said. "The one where we ran with the bulls at Pamplona."

Suddenly we were all crying. Even Dad. Pamplona was our best holiday ever. The most fabulous. The most legendary.

I felt good, even if I was crying. I knew in my heart that it wouldn't be long before I'd be disappointing them: not living up to their expectations; screwing up somehow; being less than the ideal they deserved.

I believed that, in their hearts, they also knew we wouldn't be sharing any more growing up experiences. I'd be graduating in June, and starting a life they wouldn't know everything about.

That's why I made them promise that *City Slickers* would be our family movie: the way we resolved Dad's mid life crisis; my moment to learn I could run with the bulls.

Pamplona is where we could always go in our memories to recall our legendary days together.

Dear Emily Arbutus

Our boy has lost the sheep riding bet but is not trying to wiggle out of the consequences. Keith now sees Chet as a potential danger. He's no longer just a boy he can bully – he's somebody to keep an eye on. Chet's determination is about to pay off as he gets a glimpse of Keith's dirty side.

BUCK OFF

ACT II SCENE 1
THE REVEAL

INT. THE SAMSON BARN - TWO DAYS LATER

Chet is shovelling the manure from an empty stall into a wheelbarrow. Keith comes up to him.

KEITH

So Chet, why you such a momma's boy?

CHET

What makes you think I am?

KEITH

Always holdin' on to those apron strings. I hear ya got grounded.

CHET

(embarrassed)

I'm not grounded.

KEITH

Ok then, why don't you and Jonah come by the barns tonight and have a beer, or don't your mamma let you drink?

CHET

I drink beer. I'll be 18 soon.

KEITH

Okay we'll see ya later then.

Keith walks away. A goon follows him.

A GOON

What's that all about Keith? Why'd you invite that little candy ass over to drink our beer?

KEITH

I need to keep an eye on the little fucker. I think he's smarter than we give him credit for.

INT. THE SAMSON BARN - LATER THAT MORNING

Chet walks by Keith's office. Keith is on the phone, we hear what Chet hears.

KEITH

Yeah yeah I know there's a ban on bringing cattle across the border from Canada to the US. What the hell is Mad Cow Disease anyways?

Pause ... do ya think I'm stupid? (pause) I don't give a shit. We need all the bulls we can get. Screw the border, you figure it out. (Pause.) If you can't do it I'll find someone who can. (Pause.) I don't give a shit. I'll give ya more money, but get it done. I told ya I don't give a shit. Put them in a horse trailer and tell those stupid customs jerks that they're horses. They don't know their ass from a hole in the ground. (Pause.) I said do it ... you whisper a word to anyone and you won't be kissin' your kids goodnight ... got it!

Keith slams the receiver down. He looks up and sees Chet walk past the door. He jumps up from his chair.

KEITH

Don't you have enough work to do?

CHET

I just wanted to tell ya that I'm done and Jonah and I will be over later for a beer.

Keith looks relieved.

KEITH

Ok then Goldilocks. We will see ya later.

(**Reminder to self** - write these scenes later: Just as Chet is beginning to gain confidence in himself he makes a mistake. He gets drunk at Keith's barn that night and Marlena overreacts. Johnny, his uncle who is falling apart slowly as he tries to hold back his own guilty secret, brings Marlena to the barn.)

JOHNNY

(to Marlena)

Chet's drunk at the Samson's barn and Jonah has soiled himself and barfed all over the place. His mother's taking him to the hospital.

Marlena and Johnny walk into Keith's barn. Marlena walks up to Chet and grabs his arm.

MARLENA

(yelling)

You are coming home, now!

Keith walks over, Marlena turns to him.

MARLENA

How dare you? Supplying these under age kids with booze.

Keith laughs.

KEITH

(laughing)

Just because these pansy ass kids can't hold their booze ain't my fault. Now get the little asshole outa here.

Chet stumbles out with Marlena.

CHET

Mom relax, I'm ok (slurring his words) Jonah just had a little too much to drink.

INT. THE MOTOR HOME - NEAR MIDNIGHT

MARLENA

(to Chet)

Go to bed.

Chet walks into his room. Marlena goes to hers.

INT. THE MOTOR HOME - EARLY MORNING

Marlena is on the phone. Chet stands at the door of his bedroom and listens.

MARLENA

(to George, Chet's grandfather)

It's just not working out here George. Your grandson is in all kinds of trouble, he is acting out and I can't seem to control him. We are supposed to be setting up in Edmonton next week. But I think I have to come home. (Pause.) No, you're right, I can't afford it but my hands are tied. George, I don't know what to do. (Pause.) That would be great. I can get Christina to help me with the ice cream truck and I'll put Chet on the bus. (Pause.) That would be great if you could pick him up.(Pause.) Yes, he could stay with you in the big house for the summer and work on the ranch. Do you think Jean will mind? (Pause.)

Dear Bull Rider

You have good instincts, listen to them. You have forced Chet to acquire some backbone with Keith. What I like is that Marlene thinks sending Chet to his grandparents' ranch will remove him from danger. By forcing Chet to go to the ranch, I suspect, Marlena is unwittingly forcing her son to make some independent decisions about his life. Is Marlena's manipulation going to backfire on her?

I'm hooked.

Emily Arbutus

PS. Get Chet into some rodeo action soon. This is meant to be an action-based film. It is getting a bit too sensitive.

GRADUATION

I don't suppose I'll ever spend a more carefree six months than those between January and June of my grade 12 year.

I started my last semester of high school with a 71 per cent average, brought down by a 60 in physics. Major concern expressed by The Commotion and Mashed Potatoes.

Kayden got a 72 in Math 20 and made it into Math 30 and would probably be getting into university. We could guess Willie's 90s and didn't want to snoop into Stevie's business. We all signed up for Emily's second semester Film Studies course: Hollywood Heroes.

I had a routine and I had a purpose. I attended classes, worked out and rode bulls. Reese motivated me to get my marks up so we could start at the University of Calgary together. She was sure she would become a lawyer. She was just as sure my Rockin' R friendships would fade away when I moved into the Academia Arena. She did not know that my heart was in making a statement in film, not in writing financial statements. I cannot imagine how she would have reacted if she'd known Emily was helping me with *Buck Off.*

Dear Emily Arbutus

Chet has been getting into shape working at the ranch and has been helped getting onto bulls by his uncle (Bruce) and grandfather (George). He's starting to show promise and they're proud of him. Marlena suspects Chet has been riding bulls without her permission and now she's wheedled the truth out of George.

Nathan

BUCK OFF

ACT II SCENE 2
MANIPULATION

GEORGE

Soul-breaker is the most athletic Brahman we've ever had on the ranch.

MARLENA

Chet hasn't tried to ride him, has he?

GEORGE

He's tried (he laughs) maybe for two seconds. No one will ride this one soon ... he's the fastest bull I've ever seen. Chet's been training on all our rough stock. He's a natural, Marlena.

Marlena looks at George, tears are in her eyes.

MARLENA

George I don't understand ... I don't want this.

GEORGE

It's Chet's dream Marlena ... he is determined to follow it. We could hold him back but you know that won't work. He went to the Camrose rodeo with Bruce and the other boys from the Ranch. Chet was amazing, he nailed it. He came in third in the Novice. They want to go to High Prairie for the long weekend.

MARLENA

No George ... he's smart, he's going to university this fall. We've worked hard for this. He won the Rutherford Scholarship. He is going to business school. He will get a good job. This rodeo life is not for us. You said you'd help me!

GEORGE

He wants to go to Olds Agricultural College, and then manage the Ranch when I get too old. I'm 72 now. He'll have time for all that. Right now he just wants to train to be a cowboy. Marlena he's 18. He can do what he wants.

MARLENA

I won't have it! He needs to come home and get himself ready for school. I'll sell everything to make sure he gets there.

Marlena walks out, gets in her old Ford Explorer and drives off. She pulls over on the side of the road; she grabs her cell phone from her purse and calls her sister. Johnny answers the phone.

MARLENA

Hi Johnny, is Christina there?

JOHNNY

Nope, she's out with boys. You sound upset Marlena, what's up?

Marlena can't help herself, she begins to cry.

MARLENA

Johnny, I'm scared. (she cries) George has Chet riding bulls. He even went to the Camrose rodeo. I'm so angry. Now Chet thinks I don't believe in him, but I do. I've seen the way he handles himself. He is just like his father. But he is also naive like his father. He should be somewhere safer. He should be in university.

It's dangerous out there and I don't mean the bulls. People are more so, like that asshole Keith Samson. It's people that are so dangerous. I'm not stupid, I know something went wrong that day. It had to do with Keith and you know something that you're not saying. Keith was somehow involved in the death of my husband, and he already has a grudge against my son.

JOHNNY

(feigning confidence)

That's nonsense Marlena. But I agree Chet shouldn't be bull riding. He ain't like his dad, he'll get hurt in the arena for sure ...he's not focused and he ain't got what it takes. George and Bruce should tell the kid to go off to school. Make something out of himself. As for Keith, I don't know a damn thing about what you're talking about. But don't you let these crazy ideas, of what you think happened all them years ago, get into your head. Get that nonsense out of your head. Do you hear me?

MARLENA

I hear you loud and clear. Chet will go to university but not because you think he is not good enough. But because I know you're lying about Keith. You're scared shitless of him, but I don't care. I'll tell Chet whatever I need to, to keep him safe, and you'll back me up, because you know as well as I do that I need to protect him from the Samsons.

Marlena puts her phone down and heads to the

Ranch.

EXT. THE ROUGH STOCK RANCH - LATER THAT MORNING

When Chet sees her truck drive into the ranch, he runs to meet the truck. Marlena gets out and he hugs her for a long time.

CHET

Momma! I missed you sooooo much!

MARLENA

Oh, I missed you too Chet.

CHET

Mom, I've been riding all summer, I can't wait to show you. Thank you so much for sending me here. I've had the very best summer. I'm so glad you're here. Uncle Bruce is the best...

MARLENA

We need to talk.

CHET

Please don't spoil the moment. You just got here.

MARLENA

Chet you're coming home today. We'll get you ready for university and then Monday we'll leave to get you set up in residence. I checked the mail and you're all set to go.

CHET

Mom, I'm questioning whether I should go to university at all. And especially business school? I'm just not a suit kinda guy. I'd like to be on the rodeo circuit, qualify for the Finals and the Stampede. I want to follow in Dad's footsteps. Everyone thinks I've got the talent.

I can go to school later. Maybe later I'll go to Olds College. Learn more about ranching.

Marlena is struggling to keep it together. She doesn't want to cry. It would lessen her position.

MARLENA

I talked to Uncle Johnny, he says rodeo is too competitive nowadays. You don't have what it takes. And he thinks you'd be better off at school. He knows the rodeo Chet.

CHET

(He looks defeated)

He said that? What about Bruce?

MARLENA

Bruce is out of touch now Chet. He hasn't been on the front line of rodeo for 17 years. I'm so sorry, but I think Johnny would be the one to know. I'll tell you what; you can come back to visit the ranch. Your grandparents will be OK with that. So let's get real here, pack up your stuff and let's go.

INT. THE RANCH KITCHEN - LATER THAT DAY

MARLENA

(across the table to George)

I've done it. Chet's going to university.

GEORGE

That's your decision, Marlena, not his. You'll have to live with the consequences.

MARLENA

I know. I hope I'll forgive myself

```
      if I've taken something away from
      him.
            GEORGE
(with disappointment)
      You can always claim best
      intentions. Lots of mothers have.
```

Dear Bull Rider

Nice twist, having Marlena yank Chet out of his rodeo dream and send him off to Reality University.

The viewers are going to be disappointed in their hero: he's made good progress and is ready to be riding and winning. Now he's giving up that dream. And for the wrong reasons. Marlena has lied to him about George's, Bruce's and Johnny's confidence in his potential.

I can hear the audience: "Don't give up, Chet!"

I hope Chet is unlikely to give up too easily. He's coming back! You'd better have some good ideas up your writing sleeve to get him on his feet again.

I admire the way you are handling the conflict between Chet and Marlena. If I had a boy, I'd want him to be like Chet. I might not like it, but I hope he'd know that all mothers are afraid of losing their children to the dangers of the world. Maybe Marlena will come to accept that her son is going to have a life of his own very soon, and she shouldn't protect him from Keith Samson or the secret of his father's death. It's time for those issues to be settled.

Emily Arbutus

PS. Don't let Marlena forgive herself too early for lying to Chet, at least not until Act III. Keep the audience wondering if this miracle can happen.

I rode my three steers in a row in February and Grandpa John promoted me to the young bulls that Kayden or the Jacksons had tested. I was those bulls' last chance. If they bucked me off they got a reprieve. I rode most of them and the neighbourhood freezers filled with No Buck Burgers.

By early May I had graduated to bulls that were showing promise. They still hadn't learned the high kicks and spins that rodeo bulls need, so I made my 8s without too many bruises. The oxygen bottle hanging on the rails became my reminder of how I used to be.

Kayden coached me on my form; keeping my back straight, staying in control and timing my spurs. Then he moved on to scoring points.

"If you're not exposing yourself, taking risks, then you might as well be a monkey tied on a bull," he would say. After that, he'd yell "Monkey" every time he saw me riding too safe.

We'd see Ron Atkins at the rodeos where Kayden and the twins had become the riders to watch. They were almost guaranteed an invitation to ride for $100,000 at the Calgary Stampede in July. Stevie and I got to know the other competitors. Ron tried to get Stevie to enter the girls' cow riding. Willie hung out with the bullfighters, learning from them and joining in whenever they asked, and they always did.

Ron pestered Grandpa John to bring Uncle Spencer and TwoBlackEyes to a rodeo. "You've got to let the judges see them if you want them to be considered for the Stampede."

"When's Nathan making his ride?" Jimmie Jackson asked me every weekend. "Time for talking's almost over."

"You can take your pick of our bulls," Grandpa John offered, "except TwoBlackEyes and Uncle Spencer. You're not ready for them."

Other than Jimmie's kidding, nobody seriously pushed me to make my ride. In fact, I knew in their eyes I'd already done more than they expected. I could have quit any day and been proud.

I made my decision on June 1. That afternoon I phoned the Claresholm rodeo grounds with my entry for a competition on the June 27th weekend. Nathan Munro. I don't suppose Adriano Moraes would be losing any sleep when he heard about the rookie at Claresholm. I don't suppose he had ever heard of Claresholm.

My plans were to finish writing my final exams that week and then head straight there for the Friday night performance.

The only person I told was Uncle Spencer. "I'd like you to clear it first with Dr. Sara," he said. "I've got no say otherwise. It's up to you."

Dr. Sara sent me for the usual x rays and blood tests before my appointment.

"You look like a bull rider," she said afterwards as I lay in my underwear on her examination table. "Well developed muscles. No fat. And more bruises than I can count." She listened to my chest and told me to get dressed.

"He's all man now," she told Uncle Spencer. "He's kept his word about getting into shape. If it wasn't for the lung x rays, I wouldn't believe he's the same Nathan I saw last fall."

She folded her hands neatly on her desk. "Here's the situation, Nathan. You're a dream patient. You'd pass any physical I've given to hockey players. You must have pushed yourself to have make this kind of progress in ten months."

"I had help."

"But … the fluid is still accumulating in your lungs. Do you spit it up?"

"A little. I haven't had to use oxygen since Christmas."

"And the sleepiness."

"When I get hit hard or am stressed."

"We'll deal with that later. Right now, do what's important to you. Go ride your bull." She laughed. "That sounds like a motivational line from a Tom Cruise film."

Emily ended Movie Club a bit early the next day. "I hear you've entered the Claresholm rodeo," she said to me. "I'll be there."

"We'll all be," Stevie said. "Good for you, Nathan."

Willie promised to be the bullfighter when I rode. Kayden said what I hoped he would say: "You're going to be nervous. I'll be right there with you. I won't let the chute open until I know you're ready."

Grandpa John phoned me that night and asked if I was alone.

"Yes."

"There's a problem. I didn't know you'd entered Claresholm when I entered Uncle Spencer and TwoBlackEyes. There's a chance you could draw one of them. I don't want you riding either of them."

"I can't back out now. When I entered I decided I'd ride whatever bull I drew. It has to be that way. I can't pick and choose. That's not the way I want to do this."

"Kayden's been right about you all along," Grandpa John replied. "You're on a mission. Grandma Lillian says she expects to see you beat those Jackson rod burners." I could hear her cheering in the background.

"We're proud to know you," he said and hung up.

We had a final ranch practice the weekend before Claresholm. Kayden gave me a duffle bag for my boots, spurs, chaps, rope, rosin and bell. "I won my first buckle with this bag. It'll bring you luck."

I was too wound up to study so I didn't even try. I was going into the final exams with a 75 average. Any exam marks in the 70s would guarantee me a university acceptance. I could even handle a 60 in physics.

I must have written my exams that week. I remember going to the auditorium and going home afterwards. Mom kept pestering me after each exam. "How do you think you did? Was it harder than you expected?"

I gave her the only answer I had. "Don't worry."

Kayden and I arrived early at the Claresholm Agriplex. I had ten texts from Reese on my phone. "Where are you?????????"

I knew my way around the arena and chutes but stayed near Kayden. I thought I was going to puke like the first time I rode a steer. I peeked into the first aid room and saw they had an oxygen bottle beside the stretcher. When you're scared, little things like that are reassuring.

Jimmie and Alex's welding rig rolled in. They slapped me on the back. "Ride 'em Pretty Boy!"

The draw for bulls went slowly. The more points a rider had, the sooner he drew. I was last. Number 25. Jimmie kidded me. "You'll be riding a leftover. All the good ones will be gone."

Dakota Tallboy drew Uncle Spencer. Kayden congratulated him. "You could win. He'll make you look good."

The countdown draw continued. 18, 19, 20. Five riders left. Five bulls. TwoBlackEyes still hadn't been drawn.

Number 24 drew Three Aces.

That left TwoBlackEyes and me.

What I'd wanted, and not what I wanted. I ran outside. Kayden found me sitting on my heels by the door and wiping breakfast off my shirt.

"How goddamn lucky are you? You drew the best bull! You could win on his points alone."

I smiled a little. "Want to trade?"

He pulled me to my feet. "Listen to me. Quit thinking about what might happen. Don't look so far ahead. Think about what you are going to do for 8 seconds. The ending will take care of itself."

I thought I was going to pee my pants as we paraded into the arena.

Ron Atkins introduced us to the crowd. Willie gave me a wave of his towel. Emily's sequined shirt shimmered telling me I could do this.

After that, I had to wait an hour for TwoBlackEyes to be loaded into a chute where he slung his head from side to side, that long drip of snot dancing just above the dirt.

"We've heard a lot of rumours about this new bull," Ron drawled. "He's bucked off the best riders at the Rockin' R with his back breaking, stiff leg landings. They tell me it's like getting dropped onto concrete every time he hits the ground.

"Climbing on board today is a youngster, a Rockin' R protégé, Nathan Munro, who if I had my way would be up here right now announcing with me. He's got a heck of a smooth patter. Let's see how that smoothness sits with a back alley thug like TwoBlackEyes."

A back alley thug. Ron was using my line. A compliment.

"Pay attention. Stay focussed," Kayden urged. "We've gone through this hundreds of times. Stay forward coming out, lean back on the high kick. Stay with him and he'll run up all the points you need."

He pressed my chest between his hands to steady me. "Watch his shoulders. He comes out slow and goes high. He'll spin away from your hand. Keep those spurs on him."

I took a deep breath. "Again," Kayden said. "Take a couple more."

Two more. Calmer now.

"Is Jack Sparrow ready?" Kayden asked.

"That's *Captain* Jack Sparrow," I answered, bit down on my mouth guard and nodded. I think this was the first time in my life I felt really determined. I wasn't scared by this shark eyed sonofabitch's plans to end my days.

The gate swung open.

TwoBlackEyes did exactly what Kayden predicted. Slow out of the chute. High rear. Bone jamming landing. Then spinning away from my hand. I kept pulling myself forward, pressing with my spurs and waiting for the turn I knew was coming. The fast change in direction that had flipped Jimmie off.

I felt his fast turn coming and let my right leg swing out and spurred the bastard hard in the guts to straighten him out. That surprised him. I jammed his guts again. He bucked straight ahead.

The buzzer sounded just as he landed stiff legged, his front end jarring my hand loose. As he came up again I somersaulted over his back. I was pure mad when I felt his hoof clip my right leg. "You dickhead!" I shouted as I landed. I found out later his next kick ripped my helmet off. I remember seeing Willie's cleats and hearing him slapping TwoBlackEyes with his towel.

I woke up on the stretcher behind the chutes. "The ambulance is coming," somebody said.

The next time I completely woke up I was in a hospital bed, my head supported by two pillows, my nose stitched and my leg in a cast.

The room was full of my friends. Nobody seemed to care how dazed I felt. They just kept laughing and talking about how I'd spurred TwoBlackEyes.

"82. You got a goddamn 82," Uncle Spencer smiling like I'd never seen him before. "Par, Nathan. Par!"

Stevie said Willie had to beat TwoBlackEyes off me. "You really pissed that bull off. He wanted to grind you. The back of your flak jacket is covered with snot. That's how close he got."

Kayden and the Jacksons had made the final ten. They'd ride later that night. Dakota Tallboy, again, was in the lead with a 94 on Uncle Spencer.

"I've already had three offers on TwoBlackEyes," Grandpa John said. "He could be voted best bull." He gave me a wink. "Your ride made me some money!"

Ron Atkins leaned over and, in a low voice, said, "You did something tonight nobody can ever take away from you. You didn't just ride that bull. You beat him. Nobody knows how you did it. The promoters have been showing your replay nonstop."

The intern came in and wanted to clear out my friends. "Nathan's doctor in Calgary wants us to give him a couple of tests."

"Let them stay," I said. "I wouldn't be here if it weren't for them."

Big laugh.

In the morning, The Commotion arrived and cleared the room.

Mom exploded. "A concussion, a lacerated nose and a broken leg. What the hell have you been doing Nathan?"

It didn't get better. She'd ordered a private ambulance to take me home. Willie, Stevie and Kayden held the emergency doors open as the attendants wheeled me out.

Our Elbow Park neighbours watched the ambulance unload me. I was prepackaged cocktail party gossip ready to be served on a silver tray.

"Goddamn humiliating," Mom muttered. Inside, she locked the front door and disconnected the house phones. My phone was in my duffle bag. Somewhere. Claresholm probably.

"Nothing but rest and quiet for you," she ordered.

"I'm not a little kid any more," I replied.

"I have to protect you from your own recklessness. That's what mothers do. You could have been killed by that bull."

"It was worth it."

"That's your irresponsible friends talking."

"It's me."

"No. The Nathan I raised listens to his mother's advice. We'll talk about this when you're feeling better."

Mom let Stevie in for a short visit. She told me Dakota Tallboy had won. Kayden came second, Jimmie fourth and Alex eighth. She hid a small box under my pillow. "For later," she whispered.

Inside was a silver belt buckle decorated with a bull and a gold 82. The note said, 'Pretty Boy No More.' Kayden, Grandpa John, Grandma Lillian, Emily, Stevie, Jimmie, Alex, Aubrey, and Uncle Spencer had signed it.

She had signed it Emily, not Emily Arbutus.

My Palaeolithic dream returned that night. The Great Bulls paw the ground. Kayle and Axel fire their bows. Arrows dangle from the bulls' shoulders. Two yearling bulls charge. Kayle and Axel race away, dodging between the glacier scattered boulders. The narrowing way forces the bulls to run single file, directly into the narrow trap. The bulls roar, unable to turn back. They bang their long horns against the boulders and kick as Jens, Stel and Norn dart into the trap with their spears. The weaker bull stumbles as Norn strikes. Norn fights to pull out his spear. Blood pours from the bull's mouth. The stronger bull twists free and charges over the fallen one. Norn is slammed against a boulder. His leg snaps loudly.

The hunters carry Norn for two days. They cross the river and enter the tent of Engelle, the One Who Knows. The tent is painted with a bull's head. She is more fair skinned than the hunters.

Kayle lays Norn on the robes beside the fire. "His leg is broken," he says to Engelle. "He killed his first bull."

I didn't answer a phone call or a text that week. No email. No computer. No more cowboy birthday cakes. Jewel's Restaurant was closed. I had a concussion. The Little Prince needed to feel better about himself.

Finally, Aubrey brought my phone. "Kayden found it in your duffle bag. He said he'd keep your gear until you're ready to ride again."

"Nathan won't need it again," Mom lectured. "And you've let me down. My own niece. If you'd been honest with me all this could have been avoided."

As soon as Mom left us alone I showed Aubrey the buckle Stevie had brought me.

"Would you give this to Stevie for me?" she asked handing me a sealed envelope with what felt like a card inside.

I agreed.

I watched a lot of television that week. Classes were over at Western. I'd missed the graduation parties. Reese sent me flowers with a card. "I hope you've learned your lesson!"

Everything around me seemed weird and ordinary. I'd changed, but nothing around me had changed. I'd gone to Claresholm, scored an 82 on TwoBlackEyes and now I was back where I had started.

I was so bored I even stayed up to watch the late news after the Stampede updates. A reporter said an 18 year old boy had been run over and killed by a car on 11th Avenue that evening.

"It appears he ran out from between two buildings. The police are investigating, but it is unlikely the driver of the car will be charged. The boy's name will be released after police have notified his next of kin."

Twenty minutes later I heard a car pull up in our driveway. Dad must have been near the window because he opened the door right away.

It was the police. They were looking for Wilfred Mercury's next of kin. Wilfred was the boy killed on 11th Avenue. Willie. He'd given Dad's name to Family Services.

I bobbed on my crutches to the front door.

"Willie's been killed," Dad told me.

We invited the policemen in. "I was Willie's friend. Tell me what happened."

"So far all we know is he ran onto the street from an alley. The driver said he was a blur."

"Was he wearing a blue shirt with white fringes?"

The policeman checked his notebook. "Yes."

"Was he being chased?"

"We don't know. The driver said he saw a heavyset man run off when the ambulance came. It was too dark to get a better description."

"Willie had a foster uncle or something like that who was after him for money," I said. "Dad got him on video the day he threatened us here."

Mom listened and then went to the bedroom and closed the door.

I went back to my room as Dad got out the videotapes. He came in afterwards. He was almost crying. He liked the surprise of Willie, the scrawny math whiz kid on his way to Harbour University.

"I'm sorry," he said to me. "You were lucky to have had a friend like Willie."

"All my friends. They're good friends, Dad."

"I know. And I know why you rode that bull. I understand it. Except it was a bad idea. And you lied to us. I wish you hadn't thought you needed to."

Lie, or ride a bull?

He smiled, momentarily boy mischievous again. "Mister Nathan 82." The way Willie would have said it. Dad loved me and I loved his legendary attitude.

Dad paid for Willie's cremation and offered to pay for the catering. I told him Willie's friends had it covered.

We held Willie's bull slap goodbye in the school parking lot on Friday morning, the day all of Calgary gets a holiday to watch the Stampede Parade. Splendiferous Marie parked her Lovely Golden Fries truck in the lot and we pulled two picnic tables beside it.

Mom had to let me go, so she came along with Dad. To make sure my irresponsible friends didn't lead me astray again.

Uncle Spencer came. So did my cousin Aubrey. Mom and Dad were there. Very quiet. The Montgomerys. Ron Atkins. Emily.

Apparently Willie didn't have any family or friends, except us. Me. Kayden. The Jackson twins. Stevie. Five Great Bull Hunters. The sixth didn't return to camp. Stevie asked us if she could look after his ashes. Kayden said okay and we agreed.

I'd never seen Stevie wearing a jacket and skirt before. She looked different. Missing Willie. Lonely. Not so tough. She had a white towel tied around the strap of her purse. Mom was right, when Stevie wanted to, she could look attractive. Was this for Willie?

"Quit looking at me like that," she said. "If you want a hug, ask your Mom."

Mom tried Marie's complimentary fries and coffee.

"Willie said fat, sugar, and starch were the North American cultural foods," I told her as I handed her an order of my usual: large fries, coffee with cream and two sugars. "It's our way of handling emotional upheaval. We need it today."

Emily, wearing dark blue, was the only one who spoke: "I talked to the principal yesterday. Speed of Light Willie got his Harvard scholarship." Stevie started to cry.

We stayed off the school topic. Kayden and the Jacksons had been invited to compete at the Stampede. Uncle Spencer and TwoBlackEyes would be in the chutes. Stevie didn't have any plans. We didn't talk about what would happen to us next fall.

I bobbed to Mom and Dad's car on my crutches. I saw Stevie talking to Marie by the food truck as I opened the door. Gerry was supposed to be picking her up.

"Wait a minute," I said to Mom. "I've got some calls to make."

That was an invention. I only had one call. To Uncle Spencer. He agreed to meet me at the Glencoe Club.

Mom and Dad dropped me off at the main entrance and I went up the elevator to the lounge where Uncle Spencer was waiting.

I ordered an orange juice then got straight into my questions.

"Is Mom as mad at you as she is at my friends?"

"Probably madder," he answered. Not concerned.

"Sorry."

"Don't be. I knew what I was getting into."

"What about Kayden? Have you heard if he made it into university? We didn't talk about marks at the funeral."

"Emily had a peek at his unofficial results. He's in."

"Thanks to Willie and you," I said.

"There's more to it," he said. "I looked at the will. He doesn't have to go to university. He's only required to attend a post secondary education institute. The way the lawyer had explained the will, it had sounded to them like university.

"Now Kayden has to decide. He can do what he thinks is best for himself. He can go to business school at university, or take the Olds College agricultural program."

I caught myself twisting my orange juice glass nervously. Uncle Spencer was watching my hands. His didn't move. I took a bull rider's deep breath.

"You changed my life Uncle Spencer. You helped me a lot. I want to apologize."

"For what?"

"For naming that rank bull Uncle Spencer. He's going to be in the Stampede line up next week. You might get some calls!"

His smile reminded me of Dad's little mischievous boy look. Brothers.

"I accept the apology. Anything else on your mind?"

"What's the deal with that buckle everybody gave me? And the note: Pretty Boy No More. Was everybody in on getting me to ride TwoBlackEyes?"

"Emily and Kayden saw something in you nobody else had seen. I know I hadn't. They nudged you into your Act II. Bull Riding. Then they asked the rest of us to help you write the script. We had a helluva good time watching you. The bets were 50:50 on whether you'd make the 8 seconds at Claresholm. The odds went up to 100:1 when you drew TwoBlackEyes. I bet against you. Grandma Lillian and Willie cleaned up."

"You bet against me?"

"Sure. You'd never done anything worth talking about before."

"What about Emily?"

"She said she was betting on something else. It sounded mysterious to me."

"Stevie says she's smoky and mysterious."

"Stevie's right," he said. "Emily knows more than she reveals."

I almost said, "And so do you." Uncle Spencer: the smartest persona reader I know.

Instead I changed the subject. "What am I supposed to do now? I can't go back to living the way I used to, being bossed around by everybody."

"That's up to you. Write your own Act III."

I didn't say anything, but I was getting a bit tired of hearing those types of remarks. It felt like a conspiracy. Which it was.

I got a few texts from Aubrey who was sitting behind the Stampede chutes cheering for Kayden and the Jacksons. Nothing from Stevie. I tried watching the late night TV replays, but seeing the bullfighters reminded me of Willie and I couldn't watch after that. Besides, everything was over for me. No Act III in sight. No ending. No pirate ships.

It was obvious that Mom and Dad were giving me a teenage form of time out, being polite and waiting for me to apologize. Willie was dead. I had a concussion, a broken leg and had maybe ruined my modeling career with a gash across the bridge of my nose. Kayden and the Jacksons had a $100,000 prize on their minds. Aubrey had soccer practices.

Gerry came by once, wanting to know if I'd heard from Stevie. We talked on the sidewalk.

"I haven't heard from her since Willie's funeral," I told him.

"Me, too. Nothing since the funeral. I was supposed to pick her up there, but she was gone."

"I expect she's broken up about Willie," I said. "They began hanging out together after school instead of studying. Maybe she's worried about her marks."

"That's the strange part. Mom opened her results. Stevie got a 94 average. She could have gone to Harvard with Willie. Nobody guessed she was that smart. She never studied. I guess I don't know much about her at all."

I told him about Stevie's steer riding, her horse Sunshine, headlocks, Kayden, Grandpa John's tractor. He was impressed.

"Maybe Willie was the only one who could see how smart she was," he said. "I sure didn't."

"Neither did I."

I promised Gerry I would try to find Stevie. Maybe Grandpa John and Grandma Lillian had heard from her. I felt sorry for Gerry, asking strangers to help him find his sister. Not knowing where else to look. Maybe when we're inside a family we can only see what we expect to see. Maybe we stand too close to see the changes going on in the people around us.

The Stampede Finals ran Sunday afternoon, with the bull riding the last event. I was alone in the house. The Commotion had gone to Banff for the weekend. The days when we Stampeded together at the grounds were obviously over. Mom was so embarrassed by all the questions about my bull riding that she wouldn't wear her western clothes. No backslapping corporate barbeques for The Jewel. No tickets to the Grandstand show and beer in the barns for Dad. No mention of the Rockin' R and the Munro Homestead.

Aubrey texted me that evening: "Coming to see you. Somebody else won."

I bobbed onto the sidewalk as Kayden's pickup turned up our street. Aubrey sitting over the shifter. Jimmie in the passenger seat. Alex in the back.

"The Jewel still pissed at you?" Aubrey asked with her straight smile. "Don't worry, moms can't stay pissed forever. Besides, perfect moms forgive their children. That's a Law of Nature. Listen, I'm running home from here in a few minutes. Training. UBC next year. These cowboys want to see you before they head off to Great Falls."

"Too bad about your leg," Kayden said. Jimmie pretended to kick my crutches out from under me. "You sure rode that sonofabitch."

"Thanks. How's your arm?"

He held it up. "Tylenol 3. You should try it."

I nodded. "When my cast comes off."

"I meant for your nose. You've got a lot of stitches there. Lucky the bull didn't kick your dick!"

Aubrey whacked Jimmie's shoulder. "There's a girl here, okay."

She straight smiled at me and asked if I'd heard from Stevie.

"Not lately," I answered. She shrugged, tied her hair into a ponytail and jogged toward Elbow Drive.

"Too bad your cousin doesn't like us bull riders," Alex said. "We sure like her."

Kayden shook my hand. "We've got a long drive tonight. Good to see you."

That was Kayden. Nothing volunteered. No questions about Stevie. Nothing about Willie.

I bobbed beside him to the driver's door. He got in and rolled down his window.

"This is only the beginning," he said. "Wait for the ending."

The way of the quest. Nothing mattered but the end.

The Great Bull Hunters drove into the Land of Ground Thunder Running. Without me. Without Willie. Without Stevie.

"Assholes," I yelled into the twilight as the pickup gained speed.

ACT III

I told Mom to wait in the hall while the doctors peeled the tape from nose. She went ballistic when she the saw the five stitches with loose ends hanging from the knots. Hard not to notice.

"It's a mess," she said. "We're going to need reconstruction. The best surgeons in the country. All my hard work to keep you safe ... and now this. Totally irresponsible behaviour!"

That night, Reese came over for dinner to discuss plans for our future. She and Julia had everything scheduled for me.

"This summer," Reese told me, "you'll be working in an accounting office with a career advisor. It's all set. Julia arranged it for you. You won't get any academic credits, but it will go a long way to making up for that silly Film Studies course you took."

"Sounds exciting," I answered. "I'll be getting crunched by numbers instead of by bulls."

Reese didn't laugh.

I tried going to the Glencoe gym a couple of times but it was complicated getting there without a car, and too far to walk on crutches. I was bored and restless. I couldn't stop thinking about Kayden and the Jacksons rodeoing in Montana. Wondering where Stevie had disappeared to.

I made an appointment to see Dr. Sara. I hoped I'd get her go ahead to start living again.

She sent me for the usual tests and then we met in her office. She checked me over and told me to put my shirt back on.

"You're still a handsome cowboy," she laughed. "Women really go for that scarred, returning hero look. The hospital did a good job on your nose. I'm surprised it wasn't broken. You're lucky it only needed stitching."

"My friends said a handful of Tylenol 3s was all I needed."

She leaned forward on her desk, hands on either side of a writing pad. "I've got bad news for you."

"How bad?"

"You're not getting better. In fact, you're slipping backward. Your lungs are deteriorating and there's nothing I can do about it. You're dying."

I tried to shrug it off. "I've got 8 seconds, don't I?"

"You've earned more than that. But you can't count on anything past the end of the summer."

"What can I do until then?"

"Anything you want," she said with a smile that said more than her words. "You'll feel fine until the end, the day you fall asleep and don't wake up."

She paused, waiting for me to respond. When I didn't, she continued: "You have time to make some decisions."

Treating me like an adult. Straightforward Dr. Sara.

We talked a little more. She was good about offering to send me for experimental treatments, second opinions, and everything else people reached for when they got this type of news.

"I've got to take the bull I draw," I told her. "I'll ride this one the best I can."

"A big Act III ending?"

Who'd she been talking to? Uncle Spencer?

I promised her I would call if I had any questions. We said goodbye in a temporary way.

I phoned Uncle Spencer and said I had something for him. He picked me up outside the clinic and we drove to his house. Aunt Jean was out. We sat on the same chairs where we had first talked about bull riding.

"You've won a lot of trophies," I said. "I want to give you a different one.

"Remember when I said if I make 8 seconds on a bull you'll have helped me prove I'm not a total screw up? I said you could claim that as the redeeming deed of Mean Uncle Spencer."

"I remember."

I handed him my 82 buckle. "Here's your proof."

He held it in his loose wristed hand, gently. "The start of your Act III?" he asked, glancing between the buckle and me.

I nodded, yes, and then said, "I suppose Dr. Sara called you."

"She did."

"Keep it to yourself."

I stood alone on the river bank, imagining the Palaeolithic life on the other side. The gentle current tempted me to cross, cast and all. I was considering the possibility when Stevie texted me to meet her in the morning at the international flight arrivals. One hunter was returning. I didn't feel alone anymore.

The bite in Stevie's straight talk had always pushed me. She was my Chili Palmer daring me to do something I could talk about. I could still hear her laughing at me the first time we met:

"Kayden says you want to write movies. That true?"

"Maybe."

"Maybe? Got something better to do?"

"Sure. I'm going to be an accountant."

"Great. I always wanted to meet one. My life's complete."

Maybe now was the time to finish *Buck Off.*

"Where are you parked?" Stevie asked. All she had was a backpack.

"I took a taxi. I'm not supposed to drive?"

"Jesus, Nathan," she said. "You're not supposed to do this ... You're not supposed to do that. It's been almost a month and you're still dragging that pathetic cast around. We're cutting it off this afternoon. I'll tape your leg and you'll be fine."

"The doctors said it should stay on at least another two weeks."

"And you're listening to them? Adriano Moraes is riding this summer with a torn knee cartilage and ligaments, and torn triceps."

Same dark eyes with the soft slant that didn't go with her tough persona.

She gave the driver her address and leaned back on the seat. "What's everybody doing?"

I told her that Kayden and the Jacksons were in Montana, as far as I knew. "I haven't heard from them since the Stampede. They all made the Finals."

"The Jewel still blaming everybody but you?"

"Mostly Uncle Spencer," I answered. "She's giving him the polite treatment."

"That's sad. What have you been doing?"

"Taking it easy."

"Exciting!"

"What about you?"

"Mostly getting drunk with Willie and the Harvard girls and boys."

"Willie?"

"That's what I said." She opened her backpack and pulled out a can painted Harvard's deep red. "It's an empty Pennzoil can I soldered closed." On the back a cartoon bullfighter waved a white towel. "Willie's been hanging out with me for a while."

"How did you and Willie like Harvard?"

"Everybody wants to be the next Stephen Hawking. Willie and I decided there's a limit to how many action packed discussions you can endure about what might have happened 14 billion years ago. We'd rather eat fries, drink coffee and go to rodeos."

"Gerry said you had a 94 average. You could get into any university you want. Easy. Don't you want to be the best you can be? Live up to your potential?"

"What are you? A guidance counsellor? If I'm smart enough to get into any university I want, then I'm smart enough to know that isn't what I want to do. That's living up to my fucking potential."

She invited me into her house. "Mom's in rehab. Dad's got an apartment downtown. Just me and Gerry living here, and he's at a football camp all summer. I know where Mom's car keys are. We can have some real fun. Come on, let's cut that cast off so you can drive."

"There's something you should know." I told her about my visit to Dr. Sara.

"That's it? You're dying. I suppose you'll be staying home for the rest of your life."

"No. I'm not giving up and I'm not staying home. I've drawn the rankest bull at the rodeo. I plan on spurring the guts out of him. I've got nothing to lose."

Stevie's slanted eyes laughed momentarily. "Nothing to lose? There must have been some no quit testosterone in that glob of snot TwoBlackEyes pasted on you."

She punched me hard on the shoulder. "Quick. Name your chivalrous love."

My answer was always there. "Emily Arbutus."

"Correct. Lucky you didn't say me, by the way. I'd have twisted your head off. I'm calling her right now to see if she wants to come over." She held up her phone before she dialled: "Is Jack Sparrow ready?"

"That's *Captain* Jack Sparrow," I answered, biting down on my mouth guard and nodding. She dialled. The gate opened.

"Willie and I are back in Calgary," she said to Emily. "I'll tell you about Harvard later. I've got the house to myself until Mom gets dried out. Want to come over for a couple of days, have some fun? Nathan's here. He says he's dying. Ha ha. Not to see you! Literally."

She hung up. "She's coming over. We'd better cut that plaster off."

The night with Emily would have been less Palaeolithic with my leg in a cast.

Norn and Engelle are sitting on hides outside Engelle's hut as the sun rises.

"I dreamed about a Shining Yellow Bull," Norn says. "It looked on fire. The biggest bull I've ever seen."

"I know about this bull."

"Can it be killed?"

"It runs in your dreams."

Kayle, Axel and Stel rush up, excited.

"We camped with the Horse Hunters last night," Kayle says. "A great bull ran through their tents when the moon was empty. A huge bull. A family trampled in their hut. Now they're all afraid."

Stel, almost breathlessly, pleads: "You must come, Norn. You, too, Engelle. The Horse Hunters will give us dried meat if we kill the bull. We can do it."

The dream was as real as anything I'd ever seen.

Stevie tracked Kayden and the Jackson twins to a Saskatchewan rodeo. Emily, Stevie and I met them there on Friday and had a good time until Monday.

"You're in my dreams," I told Emily after we drove home.

"Not one of THOSE dreams," she said with a blue eyed try something else smile.

"Reality replaced THOSE dreams," I replied. "These are what I call my Palaeolithic dreams. They're about Stevie, Alex, Jimmie, Kayden, you, me. And Willie. We're The Great Bull Hunters who lived 10,000 years ago."

I gave it all to her, beginning with the bulls and red hand stencils in the Lascaux caves. "The Yellow Bull is as far as I've gotten in the story," I said.

Emily kissed me. "I am blinded by your imagination ... an entire story being told around red handprints. We were here. I am overcome by your generosity. Nobody but Nathan Munro would make his friends the heroes of his own story. You are more than I suspected."

"Do you think we can kill this bull?"

"I don't know. I'm like Kayden. I'm happy to wait for the ending."

I laughed. "Kayden is my beginning. Until I met Kayden, I was just going along."

"Well, you're not going along any more," she said kissing me again. "You're talking like a scriptwriter."

She turned to Stevie. "Are you still using the school's video camera?"

"It's in the house."

"Get it. I'll call Uncle Spencer. We need the buckle. He'll love this."

When I saw what Stevie did with the video we made, I cried a little. Not totally a Great Bull Hunter, I suppose.

We spent the next weeks going to rodeos on the weekends then back to the Rockin' R or Calgary during the week. Kayden and the Jacksons usually placed in the top ten and were making enough money to pay their way. I wondered if one of them would ever win. Kayden didn't seem to care, and the Jacksons never thought of giving up.

When I told Kayden and the Jacksons about the short ride I was on, Kayden shrugged. "There goes your accounting career." That was an Act III finale I hadn't considered.

The Jacksons were more pragmatic. "So what are we supposed to do about it?" Jimmie asked. "Keep you awake?"

"Nothing anybody can do," I said. "I'm just hoping at least one of you makes enough money this summer to throw a No Buck Burger party for me."

That was as theatrical as it got.

They all knew I was working on *Buck Off.* Hanging out with them at the rodeos was the best way to keep the atmosphere of bull riding alive in my script. I only talked about the script with Emily. For no specific reason, I continued to email her my new scenes. Maybe I liked keeping the screenwriting relationship the way we had started it.

Dear Emily

In the previous scenes (still not written) Chet has flunked out of university (self sabotage). Even his strongest supporters at the ranch – his grandfather (George) and his uncle (Bruce) – are ready to give up on him. Time for him to get his act together. Fortunately, he gets a second chance at the ranch where, out of Marlena's control, he's starting to Cowboy Up as they say in the rodeo world. In this scene he's ready to test himself at the Greatest Outdoor Show On Earth.

BUCK OFF

ACT II: SCENE 3
KEITH WINS AGAIN

THE CALGARY STAMPEDE

INT. THE RANCH MOTOR HOME - MORNING

Chet and Bruce are in the Montgomery motor home, one of many behind the rodeo barns.

BRUCE

Here's your breakfast, eat up and then head down to the barn to do some stretches. After we draw our bull, we'll talk about strategy. There are lots of great boys here. The competition is tough.

CHET

Is Uncle Johnny here?

BRUCE

Yup. And still hanging out with Keith Samson.

Chet walks out of the motorhome and runs right into Keith.

KEITH

Well if it isn't Suzy the Smoothie again. Think you're a cowboy because you won some dough do ya? Well to most of us you're still the Ice Cream Queen. They'll give anyone a card these days.

CHET

Nice to see you too Keith.

KEITH

I just want you to know boy, the rules are the same. I run the show.

CHET

If that makes ya feel big Keith. Makes ya feel important. I know you're nothing but a shady crook and an over the hill cowboy.

KEITH

Watch your mouth Chet I'm still ranked Number One.

CHET

This is what you don't get; I don't give a shit who you think you are. I'm not afraid of you.

Keith moves closer, Johnny Anderson comes around the corner.

JOHNNY

Hey Keith, let me talk to the boy. We all get it, he will too. If he wants to compete, he'll learn the cowboy etiquette.

Keith spits at Chet's feet and walks away.

JOHNNY

What on God's green earth do you think you're doing? You're not here a day and you're raising hell. If you want to show you're a man then keep your goddamn mouth shut and show it in the arena. I thought you were smarter than that. You need to get rid of that chip on your shoulder.

CHET

He's a bully and I'm not afraid of any man that picks on women.

JOHNNY

Well then you're stupid.

Chet walks away.

THE CAMERA FOCUSES ON MARLENA MOMENTS LATER AS SHE PARKS BY THE BARNS. THE FIRST PERSON SHE SEES IS KEITH.

KEITH

(as they pass)

You best put a leash on that kid of yours or he could get himself hurt.

INT. THE MONTGOMERY BARN - MORNING

Marlena enters the barn. Johnny, Bruce and George are there with Chet.

MARLENA

(angrily to Chet)

I just saw Keith Samson. Did you speak to him?

CHET

Ya, he tried to intimidate me, so I told him I'm not afraid of him.

JOHNNY

He don't know when to keep his pretty little mouth shut.

MARLENA

Chet you made a deal with me.

CHET

And I'll keep it but he ...

MARLENA

No buts, Chet.

EXT. THE RODEO ARENA - AFTERNOON

THE ANNOUNCER (V.O.)

It's time for the Bull Riding Finals. And here's no surprise -

The Rookie of the Year, ladies and gentlemen, is Chet Montgomery, Junior ... the son of the famous Chet Sr. from Longview Alberta and the Rough Stock Ranch. He's been having a very good week here at the Stampede winning over $9,000 so far. This could be his moment of glory. His dad would sure be proud to see him win the $100,000 today.

He sure has a good chance to do that with the bull he's drawn: Crazy Man. He's only been ridden three times.

Bruce settles Chet onto the bull and wraps the rope tight around his hand.

BRUCE

You got this one Chet ... for your Dad.

Chet is hard-focused.

He tips his finger on his hat and nods yes. The gate swings open. Twist and turn and buck. Bruce watches closely. Crazy Man is not having his best performance. This could be a huge problem. The horn sounds and Chet swings off and lands lightly on his feet.

ANNOUNCER

Wait for it ladies and gentlemen ... a very nice ride on a mean bull and here comes Chet Montgomery's score -

```
        88 and the rookie is in the lead!

Chet jumps up on the rails beside Bruce.

                BRUCE

        Your bull didn't buck good enough
        for you to win - unless Keith bucks
        off. He's got a rank one.

Never Quit is on fire. Keith rides solidly,
spurring and in control. The fans are screaming.
Never Quit is putting on a show for them.

Chet shakes his head. Before the score is
flashed on the screen, he knows Keith's won the
championship - again.

Keith grins as he watches Chet and Bruce leave
the chutes.
```

I ran out of birthday money and began emptying the education account my grandmother had left me. What the hell?

When I stayed at Emily's house in Sunnyside we liked to watch DVDs from her collection. Directors, writers and actors had signed a lot of the cases.

Other times we read the assignments from the film course she taught two nights a week. After I read them, she let me give them a mark that we compared to hers. My marks were always lower. "I'm turning into Uncle Spencer," I said. "He's a hard marker."

"I like him," she replied. "He's a good friend to you." She flipped through the pile of scripts. "Some of these students are trying to get into the Vancouver Film School this fall. They want me to give them recommendations."

"Will you?"

"The school owes me a favour. I can recommend one applicant's script. They'll accept him or her. No questions asked."

Would it have been me and *Buck Off?* I didn't ask.

The only time I went home, Mom was at a seminar. Dad was really decent about not prying into how I was spending my summer. "We understand you're just having a good time with your friends until university starts and you have to get serious."

"Tell Mom I'm eating my vegetables."

He laughed.

I almost told him about Dr. Sara. But all I could think about was how he and Mom wouldn't sleep at night. Better for them to be worried about how good a time I was having. He left a cheque on my dresser. "For university tuition and expenses." It was his way of saying he loved me enough not to ask a bunch of questions.

The first weekend of August a half drunk bull rider in the Swift Current bar made a smart mouth comment about Emily and I punched him. It wasn't much of a punch. I had to do it off one leg. Right away his friends and my friends were involved. Physically. I'd never punched anybody before. It felt good.

Emily thought I was very knight errant and told me she was worried the rest of the rodeo girls would be after me. No chance, I told her.

The next day I bought her a silver bull rider pendant inside a heart, made by one of the girls following the rodeos ... mostly following the twins.

When we met those mouthy Swift Current riders the next week in Pincher Creek, Stevie wasted no time in challenging them to arm wrestling, if they agreed not to use their riding hands. She was left handed and most of them rode right handed. When they gave up trying to beat her, Stevie bet them a beer that they couldn't break out of her headlock in less than 30 seconds. Free beer all night. I really liked hanging out with the bull riders. To them, the future emptied into the next rodeo grounds. Same as mine.

Emily and I had no plans. It was as if she were dreaming me toward a later in the summer bull riding where I would enter the Palaeolithic event. We never talked about love because there wasn't any point. We didn't avoid the topic. It just never came up.

I liked seeing all those cowboys checking out Emily, always the best looking cowgirl at the rodeos, and knowing I would be arms around her drifting into the whispering night. Across the river and into the trees. Great Bull Hunters roaming the shadows.

Stevie noticed me deleting texts from my phone every morning. "That reminds me of when Willie and I went to Harvard," she said. "Not a discussion time. We needed to think on our own."

She took my phone, sent a text and showed it to me. "It's to The Commotion: 'The Little Prince has his inhaler. Relax.'"

We put a lot of miles on the vehicles, talking and not talking. Stevie mostly rode in Kayden's truck and the Jacksons rode with Emily and me. Kayden said he was going into the agricultural program at Olds College. Stevie said she was going with him, but into the heavy equipment program. "Got to learn to fix the ranch machinery," she explained. That was their way of telling us they were planning to stay together. A twist in their script that didn't surprise anybody, but disappointed the Jackson twins who planned to rodeo with them right up to Christmas.

"We got the rest of our lives for welding," Alex said. "Don't got a lot of bull riding years left."

By August I was starting to get nervous about finishing *Buck Off* and pushed ahead as hard as I could between rodeos.

Dear Emily

While you were in Vancouver this week, I worked on this scene almost non stop at Stevie's house. I want it to establish the two fears Chet is facing –Marlena and Keith.

I wish I were in your arms.

Nathan

BUCK OFF

ACT II: SCENE 4
THE TRUTH

INT. THE ROUGH STOCK RANCH KITCHEN - MORNING

MARLENA

I'm worried about the Canadian Finals Chet.

CHET

Don't be.

MARLENA

Keith Samson will be there. He doesn't like the fact that you're better than he is. He knows he only won at Calgary because you got a low scoring bull. He is so, so dangerous.

Chet sits opposite her, his eyes steady, unflinching.

CHET

We need to talk about Keith Samson. I want to know why you're afraid of him.

MARLENA

You've heard what he does to his wife and son, haven't you? Isn't that enough?

CHET

Everybody knows that Mom. But there's something else that you're scared of.

MARLENA

It's just a feeling I get Chet.

CHET

Mom, do you think Keith had something to do with Dad's death?

Marlena is stunned into silence.

CHET

I knew it ... I knew something was just too creepy. I heard him on the phone, talking about illegally bringing livestock across the border, and drugs. I know he was into breaking the law and doing whatever it took.

Marlena is shaking.

CHET

Mom we need to make this right. You need to tell me what you know ... the truth now.

Marlena and Chet sit down on the couch. Marlena takes a long time to gather her thoughts.

MARLENA

Around the time you were born, there was a lot of talk about steroids, and not only with the cowboys. There were rumours about contractors giving them to the bulls. Bulls that were pumped up and could really buck were worth a lot of money. Your dad believed Keith Samson was the main dealer.

He went to the Samson's barn and confronted Keith. He found evidence. He told Keith that he would give him the opportunity to turn himself in. The next day when I saw your Dad on Outlaw I knew something was wrong. He always gave a little tip to the front of his hat before he climbed onto the chute. We called it our secret Chute Salute. That day he didn't do it. He also didn't look right as he was getting on the bull. I've seen him ride a thousand times and there was something different. After I came back from the hospital to get my things from our trailer I ran into Keith. His eyes threatened me and put a fear in me that has lasted all these years.

I went to Uncle Johnny. He knows something but he's too afraid to say. He wasn't always a drunk and cowardly. Your father respected him.

I have lived in fear ever since

then. I probably handled everything so wrong. Nobody at the ranch knew anything. They just blamed themselves. Everyone is just trying to keep it together. Chet you're all that matters to me.

Now leave it be. There is no proof - it's all just a story from a grieving widow.

Chet holds his mom like he never held her before. He looks her in her eyes.

CHET

Thank you Momma, your strength will always be part of who I am.

Chet walks out the door. He drives to the Calgary airport and gets on a plane to Dallas. There he rents a car and is at Johnny Anderson's front door before nine the next day.

Christina (Marlena's sister and Johnny's wife) answers the door.

CHRISTINA

Oh my god, Chet, what on God's green earth are you doing at my door? Come on in. Is it Marlena, is she ok? Is it something to do with Marlena?

CHET

No, she's fine. I'm here to see Uncle Johnny.

CHRISTINA

He's out at the barn. I'll call his cell.

CHET

That's OK. I'll surprise him.

Chet walks out to the barn. Johnny knows why he is here.

JOHNNY

I think I'm going to be sick.

CHET

Tell me everything you know. Everything. Mom told me what she knows.

JOHNNY

Keith killed your father after your father caught him using steroids on the bulls. Your Dad gave him one chance to come clean and Keith used it to dope the bull your Dad was to ride. I was the one who told Keith your father had found the steroids. I was the one who slipped the tranqs into your father's coffee that morning.

Your dad might as well have been dead the moment they opened the gate.

I was the rodeo clown that day. I couldn't stop it ... and I knew about it.

Dear Nathan

You're starting to reveal Keith's and Johnny's misdeeds but barely touching on Marlena's. Chet's almost 20 years old at this point and his mother has been lying to him the whole time about what she suspects – the drug and Keith and Johnny's involvement. Her fears made him a figure of ridicule as a boy (Suzie the Smoothie, The Ice Cream Queen) on the rodeo circuit; and she almost destroyed his self confidence by sending him to university, telling him he had no future in rodeo. Chet doesn't need protecting from Keith; he needs protecting from Marlena's fears.

In this scene, when he needs all the self confidence in the world to test himself against Keith in the Canadian Finals, Marlena throws an emotional bomb in his face: Keith killed his father. And Chet's response is, once again, meek and mild: 'Thank you Momma, your strength will always be part of who I am.'

I understand this script sometimes reflects your natural avoidance of confrontation, but your character Chet has to stand up for himself. And now is as good a time as any for him to challenge Marlena and Keith.

Emily.

PS. In your arms, too.

Ron Atkins liked to hand me the microphone when we met at the bigger rodeos. I had begun to develop a following, mostly because I was getting to know the riders and bulls and could make the crowd laugh with some too personal insights.

At Lethbridge, Kayden drew TwoBlackEyes and Ron pulled me into the announcer's booth to give the crowd the inside story.

"Here we are folks, " he opened, "with Nathan Munro, the last rider to make 8 seconds on this bull.

"What do you think, Nathan? What are Kayden's chances today?"

"He can ride TwoBlackEyes if he wants, but that's not Kayden's way. He's not one to be satisfied just making 8 seconds. He's on a quest for the perfect ride, one he has defined for himself. He keeps his own score.

"The best way to describe Kayden is to say he makes music. He wants every ride to be as beautiful as Mozart's *A Little Night Music*. Full of risk and rhythm. You watch that free hand of his, it's like he's conducting an orchestra ... A Little Bull Riding Serenade.

"But today he's up against a bull that's got no musical ability. TwoBlackEyes jolts you hard and there's no soft landing – ask me, he broke my leg and my nose after the buzzer went!

"I'd say today we're in for more of a brawl than a concert. That's all you can expect when a conductor faces a jackhammer."

Four seconds after the chute opened, TwoBlackEyes delivered an offbeat crescendo and Kayden Montgomery lost his rhythm: Bucked Off.

After the rodeo, Ron found us packing up to drive back to Calgary. "Want a job?" he asked me. "You've got a natural ability with a microphone.

I had a lot of compliments on your performance today. Loved that Mozart concept. Very classy. You could come with me on the road for the rest of the summer. Maybe take over in a year or two."

I was flattered but turned him down. "But anytime we meet up at a rodeo, I'll sit in with you – no charge."

On the drive home, Emily teased me, asking why I hadn't taken Ron up on his offer. "You could have made some money."

I reached over and rested my hand on her thigh. "Two reasons. First, I'd rather be with you. Second, just because I'm good enough to do it, doesn't mean I should." Thanks for that line, Stevie.

"We'll be home in a couple of hours," she said softly, glancing at my hand on her thigh. "Anything new with the Bull Hunters?"

"Nothing. They're still looking for the yellow one."

Reese sent me three long texts breaking up with me that concluded with her telling me I was a disappointment and would always be a loser without her. She had a new project: Jed from private school. They would be going to U of C together. I wondered if she could keep him sober long enough to make something of him.

Gerry and I talked a little. He was keeping a brotherly eye on Stevie ... and a wistful eye on Emily. He admitted that he had been in love with her at Western, like every other boy. "Stevie says she's smoky and mysterious."

"She is," I replied. "It's like she's perfect and makes you feel that way too. That you can do anything."

"Kinda like how Kayden believes one day he's going to score the perfect bull ride."

"Emily makes you think it's possible."

"You're lucky," he said. "Most adults make you feel like crap unless you're going along with their ideas."

Stevie kept Willie's ashes on her dining room table, the Pennzoil can now decorated to look like Marie's food truck.

"It's like having Speed of Light around," she said. "He was good for us. As weird as he was with all that dancing and crazy talk, he always knew what he was doing.

"He'd decided he had to raise himself without parents and he was doing it. That's why he didn't care what anybody else thought. That was his cheerfulness. That's more than scholarship smart."

I walked to the river and sat on the bank as slow twilight turned the poplars into long shadows. The traffic on Elbow Drive faded away. I could hear the bulls running.

A few days later I understood Willie's cheerfulness better. We were having Saturday morning breakfast in Maple Creek when Stevie said, "Willie left something for you." She set the food truck can in the middle of the table. Emily handed me an envelope. I read the letter aloud.

Dear Movie Club Nathan

If you're reading this, Uncle Creeley has found me and I'm a goner. There is $25,000 in my safe deposit box I want you to have. I stole the roll of cash from Uncle Creeley after he stole it from my unexpectedly disappearing parents. This money has been looking for a purpose, and you're it. Your secret girlfriend Emily has the key to the box.

It's obvious to everybody that you're not a very good bull rider and you'll make an even worse accountant. I want you to use the money to develop the Buck Off story about Chetter and his Big Chill mother (Very Freudian. Ha ha.) and study script writing in a real school. Now you have had your brain rattled by TwoBlackEyes, I bet you'll find some good ideas you didn't know you had.

Emily told me she could get you into a good film school so take up her offer. This money will pay for your first year tuition and a few meals. After that, you'll be on your own. Get a job like everybody else.

Eat fries. Drink coffee.

Your now deceased friend,

Speed of Light.

Nobody asked what I was going to do with the money. I think that was the first time I wished I didn't have a falling asleep waiting down the road for me. Willie could have spent that money on himself. Instead, he wanted it to have a purpose, and that purpose was me.

I didn't know where to leave the sadness I felt after that, and that's why it broke loose as anger that afternoon in the rodeo grounds parking lot. Stevie and I were sitting on the tailgate of Kayden's truck waiting for the bull riding to start when a clean cut cowboy approached us. He didn't look like he could ride anything. I guessed he was part of the local rodeo committee.

He handed me his business card. "I'm a private investigator," he said. "I've been hired to ask both of you a couple of questions about your year at Western."

"We both passed," Stevie said. "End of interview."

"I wish that was it," he said. He had a slick, confidential tone. As if he had our best interests in mind. "I've got to ask you about Miss Arbutus, your Film Studies teacher. There have been complaints."

"Good teacher," Stevie said. "End of interview."

He shook his head and looked at me. "What's your personal relationship with her?"

"Shut your mouth," I said. "I'm not in school anymore. I graduated."

"But what about while you were in school?"

"She was my teacher. That's all." I stood up and faced him. "One more question like that and you'll be asking questions through a couple of broken teeth."

Stevie pulled me back. "Easy John Wayne. Smacking the bad guy won't make this go away."

The investigator continued, trusting that Stevie could control me. "That's not the only complaint. I was told she showed a pornographic film."

"Who made these complaints?" Stevie asked. "A student?"

"Parents."

"Give us a name."

"I can't tell you. It's confidential."

"And so are our answers," Stevie replied. The investigator heard the steel in her voice and left.

Emily wasn't concerned when we told her about the interview. "Don't worry about it. The principal has already told me he's not renewing my contract. I'd say some parents are trying to make a fuss – maybe see if the School Board has any liability. Creating an issue about showing a few minutes of *Deep Throat* in a provisional film class isn't going to make anybody look good. And accusing me of having sex with Nathan before the end of the term is going to get everybody a lawsuit."

"What are you going to do?" I asked.

"I've already got a contract as a script consultant in Cannes." She gave my shoulders a hug. "I'm in no hurry to start."

She changed the topic, asking me if I had a scene that would bring *Buck Off* to an end. "It's about time, don't you think?"

I told her I had decided on an ending, but I didn't think I had enough summer left to go back to the beginning and complete the scenes that would tie everything together.

"Leave that to me," she said. "You write the ending and I'll know what to do with the rest of it."

"Would you take it to Cannes?"

"If you ask me."

"I'm asking."

I emailed her the final scene three days later.

Dear Emily

Without you, I would never have written this.

Forever,
Nathan

BUCK OFF

ACT III SCENE 1
THE SHOWDOWN

EXT. EDMONTON'S SKYREACH CENTRE - NIGHT

Neon bulls, broncs and cowboys light up the electronic screens at Edmonton's Skyreach Centre. Cowgirls sway their hips across billboards. The Canadian Finals have transformed the hockey arena into a rodeo spectacular.

The camera swings down from the sky, swooping like a predatory bird through the arriving crowd, searching for its target. It zooms in on Chet Montgomery and Max Samson (Keith's son and defender of his battered mother) as they turn from the parking lot toward the dimly lit competitors' entrance.

(Reminder to self – write a scene later to explain how Chet Jr. and Max have become friends united against their common enemy – Keith.)

THE CAMERA FOLLOWS THEM INSIDE.

Chet and Max search the alleyways and pens filled with bulls, horses, and cowboys waiting to compete. A few cowboys nod greetings to them.

A BULL RIDER

Hey Chet. Checking out tonight's go-round? Heard you already made tomorrow's Final. Who'd you draw?

CHET

Biker.

A BULL RIDER

There's been a couple of 90 rides on him this year. Mostly high 80s. You'll need at least a 90 to win. Too bad Keith didn't draw him. I heard he got a real rank one.

CHET

Got to ride the bull you draw.

MAX

You seen my dad around? He's riding in this round.

A BULL RIDER

He's probably doing his secret psych-up somewhere where we can't watch. That sonofabitch must have some kind of magic spell. He's in his 40s and still winning. Think Chet can knock him off?

CHET

I'm gonna try. Thanks. Come on Max. We'll look through the storage rooms along the back wall.

They wind their way through the pens and into the shadows. Chet reaches over and grabs Max's arm.

CHET

Quiet! I can see him.

They creep closer and see Keith injecting himself. Max stumbles against an open chute gate. Keith looks up when he hears the clang. He caps the needle and stuffs it in his boot top.

KEITH

Who the hell's out there? Get over here or I'll knock your teeth out when I catch you.

Chet latches the chute gate closed, creating a barrier in front of Keith.

CHET

Still pumping the chemicals, Mr. Needles? What are you using these days?

KEITH

Nothing anybody can test for.

CHET

That's what Marion Jones thought before they took away her five Olympic medals.

KEITH

If you two dick-sniffers say anything your mommies will wish you'd kept your mouths shut.

MAX

Smack Mom around one more time and I'll call the cops.

KEITH

I've heard that threat before. It

don't scare me.

CHET

Your day is over Keith. Whatever's in that needle won't make a difference tomorrow night. See you behind me at the payout window.

KEITH

No chance. When it comes to the big money ride, you'll choke just like your old man. I'll be watching the ambulance haul another Montgomery away.

CHET

(shrugging)

Come on, Max. (Over his shoulder.) See you tomorrow Mr. Needles.

INT. THE RODEO ARENA - NIGHT

Chet, Marlena, Johnny, and Bruce are in the stands waiting for the calf roping to end and the bull riding finals to start.

MARLENA

Please, Chet. Just go for the ride. Nothing fancy. Just make your 8 seconds and get out of there safely.

BRUCE

Your Mom's right. We don't know if Keith has got to Biker. He could be pumped up crazy.

CHET

I'm riding for the win. That's why I'm here.

THE CAMERA PANS TO THE CHUTES AND SHOWS ABBREVIATED VERSIONS OF THE FIRST EIGHT RIDES. THE SCOREBOARD DISPLAYS THE TOP RIDE SO FAR: 89. THE CAMERA FOCUSES TIGHTLY ON CHET AS HE STRADDLES BIKER IN THE CHUTE.

Max pulls Chet's rope. Chet looks over at Marlena and taps two fingers on his helmet. She smiles, recognizing his father's Chute Salute.

CHET

(In a low voice to Max)

He feels ok.

Chet nods and the gate swings open.

THE CAMERA IS TIGHT ON CHET AND BIKER.

The noise of the crowd is blocked out. All we hear is Chet's breathing and Biker's grunts. He's spinning away from Chet's right hand. Chet's free hand is high over his shoulder, swinging rhythmically like a flag in a gentle breeze. His back is straight. His outside leg keeps driving his spur into Biker.

The horn sounds and Chet flips the tail end of his bull rope free and steps off Biker. The bull stops bucking and paws the dirt until he is chased from the arena.

The score flashes: 90

THE CAMERA SWINGS BACK TO THE STANDS.

Bruce is shaking his head in disappointment.

BRUCE

Too easy. That spin didn't score high enough for a championship ride. Keith is going to win again.

ANNOUNCER (V.O.)

Our final rider is Keith Samson on Jackhammer. He's only been ridden once this year. By a rookie rider who paid for it with a broken leg and nose. This bull loves revenge.

We might be witnessing the ride of the year tonight! We've seen this bull bucking harder every time out, and Keith ... well, he always pulls off a high score when he needs one.

THE CAMERA RETURNS TO KEITH.

Keith tugs his cowboy hat down and nods. The gate swings opens. Again, the crowd noise is silenced. We hear Keith's raspy breath coming in staccato as Jackhammer pounds him with jolt after jolt. Keith is staying on top, spurring him. The clock ticks over. Five seconds. Jackhammer makes his move. He appears to start spinning to the outside as Keith drives him hard with his outside spur.

THE CAMERA FOCUSES ON KEITH'S MISTAKE.

Keith's inside spur is losing its grip on the bull's hide. He's not prepared as Jackhammer pulls out of the spin with a back-jamming high kick. Keith is caught off balance but hangs on until the horn sounds. He gets flipped backward into the air where the bull's high kick drives a hoof directly into his face. He lands, crumpled, as Jackhammer turns and smashes him against the rails. The bullfighters rush in. Then the emergency crew. They don't waste any time lifting Keith's limp body onto a stretcher and into the ambulance.

ANNOUNCER (V.O.)

(trying to distract the crowd)

Look at that scoreboard folks! A 92! We'll let that scoreboard speak for itself while we give Keith Samson a championship round of applause.

The camera follows the ambulance to the hospital.

Minutes later at the Presentation of the Championship Buckle, Max and Chet are on the stage.

ANNOUNCER

Still no word on Keith Samson so we've asked his son Max to accept the Championship Buckle on Keith's behalf. First, let's get a few words from the second place rider, Chet Montgomery.

CHET

This has got to be a proud moment for Keith's family. I know Mrs. Samson is watching in her hotel room. (He hands the microphone to Max.)

MAX

Love you Mom. Don't worry. Dad will be ok.

ANNOUNCER

That's rodeo family at its best, folks. (He hands Max the buckle and a mock-up of a $50,000 cheque.) Be proud, son.

The camera moves behind the chutes as the crowd clears. Chet, Marlena, Johnny, and Bruce are talking.

JOHNNY

(elated)

Jackhammer had Keith lined up. He was dead before he hit the ground.

BRUCE

(disgusted)

The championship should be yours, Chet. All you have to do is ask for a drug test. You know what's left of Keith will test positive. Then you'll be one buckle and $50,000 ahead.

CHET

Max needs the money more than I do. If I don't say anything, his father will die a champion. His mom's going to need help and she deserves it. She took a lot of Keith's abuse to protect Max.

MARLENA

Your father would be proud of you. (She starts to cry.) I should have told you everything. A long time ago. I wish you'd forgive me.

CHET

I'll never forget some of the humiliation that Keith put me through. That you made me accept. It's a lot to forgive.

Marlene stops crying and is looking at Chet, shocked.

CHET

Every time it happened, I just wanted to prove myself more.

I wouldn't have made it here if you hadn't loved me the best way you could. So I can't forgive you. I can only thank you.

Chet stretches his arm protectively over his mother's shoulder. She looks old, tired and frail beside his strength and youth.

CHET (CONT'D)

I hope one day I'll show enough of Dad's championship style to win a girl like you - one who cares about her family the way you always have.

(Hesitation)

Well, (long pause) maybe not exactly like you.

MARLENA

I'll make a few calls.

THE END

Emily only mentioned the *Buck Off* ending once. "You needed to write that," she said. "You wrote a touching reconciliation for Chet and Marlena. Your mother will love it."

Afterwards all she was interested in was my Palaeo dreams: "They're about the boy who wandered into Film Studies from another time and is going back a man."

"Thanks to you and my friends," I replied.

I had a new dream to tell her the next morning. "The hunters have found the Yellow Bull's tracks. He's joined up with a small herd that's grazing south. The hunters aren't worried about losing him now. He's easy to spot. They're going to follow the herd until they find a natural trap."

"What kind of a trap?" she asked.

"A narrow chute in the rocks where it will be hard for him to turn around. His horns won't be so useful then."

"And Engelle? What's she doing?"

"She's with them. She's the only one who knows the Shining Yellow Bull is death. Not that it would discourage them. They're determined. I'm worried about her."

"How come?"

"I think she may leave the hunters after this. She senses they don't need her any more."

"What about Norn? What's he say?"

"He's quiet. He's got a plan he's not ready to tell Engelle."

EMILY ARBUTUS

Nathan told me his final Palaeo dream as we drove back to Calgary from Maple Creek. He'd been avoiding talking about the story for a few days.

We had just crossed the deep and dark South Saskatchewan River outside Medicine Hat when he asked if I would pull over. "I'm ready to tell you the rest of the story," he said. "Let's take a break so you can concentrate."

I turned onto a gravel road and followed it to the top of a knoll. I sat on the grass with his head in my lap. He closed his eyes and told me what he was seeing.

"The hunters are running the Shining Yellow Bull along a dry creek. There's a cut in the rock ledge ahead that looks like an opening into another meadow. But it's a dead end. Kayle has positioned the hunters on either side of the creek. They're hazing the bull toward the trap.

"Kayle begins yelling. It's the signal to spook the bull into the opening. The bull panics. The thunder rumbles as he stampedes into the trap.

"But there's been a mistake. The bull can turn around. He's backed under the ledge and the hunters can't get near him.

"'We need to force him out to where we can use our spears,' Kayle says.

"'He's my bull,' Norn says. 'I'll be the one who goes in. I have to do this.'

"Norn steps toward the trap."

Nathan stopped and took a shallow, quiet breath.

"Take your time," I said to him. He opened his eyes for a moment then, closing them, continued.

"Norn sets down his spear and pulls a pouch of red powder from inside his shirt. He places his right hand on the rock and blows powder over it. When he pulls his hand away, the outline remains. He picks up his spear and walks into the trap."

Nathan stopped and took another shallow breath. "I want Engelle to find more of our lost Great Bull Hunters. I want her to take them across the river ... to where they belong. To where they don't have to just go along."

"I will."

A week later the funeral crowd flowed into the Glencoe Club. I joined the Rockin' R bunch of outsiders at a griefless table. We didn't know private school, Elbow Park Nathan. We knew the Nathan who, like Willie, Stevie, Alex, Jimmie, and Kayden ate No Buck Burgers and swung their spurs out. Exposed themselves to danger. We would miss him. We didn't cry over Willie's goodbye and we wouldn't cry over Nathan's.

Uncle Spencer came over and gave me a hug. "Thanks for being here. Nathan would have been disappointed if all of you hadn't come. Maybe Julia and Rick will say hello later. They're overwhelmed."

He gave Stevie an affectionate shoulder rub. "I see you've brought Speed of Light. The black can is an appropriate touch. Nathan has a bronze urn."

I expect some people wouldn't have thought the black can was appropriate. They would have been surprised to know how little Stevie cared about what they thought.

The only time I'd met Nathan's parents was during the Finals in Edmonton. I knew them better as Marlena and Chet Sr. in the early scenes of *Buck Off.* Difficult to see them written differently at the Glencoe Club.

Aubrey was our only other visitor. "I think everybody but Uncle Spencer is afraid of the cowboy table." Her eyes met mine momentarily. "I cry all the time when I think about the summer you and Nathan had. What all of you did for him. Giving him what we all want, a life of our own."

"He did it himself," Stevie said. "We just showed him where the door was. He walked through. No headlocks."

Aubrey turned away and then glanced back at Willie. "Looking good young man!" She blew the can a kiss. She leaned over and whispered in Stevie's ear. Stevie laughed, stood up, put her arms around Aubrey and kissed her on the mouth. Warmly.

"Thanks for the card," Stevie said to Aubrey's straight smile. "And does that answer your question?"

The eulogies were tearful. Uncle Spencer spoke last. Nobody was prepared for what he had to say.

"Some of Nathan's friends might remember Willie from Western Canada. He was one of the four students in Movie Club. He was the foster kid who ate cafeteria leftovers, cut his own hair and got himself a scholarship to Harvard. Willie died in June, killed in a traffic accident.

"Willie left Nathan a gift. He knew Nathan wanted to be a screenwriter, so he left him $25,000 to cover his first year tuition and expenses at a film school.

"Nathan, of course, couldn't use the money, so he asked Emily Arbutus if she could arrange for it to become a scholarship fund. Today I am revealing that Emily has chosen to give Willie's $25,000 to The Commotion – Rick and Julia Munro. If they listen to what Stevie says this afternoon, they'll know Willie and Nathan would have wanted the money to go to kids who don't mind getting bucked off."

Stevie stepped into the spotlight wearing a cowboy hat, flak jacket and jeans.

"Kayden, Willie, Emily and I met Nathan a year ago when he was a Pretty Boy in Movie Club. It took a while, but he convinced us that he was something else, something so wonderful that we made a film about it."

She nodded to Uncle Spencer and an overhead screen flickered.

BUCK OFF

THE TRAILER

The trailer opens with a collage of Nathan and his friends on the summer rodeo circuit. The collage streams behind the title and the opening credits.

Written by	Nathan	
Inspired by	Emily	Kayden
	Stevie	Speed of Light Willie
	Uncle Spencer	Jimmie and Alex Jackson
Starring	Nathan and TwoBlackEyes	
Filmed by	Stevie on a camera borrowed without permission from school	
Additional footage	Courtesy of Claresholm Agricultural Society	

The camera pans the Claresholm Community Arena marquis.

BULL RIDING
FIRST ROUND TONIGHT

The camera turns to Stevie standing outside the arena. She is filming herself in the side mirror of Kayden's pickup.

STEVIE

```
This is an 8 second film that Nathan
stretched out to fifteen minutes
because he wanted to include some
really profound stuff about growing
and learning and changing. It's all
deeper meaning bullshit so I'm not
going to use it. Three minutes is
all anybody needs to describe the
best 8 seconds of their life without
boring people.
```

The camera follows Stevie's walk through the arena entrance and to the changing room where the bull riders are pulling on their vests and chaps. The sound of the announcer and the crowd echo in the hallway. Louder and closer, chutes clang as the bulls are driven in from the pens.

The camera moves into the arena and pans the crowd, stopping on a small group: Emily, Grandpa John, Grandma Lillian, Uncle Spencer. They smile.

"Look at them. They're peeing their collective pants," Stevie says.

The camera follows beside Stevie as she smart mouths the bull riders as they walk into the arena to be introduced to the crowd. Kayden and the Jacksons lift their hats as they're cheered. Nathan, the last in the line, is barely applauded.

The camera sweeps along the rails, focussing on Speed of Light Willie who waves his towel and dances.

A collage of riders buck out of the chutes. The scoreboard flashes scores. The last rider is Nathan on TwoBlackEyes.

The camera zooms in on Nathan. Kayden is steadying him while Jimmie pulls his rope. Nathan takes two deep breaths and nods. The chute gate opens. Four seconds later the action freezes on Nathan as he swings his outside leg wide in anticipation of TwoBlackEyes' inside turn.

The crowd is holding its breath. TwoBlackEyes looks like he's gathering himself for an explosion.

Nathan jams his spur into the bull's side driving him forward. He jams him again. TwoBlackEyes jolts ahead and lands hard on stiff front legs and continues into a high kick.

The buzzer sounds. Nathan somersaults backward off TwoBlackEyes who drives one rear hoof into his leg. The other rips off his helmet. Nathan lands face down.

TwoBlackEyes turns and is about to grind him. Suddenly a pair of cleats dashes into the frame. A white towel slaps the bull's face. The bull turns and chases Willie to the rails. Nathan doesn't move.

The scoreboard flashes:
Nathan Munro 82

The scene changes to Nathan standing on crutches in Stevie's driveway. The remnants of his cast are on the ground to his left. His nose is stitched. He's wearing his silver and gold 82 buckle.

NATHAN

TwoBlackEyes taught me a lot about becoming a man. He taught me I can try anything if I'm willing to take a few risks ... and if I don't mind getting bucked off, my nose smashed and my leg broken.

TwoBlackEyes taught me to spur hard.

Now I've got another monster bull to face. Last week my doctor told me my lungs are going to give out before the end of the summer. I always knew they were a pair of whiney pants.

Last fall I started writing a film called Buck Off. It's a rodeo murder mystery about a momma's boy who wants to be a great bull rider like

```
his father who was killed by a wife
beating no good cowboy.

After I got the big news from my
doctor I had to make a decision
about how I wanted my life to end.
I could either stay home or I could
go rodeoing with my friends and be
inspired by them to keep writing
Buck Off.

I chose to die proud of myself. I
chose to die spurring hard enough to
finish Buck Off and give it a chance
to be screened at Cannes.

That's all I want to say.

(Long Pause)

And if you cut any of this out
Stevie I'm going to twist your
fucking head off.
```

The screen fades. A new title builds as TwoBlackEyes pounds in slow motion into the Rockin' R arena:

BUCK OFF

Coming Soon To Theatres

The audience is as silent as Willie's ashes. As silent as a red handprint on a rocky wall. The rumble of the bull's dirt pounding fury builds. Everyone is on their feet, clapping. TwoBlackEyes is the sound of Ground Thunder Running.

BRANDON FLOCK
AND THE UNFINISHED SCRIPT

Buck Off, Brandon Flock's unfinished murder and revenge script, is an integral part of Tyler Trafford's tale of Nathan Munro, born into a privileged life in Calgary's Elbow Park, but with personal goals and ambitions at odds with his family's plans for him.

There is much of Brandon in Nathan's story. As his parents, Brad and Dena Flock say, "As our only child, Brandon inevitably carried the weight of our aspirations for him. He did his best, while, as all young people must do, he searched for his own path in life." Brandon tried to accommodate their wishes for him to follow their path into the business world, but he was never comfortable with that goal. After much family discussion, he enrolled at the New York Film Academy, eventually graduating with an MFA.

Brandon drafted *Buck Off* over several years, beginning in 2008 while he was at the New York Film Academy. During this time, watching his Elbow Park friends begin careers in business and engineering, he began to realize that his chosen path – his dream – was precarious, challenging, with great potential for failure, and that he was fortunate to have the support of his family and friends.

Shortly after graduating, Brandon and his friend Max Van Dijk started ZClay Fresh, an integrated design and production company. They used original artwork by local artists to create unique advertising and branding material for their clients.

Brandon saw the financial woes and lack of support that many people working in the arts are forced to deal with. He knew that he had been extremely fortunate. So, through ZClay Fresh, he and Max initiated an Arts Scholarship Program to help struggling arts students.

Sadly, Brandon never lived to complete his script. He passed away in 2012, leaving the unfinished manuscript in with his papers. Dena found it, and after she and Brad read it they knew their son had left them a gift, and they thought he would have wanted it shared. *Buck Off* is the story of a young man who finds something in himself that others couldn't see. It's a story of redemption more than revenge, and it's a story of how challenging yourself to do the seemingly impossible is the only way to grow.

After Brandon passed away, his friends encouraged Brad and Dena to start a foundation to continue the arts scholarship program that Brandon had founded with ZClay Fresh. They agreed, and the Brandon Flock Foundation was created.

Tyler Trafford has created a parallel world in *TwoBlackEyes and The Unfinished Script.* The story of Nathan Munro is in many ways similar to the story of Brandon Flock, yet it isn't just Brandon's story. It's the story of every young person who takes a chance and follows their dreams. It's the story of every person who understands that the only thing worse than being bucked off is not trying at all.

THE BRANDON FLOCK FOUNDATION

www.brandonflockfoundation.com

Proceeds from the sales of *TwoBlackEyes and The Unfinished Script* will go toward funding the Brandon Flock Foundation scholarships.

Brandon recognized the financial challenges many young people face as they begin careers in the arts. He knew he was extremely fortunate to have friends and family with the resources and desire to provide him with the support he needed – and that not everybody was as lucky.

The Brandon Flock Foundation offers financial aid and mentoring to students seeking their passion in the Arts. The Foundation provides scholarships to students attending The Vancouver Film School, Alberta College of Art and Design, The University of Calgary, and Emily Carr University.